Praise fo

'Elegant, thoug~~~~~~ ~~~~ powerful'
Daisy Buchanan

'A cobweb of a book: beautifully intricate and delicate'
Veronica Henry

'A truly beautiful story of love, desire, identity and
courage – Julie Cohen is at her spellbinding best'
Rosie Walsh

'Wonderfully written and evocative'
Woman & Home

'Beautifully written and thought-provoking'
Kate Eberlen

'Loved every page!'
Claire Dyer

'Simmering with passions, it is a testament to
the enduring power of love'
Sunday Mirror

'Poignant and heartfelt'
Prima

'Wonderfully evocative'
Woman's Weekly

'A must read from Julie Cohen'
Good Housekeeping

Julie Cohen grew up in the western mountains of Maine and studied English at Brown University and Cambridge University before pursuing a research degree in nineteenth-century fairies. After a career as a secondary school English teacher, she became a novelist. Her award-winning novels have sold over a million copies worldwide. *Dear Thing* and *Together* were both selected for the Richard and Judy Book Club. *Together* won RNA Contemporary Romantic Novel of the Year and *The Two Lives of Louis & Louise* was longlisted for the Polari Prize

Julie is a teacher of creative writing, a founder of the Romantic Novelists' Association Rainbow Chapter for LGBTQ+ authors, and a Patron of literacy charity ABC To Read. She lives in the south of England with a terrier of dubious origin.

Bluesky: @juliecohen.bsky.social
Website: www.julie-cohen.com

PARADISE

JULIE COHEN

ORION

First published in Great Britain in 2025 by Orion Fiction,
an imprint of The Orion Publishing Group Ltd.
Carmelite House, 50 Victoria Embankment
London EC4Y 0DZ

An Hachette UK Company

The authorised representative in the EEA is Hachette Ireland,
8 Castlecourt Centre, Castleknock Road, Castleknock, Dublin 15, D15 XTP3,
Republic of Ireland (email: info@hbgi.ie)

1 3 5 7 9 10 8 6 4 2

A CIP catalogue record for this book is
available from the British Library.

ISBN (Mass Market Paperback) 9781409190202
ISBN (eBook) 9781409190219
ISBN (Audio) 9781409190226

Typeset at The Spartan Press Ltd,
Lymington, Hants

Printed and bound in Great Britain by Clays Ltd,
Elcograf S.p.A.

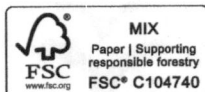

www.orionbooks.co.uk

For all my friends at the pond, and especially for
Harriet
Chris
Kathy
Regine
We miss you every summer and always.

Part One

——

Paradise Lost

Chapter One

Katie

The day of the accident

I'm floating on my back in the lake. High above, the sun beats down and paints the water with flakes of hammered gold.

My body lies at the middle of a series of concentric circles. Ripples spread out, tipped with gold. Then the dark-blue shape of the lake, surrounded by a ring of smoke-blue mountains, soft as breath. And above it all, the dome of blue sky. Circles upon spheres, time cycling once again to summer.

Here I am. Part of the water, part of the sky. I spread my fingers and toes, the water like velvet. It's the best place on earth. It never changes. Heaven. Eden. Paradise.

And then I wake up.

Everything hurts.

Everything.

Oh, God, what's wrong?

No, not everything – mostly my head.

I move a little bit and my head responds with a bolt of pain.

When I open my eyes, it hurts more. Light assaults me. I close them, but a few – seconds? Minutes? Hours? – later, I try again. I blink and squint, and can't seem to open my eyes very much, but I can just about see part of a wall, part of a grey curtain, and a cupboard.

'Where am I?' I whisper. What a cliché. If I can identify clichés, that is a good thing, right? Thinking. Also good. What is this?

Was I in an accident? Am I very hungover? I clench my hand around something soft: a blanket. I'm lying down. I'm in a bed.

It's a hospital. I can smell it.

I attempt to sit up. My head hurts enough to make me cry out and fall back onto the pillow.

'Oh, you're awake,' says a soft voice. A hand on my wrist, a hand on my forehead; brief touches. A woman I don't recognise. In scrubs. Wearing a surgical mask.

'Are you a nurse?'

'Got it,' she says and her eyes smile. 'I'm Debbie. What's your name?'

'Katie.'

'Oh, good. I'm glad you're with us again. You were awake a little while ago and didn't seem to be very together. How are you feeling, Katie?'

'My head really hurts.'

'I'm not surprised. Do you remember what happened?'

'Migraine?' My words feel slower than usual. My tongue is dry.

'Do you get migraines?'

'Sometimes.' I touch my face and wince. My eyelids feel terribly swollen and they hurt to the touch.

'You've got a couple of black eyes,' the nurse tells me.

'So ... not a migraine.'

'Not unless you normally get a migraine from trying to knock down a tree with your head.'

'Not ... what?' The light's bright, too bright, and I try to follow the nurse's words, but they seem to be spiralling around the room and their movement makes me nauseated.

'Are you going to—' Something cardboard appears under my chin. As soon as I've finished being sick, the nurse whisks it away, wiping my mouth with gentle hands. *Good service in this place. 10/10 – would visit again.* I close my eyes because it hurts less and everything goes away for a little while.

'Katie, how are you feeling?' someone says, someone different;

an overly cheerful voice. It recalls another time, a thirsty time, when I had my appendix out the day before my junior prom. I clear my throat and words come out, but they seem detached from me and I'm not really sure what they mean.

'Is there someone we can call for you?'

One number at a time, as they arise. Then back to sleep.

Kitty. From a long way away.

Kittycat. Meow.

'Kitty...' and it's my dad's name for me. It's my dad. My dad holding my hand, stroking my arm; my dad's here and it's OK.

'Dad,' I say. I turn my head a little and there he is. His hair is shorter than the last time I saw him. His glasses are crooked above his surgical mask.

'Oh, Kittycat. You're awake.' He squeezes my hand. 'We've been worried.'

'Typical Katie. Anything for attention.'

My brother, Shane, is on the other side of the bed. He is also wearing a mask. What's with the masks?

He sits beside me and I realise I've got an IV in my arm, with clear fluid going into it. 'What happened?' I ask.

Dad gently squeezes my hand. 'Do you remember?'

The last thing I remember is... 'Which hospital is this?'

'Casablanca Community Hospital,' says Shane. 'Western Maine's finest. It looks exactly the same as when I was in here as a kid.'

It hurts to think. 'We're in Maine?'

'Last time I checked.'

'When did I get here?'

'This morning.'

'The nurse... said something about a tree?'

'You were riding a bicycle and an ATV hit you. It knocked you off your bike and you went flying across the road, and hit a tree with your head.' My dad is putting on a brave face, but even with my head pounding and half his face covered, I can tell he's terrified. 'The guy's from out of state. He didn't know who you were. He called an ambulance and followed behind it. The nurse said he was beside himself. He wouldn't leave, and stayed in the waiting room until Shane and I showed up. We had to promise to call him with updates.'

'So he hit you with his recreational vehicle,' says Shane. 'But at least he's sorry about it.'

'Those things travel way too fast up there,' my dad says. 'There's a fifteen-mile-an-hour speed limit, but you can't tell me that he wasn't going faster than that to knock you right across the road. We have to do something about that – it's an absolute travesty. He said he didn't see you pull out, but—'

'Later, Dad,' says Shane and my dad shuts up.

'How's the bicycle?' I ask, because I know my dad rants about things like road safety when he is frightened and I want everything to go back to normal. I don't feel normal, though.

'We didn't ask. It wasn't our highest priority.'

'How do I look?'

'Like shit,' says Shane. I attempt to elbow him with the arm that has the IV. I can tell he feels sorry for me because he could dodge it easily, but doesn't.

'I feel it.' Now that I'm properly awake there's pain all over my body, though it's worst in my head. 'Why are you wearing masks?'

'Just to be safe,' says Dad. 'There are a lot of sick people here.'

'Well, yeah, it's a hospital.'

'I'll go call Brian,' says my dad, and gets up and goes into the hallway. I'm not sure who Brian is – maybe one of his golf buddies. Maybe Dad interrupted a game to come here. For the first time, I register the absence of someone who should be here.

'Where's Nic?'

My brother, beside me, shrugs. 'I don't know.'

'Why isn't she—'

The masked nurse appears again, checks my temperature and

blood pressure, and looks into my eyes. Once my father returns, she informs everyone that I don't have any broken bones and that I'm showing no signs of internal bleeding or brain swelling, but that I was unconscious for a couple of hours and most likely have a concussion, and that she expects the doctor will do some neurological tests and order that I stay in the hospital for at least a night for observation. She calls me lucky and asks me if I want any pain relief.

I say yes.

It seems as if I should deserve the heavy guns when it comes to painkillers, but the nurse gives me two Tylenol. I'm so exhausted by these simple conversations that I go back to sleep soon after taking the pills. But this time, as I close my eyes, despite the pain, I feel safe.

I'm woken up, I don't know how much later, by being hugged. Somehow I can tell it's a man, and, by instinct, my arms go up to hug him back. It feels good. At first I think it's Shane, but then I open my eyes, see dark curly hair, smell an unfamiliar shampoo.

'You had me so frightened,' says the man into my shoulder. 'I thought you were never coming back.' I can't see his face. I drop my arms.

'I'm back,' I say, as cheerfully as I can. He straightens up, one hand still on my arm. He, too, is wearing a mask, so it takes me a minute to put things together – the brown eyes, the curly hair – and recognise him.

'Bryan?'

This was who my father said he was going to call? My neighbour, the guy in the apartment next door to my rental in Philly, the one whose pizza I was delivered once? We say hello in the hallway, talk about the weather. I don't even know his last name. Just Bryan with a y, from Number 212.

There are tears in his eyes. One falls and wets his mask.

Why does he care? Why is he here in the hospital?

'Don't worry,' I say. 'I'm told I'm going to be OK.'

'Thank God.' He squeezes my arm. Shane gets up from a chair and pushes it towards the bed so this guy can sit beside me. I shoot Shane a look. To be honest, I'm still feeling awful and I could do with not having to reassure someone who's basically a stranger. Also, even with a mask on, he's quite good-looking, and Shane has already told me that I'm not at my best.

'I found your bike when I came back from the cemetery,' Bryan says. 'It's a wreck. I've been going nuts, trying to find out what happened. And then your father called—'

'I didn't have your number,' Dad says to him, apologetically. 'I had to look you up and call your office. That's why it took so long.'

'Why...' I start to ask, but it all seems like too much to work out.

'That's OK,' says Bryan. 'I'm just glad you got hold of me. And you've got my number now.'

'Are you the person who hit me?' I ask. My head is pounding. I wonder when I can get more Tylenol, or something stronger. I wonder if I shouldn't say anything about not blaming him for the accident, for insurance purposes or whatever. But what are the chances of my neighbour in Philadelphia hitting me with an ATV by mistake in Maine?

I scrunch my swollen eyes shut, trying to remember what happened. I can sort of imagine it, purely from how I feel: an ATV going hell for leather on the main road, Bryan driving it, maybe talking on his phone so he's not paying attention. The ATV was green. Or maybe red. It would have been really noisy – those things make a huge racket, so how did I not hear it? What was I doing? Did I have headphones in?

I don't remember.

'Me?' says Bryan. 'No, I didn't hit you. I was looking all over for you. The bike was ruined and I didn't know where you'd gone. I thought you'd wandered off and you were hurt...'

His hand is still on my arm, which is weird. I extricate my

arm, but gently, so I don't offend him because he also seems to be having a shitty day.

'I should have waited for you,' he continues. 'I can't forgive myself. If I'd waited, this would never have happened.'

'Why are you in Maine?' I ask him.

'Don't you remember?'

I don't. Not the accident, not coming to Maine, not anything to do with my neighbour. And this ...

I've been in pain, but now I start to feel frightened. My brain is slow, dull, throbbing.

'Kitty, what's wrong?'

'How did I get here?'

'You were in an accident. The man who hit you called an ambulance.'

'No. I mean – how did I get to Maine? And why was I riding a bicycle in the middle of winter?'

My brother laughs. He's the only one.

'And why are you all wearing surgical masks? Have I got some sort of contagious disease?'

'You shouldn't joke like this after knocking your head,' says Shane. 'You'll get people scared.'

Bryan seems to be speechless. So I turn to the one person who I know I can trust, who I know has never lied to me: my dad.

'Why did you have to call my neighbour?'

Dad walks over to my bed, Shane and Bryan stepping back to give him room. He puts his hand on my forehead – the way he used to do to me when I was a little girl and I had a fever, or to my brother when he was sick from chemo. I notice that his hand is shaking a little.

'Kitty,' he says, and his voice is so loving, so careful, and above his mask his eyes are so kind, and that's what he was like when my brother was sick, when he thought that Shane was going to die, and I can hardly breathe.

'Kitty, sweetheart,' he says. 'It's summertime. You and Bryan came up to Maine yesterday. You drove up from Philadelphia.'

Now I am shaking a little, too.

'Why did Bryan come with me?'

My dad looks at Bryan.

'To meet your family and to see the place you grew up,' Bryan says.

'But ... why?'

'Don't you remember?' says Bryan. He sounds upset. 'We're in love with each other.'

'You started dating during the pandemic,' says my dad gently.

'What do you mean "during the pandemic"?' I ask.

And I can't see their full faces, but I know I have said something very wrong.

Chapter Two

A neurologist comes and I have tests, both verbal and physical. Everyone is muted, worried, but the doctor seems more intrigued than anything, so I try to answer his questions as fully as I can.

My head still hurts, especially when I sit up or try to move. The Tylenol doesn't touch it. But I'm alarmed enough to force myself to stay awake and alert, and attempt to figure all this out.

Bryan, whom I am supposedly dating, stays in the room with my dad while I go off to get a CAT scan. If it were just me, I would send Bryan away. He's always seemed like a nice guy, but I don't know him.

But Dad knows Bryan. He agrees that Bryan and I have been dating for about a year. And my father has never lied to me in my life. Not about good news (Shane's remission) or bad news (my mother leaving). Not even when I was about six and asked him how babies were made. I've always known that if I call him up and ask him his opinion about something, he will ask me if I really want to hear it, and, if I insist, he will gently, kindly, tell me exactly what he thinks and why. *No, you should not buy that car. Yes, you should see a doctor. No, that job isn't worth your time.*

Maybe Bryan has convinced my father somehow, too.

When he's asking questions, the doctor notices that I keep on looking at my dad and Bryan instead of paying full attention to him, and he asks them to leave the room for a little while and go get some coffee.

'It's clear that you have some memory loss,' the doctor tells me. 'This isn't unusual following a head injury. The good news is that you don't have any anterograde amnesia, which is the inability to form new memories, which is a more common long-term problem. You're able to follow conversations, your short-term memory since regaining consciousness is intact. The other good news is that I've had a look at your scans and I don't see any brain damage.'

I let out a great breath of relief.

'So any memory problems you're experiencing are likely to be temporary.'

'I don't really have amnesia?'

'No, you do. You don't have anterograde amnesia. What you're experiencing is retrograde amnesia.'

'But that's when people forget everything about themselves. I know everything. I know my name and my birthday, and where I went to school, and my social security number, and what my job is and who my family are. I know everything except about the last … I don't know how long. I missed a global pandemic. And dating my neighbour.'

The doctor's eyes smile kindly above his mask. 'It's much more common for people to only lose more recent memories when they experience trauma. Many accident victims, for example, never remember the moment it happened. It's almost as if the brain protects itself.'

'I don't remember the accident,' I say.

'And you may never recall it. But you will most likely recover the memories you've lost. Retrograde amnesia due to head injury is usually temporary. It only lasts hours, or perhaps days.'

'My dad is scared.'

'Are *you* scared?'

I bite my lip. 'Frankly, I don't believe a word you're saying, so it's hard for me to be scared. It seems to be a much simpler explanation that all of you are making this up.'

The doctor nods. 'It's natural to want to believe that you're not mistaken and sometimes our brains prefer to invent fictional explanations rather than acknowledge that there is a deficit. But your family will be able to show you documentary evidence of what you've forgotten, which may help.'

'I don't mind missing a pandemic. But I would like to remember falling in love. It feels as if I've missed the whole fun part. And why did I fall in love with him? I'm not a relationship person.'

'I can't really comment on that,' says the doctor. 'But I will suggest that you and your family spend some time talking about what you do remember, and how much they can corroborate. Pinning down some dates might help you. And I really do think that once you're home, in a familiar setting, you will find that you remember more and more.'

'You're sure?'

'Well. It's neurology, not mathematics. Everyone heals at a different rate. But you're young and healthy, and there's no reason to suppose that your memory won't go back to normal.'

'What if it's not my brain? What if something horrible happened to me – not the accident or the pandemic, something else – and I don't want to remember it, for psychological reasons?'

I don't even know that I'm going to ask that until I do.

There's the answer to his earlier question: I am scared. Because if I don't remember everything about who I am, how do I know I'm still me?

He considers. 'People do suppress painful memories, in order to function. But with therapy and time, people can recover. Do you have any reason to suspect that might be true?'

'If I did, I wouldn't remember it. So how do I know?'

His phone buzzes and he glances at the screen. 'Get some rest tonight. You should be able to go home tomorrow, or the next day. Odds are, your memory will come back before those black eyes have faded.'

Then he leaves, and visiting hours are over, and I'm left all alone with a pounding head and my fear.

*

The doctor told me that people tend to sleep a lot after a head injury, even a relatively mild one, but that night I sleep very little. My entire body hurts, the hospital bed is uncomfortable, the ward is noisy and someone comes in to take observations every few hours. But that's not why I'm awake. My brain, injured or not, is too busy. I keep on trying to put together what I know for certain, and what others have been telling me, and the gap between these two things is black and terrifying and incomprehensible.

How could I have done things that I don't remember? Is there going to be a big blank space in my life for ever? What if it happens again, what if it gets worse, and I forget my brother, my job, my best friend, my father, myself?

My throat keeps closing up. I feel as if I've drunk a million cups of coffee and also fallen off a building. I'm on the verge of a panic attack and I only fend it off through concentrating on each breath, one by one.

Every time my heart slows a little, I try to think back to the last thing I remember. Try to pinpoint the exact time and place my old life ended.

It's difficult to know what your last memory is. I've never had to do it before. Usually, life is a continuity from one moment to the next and if someone says, 'What's the last thing you remember?', it's referring to a specific incident in time. They want to know what's the last thing you remember about Friday night's party, or the last thing you remember before being abandoned by your mother. There are signposts to help you contextualise that moment. There's a story that makes sense.

It's entirely different when you're trying to remember the last thing you remember before there was a massive hole where you remember nothing.

When the doctor asked me this afternoon, I said that I remembered being in my apartment in Philadelphia. Although it's not strictly *my* apartment; I'm on a short-term lease while I work for Franklin Bank. I don't even own the furniture.

When I try to recall, I get more of a feeling than a memory – the feeling of something ending. It's a familiar feeling, though usually it's associated with Maine, not anywhere else. For all of my life, the lake was where I began and ended my summers. It was the feeling of school vacation, summer romances, adventures with my best friend, and watching those things pass by with every sunset over the water. I've lived in dozens of places, but I only ever regret leaving the lake.

So when the doctor asked me what time of year it was, I said, 'Autumn.' And it felt right, because that's the season for that feeling of ending. But then I thought a minute, remembered snow outside the window, falling down between the brownstones, and said, 'No, it's winter.'

But then my dad said, 'Kitty, sweetheart, it's June.' And when I told him it wasn't, when I said no, June was my favourite month, I'd know if it were June, he showed me his phone with the date on the lock screen. It's midsummer day, 2021, and about seventeen months after the last memory I've just been talking about.

Everything seems slippery and untrue. Even June.

Chapter Three

I must have slept, because I wake up to the nurse swishing back my curtains and saying, 'Breakfast!' And maybe it's because she's so cheerful, or maybe it's because my head hurts a little less, or maybe it's because I've finally figured it out, I don't feel frightened. Everything makes sense now. Occam's razor: the simplest solution is the true one.

Everyone has been lying to me. This is a practical joke. Shane's orchestrated it, somehow. He used to love practical jokes. He used to bring a fake hand to chemo to freak out the nurses. One time, growing up in Connecticut, he charmed his entire sixth-grade class into turning their desks around so that when his teacher walked into the room after lunch, she was confronted with twenty-seven children facing the wrong way.

And if I can remember such a silly and long-ago memory, this is proof that my brain has nothing wrong with it and it's all my ridiculous younger brother's fault.

There are some holes in this theory, I will admit. For one: why would Shane keep on with the joke if he knows that I'm frightened? His jokes have always been harmless. And he hasn't really done any pranks since he was a little kid. Also, why would Bryan look so sad? Why would my dad go along with it?

And of course there's the big one: why, when I look out the window, can I see summer leaves on the trees?

But all of that can wait until I get a chance to call Shane out, and he can have his laugh, and stop it, and we can all go back to normal. Meanwhile, a volunteer brings me a tray with toast and cornflakes, and a cup of orange juice, which I drink gratefully.

I'm attempting to spread grape jelly on toast when I hear a slight sound nearby and look up.

It's Nic. She's wearing a mask but I'd know her anywhere. She's in a T-shirt, shorts and sandals, short dark hair pushed back from her face, her skin freckled and tanned, her arms full of beaded and woven bracelets. My best friend, my person.

'It isn't visiting hours,' she says. 'But I came now so I wouldn't run into anyone.'

'Thank God you're here,' I say, in relief and joy. 'What took you so long?'

She takes a step forward. I can't see her expression, but her arms are crossed over her chest as if she expects to be struck.

'I'm OK,' I tell her. But she doesn't come any closer. 'Listen, tell me something. Is this all one of my brother's pranks?'

'I wouldn't know,' she says.

'What day is it?'

'It's the twenty-second of June.'

Shit. Like my father, Nic also does not lie as a rule, and she has never enjoyed a practical joke.

'What year?'

'2021.'

'Was there really a global pandemic and lots of people died, and we weren't allowed to leave our houses for months and months?'

'Yes.'

'Is it over now? Why is everyone still wearing masks?'

'To be safe, I guess. Everything has opened up, but it's not over. Just the worst of it. We're still dealing with it.'

'So ... everything is different.'

'That's an understatement.'

She is not looking at me. She's looking at something behind my head. I try to see what it is, but twisting my neck hurts.

'Are you OK?' I ask.

'Are *you* OK?'

My throat is clogged with dread and I'm not sure what's going on. 'Can I have a hug, please?'

She comes no closer. 'Shane says that you've forgotten every-thing since like the beginning of 2020.'

'That's what they tell me.'

'Is that real or is it bullshit you've made up so you don't have to deal with stuff?'

This is typical Nic. At least one thing hasn't changed.

'It's real. Does it sound like something I'd make up?'

'It seems . . . very convenient.'

'It's not convenient. It's really scary, Nic. Did Shane tell you that I've forgotten that I have a boyfriend?'

'I met him.' Her voice is flat. 'The day before yesterday.'

'What do you mean by that?'

'By the fact that I met him?'

'By the way that you sound. You don't like him?'

'I have no opinion one way or the other about him.' She looks at her watch. 'Shane said you were asking about me, so I came.'

'Is your mother all right?'

'How do you mean?'

'I mean, with the pandemic. Is this why you're acting weird? Is she OK?'

'She's healthy.'

'What's wrong?'

'What do you mean?'

I put my hand to my aching head. 'I don't – this conversation feels slippery. Not normal. Are you not telling me something?'

Nic sighs and leans against the wall. 'What do you remember about me?'

'You? You're my best friend. We've known each other since we were nine. We spent every summer together growing up. We know everything about each other.'

'Do we?'

'Well, I seem to have forgotten the last year and a half, but, aside from that, yes.'

'Hmm.'

'And you're dating my brother.'

Nic doesn't answer, and after a moment she rubs her eye and I realise she's crying.

'Harriet,' I say in alarm. 'What's wrong?'

'Don't call me that.'

'Are you all right?'

I push aside the breakfast tray and start to get out of bed, but she shakes her head and steps backward, wiping away tears.

'Do they think you're ever going to get your memory back?' she asks.

'The doctor says I probably will, eventually.'

'Like, tomorrow? Or ten years from now?'

'Nobody knows. Nic, tell me what's wrong. Am I hurt, more badly than they're telling me?'

'No one has said anything about that.'

'Why are you crying? Tell me what happened.'

'Do you remember what happened before the accident?'

'No. Did something happen?'

She's shaking her head. 'I can't deal with this.'

'Deal with what?'

'This. Everything.'

'I need you, though, Nic. I can't remember any of this by myself. I need you to help me.'

She's shaking her head. 'I can't.'

'You know everything about me. Right now, you know more than I do myself. Why can't you help me?'

'This is too much,' she says. 'I have to go.' And before I can say anything else, she turns and flees.

Chapter Four

I first met Nicole Leblanc one June day when she paddled a canoe up to our side of the lake. I was nine years old, and my younger brother, Shane, had leukemia, and I was desperately, desperately lonely. We were in Maine for the summer like we always were, but Shane was in Casablanca hospital after taking a turn for the worse. My mother had left by then. I suppose my grandmother came to look after me – I don't actually remember. I only remember everything being hushed. I had nothing to do but sit by myself and read.

I was so scared. Every time the phone rang, I thought it would be bad news. I went down to the beach so I wouldn't hear it. And then came a girl in a canoe, paddling around the point all by herself and totally not afraid of anything, and I knew right away that I wanted to be like her.

That's the thing about best friends, especially the ones who have known you for most of your life – they teach you how to be a better version of yourself.

I'm impulsive; Nic is introspective. I'm outgoing; Nic is shy. I like making money; Nic likes music. I take risks; Nic likes to play it safe. On paper, you wouldn't put us together. But friendship is more than similarities or differences. It's about knowing everything about each other. Being fierce for each other. Always taking each other's side.

Growing up, I had a large group of friends where I lived in Connecticut – schoolfriends, cheerleading friends, family friends, neighbourhood friends, softball friends, sleepover friends – and then, in the summers in Maine, I had one *real* friend. We packed more fun and adventure and togetherness into those eight weeks of summer vacation than I had in the whole rest of the year. And those years of childhood and adolescence, spent mostly in two different states, meant that when we grew up, we stayed close when most other childhood friends would have drifted apart.

I work in finance and I'm good at it. I've spent my adult life travelling from city to city, country to country, working for whoever can afford me. I might spend the winter in Kuala Lumpur and the spring in Vancouver; my homes are a series of short leases. But every June, for a month at least, I come back to Maine, to my family's old lake house that we've named Paradise. So that's my real home – the thing that never changes, the touchstone that makes me myself. The old wooden house by the lake and the stream, full of my grandmother's furniture and books that I've read a million times. With my dad, and my brother, and Nic.

Except there's something wrong between Nic and me. And I don't remember what it is, and she's not telling me.

Chapter Five

I'm in the passenger seat of my dad's car. Dad is driving. Bryan isn't in the car with us; he's following us in another car.

This has taken more negotiation than I feel capable of dealing with.

When a nurse came in and said, cheerfully, 'We're discharging you!' my response wasn't relief, but dread. In a hospital, you don't have to make any decisions. They are also places where strange things are normal, or at least normal-ish, and have reassuring scientific explanations.

In contrast, right now I'm not even sure what normal is.

More thinking time has given me a clearer sense of what my last memory is. It's nothing to do with a bicycle or an ATV. The last thing I remember is standing at the window of my Philly rental. It was a weekday afternoon, early January. I was wearing a fluffy bathrobe, after coming back from work and having a shower. My hair dripped down my neck, but the apartment was warm and I was barefoot. Outside, it was dark already, and I was at the window because it was starting to snow, something I was excited to see, since I'd spent the last winter in Singapore for work. I remember thinking it was nice to start the new year with a blanket of snow covering everything, like a fresh start.

This is the last thing I remember. It's clear enough that it could have happened yesterday. To me, it feels as if it did happen yesterday – or at least directly before I woke up in the hospital.

It's strange, though, because when I first started trying to work out what my latest memory was, I felt a sense of an ending, whereas this memory is of clean beginnings.

In any case, figuring this out is the only thing I have accomplished in my two days as an in-patient. I haven't figured out anything else. I haven't even slightly managed to get my head around the idea that I've lost eighteen months and that the world has changed, let alone the strange way that Nic was behaving yesterday.

Dad and Bryan both turned up expecting to take me home. They arrived independently, at about the same time, and looked surprised to see each other, which would have been funny in another context. They also each had a bag for me. Bryan had a reusable canvas shopping bag with my own clothes, and Dad had a plastic bag from Walmart with new clothes.

They proceeded to have an incredibly considerate argument.

'Bill, it's fine,' said Bryan. 'Of course you want to take your daughter home.'

'I'm so sorry, I'm used to doing the dad things.'

'No, it's completely understandable. Plus you probably want some time together.'

'She remembers me. It's you she needs some time with.'

'We've got plenty of time. You go ahead and I'll follow.'

'I just think that if it were my partner, then ...'

You know – real alpha-male sort of stuff.

I took both the bags of clothes and went to the bathroom to change while they thrashed things out. I was dreading opening Bryan's bag and seeing a set of strange clothes in my size – clothes that belonged to some mysterious other woman who was not me. But it was my favourite pair of white shorts, a well-worn blue T-shirt, and a familiar bra and pair of underwear. The tennis shoes might not be the same ones I remember wearing last, but they were at least the same brand.

On the other hand, my father's bag didn't contain a bra, but did have a pair of leopard-print leggings.

I don't blame my dad – Walmart probably didn't have much of a selection and I used to wear leopard print in college – but I wore the clothes that Bryan brought. They made me feel more like myself.

When I came back, they were still busy deferring to each other. My dad turned to me. 'Which do you prefer, Kitty? Do you want to ride home with Bryan or me?'

I opened my mouth, but I could not answer his question. In truth, I wanted to go with my dad. I didn't feel that I knew Bryan well enough yet to face the pressure of being alone with him for a whole car journey. It was stressful enough leaving the hospital with a big gap in my memory, without having to make conversation.

But even though I didn't know Bryan, I didn't want to hurt his feelings. From the little I've seen of him, he's always seemed like a nice guy.

'Um,' I said. And nothing else, because it was all too complicated and it was only a car ride. And because Bryan was biting his lip and clearly I was already hurting his feelings, though he was trying not to show it.

Finally, Bryan said, 'Well, I've enjoyed arguing with you, Bill, but fair's fair. She's wearing the clothes I brought, so you take her home. That OK with you, Katie?'

And I knew that he understood my conflict. Which means that maybe he does know me, at least a little.

My dad drives out of town, towards the twisty and hilly road that leads to Morocco Pond. He's driving much more slowly and carefully than usual, and his hands grip the wheel tightly.

'You can drive normally,' I tell him. 'I'm not traumatised by the accident. I don't even remember it.'

'OK,' he says, but he doesn't speed up. At least we're not wearing masks now, so I can look at his face.

'Dad,' I say. 'Is there something wrong with Nic?'

'Why do you ask, honey?'

'I thought she'd be here today.'

'Well, she is a busy person, you know. It's high season.'

'Did she have a fight with Shane? Did I take sides?'

This is the only explanation I can think of, for Nic acting so weird and keeping her distance while I've been unwell. But whose side would I take, between my brother and my best friend? How could I choose one over the other?

'Oh, Kitty, I couldn't really say. Shane doesn't tell me much. You know how he is. Anyway, you need to concentrate on your own healing now.'

My dad, like my brother, is not a person who likes to talk about difficult or unpleasant emotions. He prefers to be stoic, live and let live, and get on with it. This has usually been easy enough to get along with, but in these circumstances it's frustrating.

'How's Tessa?' I ask instead.

'She's OK. We've been staying in town. She was feeling sick so she didn't want to come into the hospital in case she spreads it. She hasn't been able to eat anything for two days.'

'Oh, no, Dad. Poor Tessa.' My stepmother and my dad both took early retirement and have been walking the Appalachian Trail in stages for the past two years. Wait ... 'Did you finish the Trail and I forgot it?'

'We're supposed to go down to Virginia in September. I'm not sure we'll make it.'

'Is she feeling any better today?'

'This morning she had a few Saltines and some ginger ale, which gave her a little colour. She's been worried about you, though. She wouldn't let me come upstairs in case I got it and gave it to you, so I've been sleeping on the sofa bed. It's pretty comfortable.'

I have slept on that sofa bed. It is not comfortable.

'Have you made her soup?'

'Freezer's full of it, in single-serving portions.'

There, at least, nothing has changed. My dad held down a full-time job as a lawyer while being a single parent to two kids, one of whom had leukemia. He is the king of batch-cooking.

'As soon as she's better, we'll come up to see you,' he says. 'We have a lot to talk about.'

'Why aren't you staying at Paradise?'

'Well,' he says, a little awkward. 'You and your boyfriend don't want your old dad and his wife hanging around.'

I kind of do want my dad and his wife hanging around. They're my security blanket.

Then I think of Bryan's hurt face.

I turn on the radio, which is set to the eighties music station, as usual. 'Big Shot' by Billy Joel comes on. 'I sort of hate this song,' I say, because I always say that when I'm in the car with my dad and it comes on the radio. When it comes on the radio when I'm not with my dad, I say it aloud sometimes anyway.

'Yeah, but it's catchy,' he says.

'Yeah, but it's either about his girlfriend, which means he's mean, or it's about himself, which means he's an asshole.'

'You can just listen to the music and relax.'

'I can never just listen to the music.'

'That's why you're such a terrible dancer.'

This is exactly what I wanted. I laugh, and then he does. We drive through the woods. The song ends.

'How come my brain can hold all of the words to songs recorded before I was born, but I get conked on the head and I can't remember the past year and a half?'

'I don't know, Kittycat,' says my dad. 'It's a mystery. But you're going to be OK.'

I hope so.

'Do you like Bryan?' I ask.

He glances over at me. 'Well, I just met him, but he seems very nice.'

'He's the first boyfriend I have ever brought to Maine.'

'Yes, Tessa pointed that out.'

'Is she already marrying us off?'

'You know Tessa.'

'What if I never get my memory back, Dad?'

'Sometimes things happen,' he says. 'And we just have to adjust.'

Another song comes on the radio.

Chapter Six

When I call my family's summer home 'Paradise', people tend to think that it's much grander than it is. They picture a huge house, suitable for the Great Gatsby. I then have to explain that in Maine, there are a lot of lakes and although property on the coast is incredibly expensive – because out-of-staters like to vacation there – lakeside property is more affordable and Maine families have owned summer houses by the water for generations. Some of these are in fact very grand, but most of them aren't. They range from McMansions to tarpaper shacks. Many aren't winterproofed, though some are used as hunting lodges in the winter. They're places for families to gather, for couples to take a little alone time, for children to learn to swim and bike and fish. At Morocco Pond, a smallish lake in Western Maine, there are some rentals for out-of-staters and one grand house where the hotel used to be, but most of the houses are owned by local people, who either take a week or two there in the summer or who move up for the whole summer and commute to work.

These summer houses are called 'camps' and the correct Maine term for visiting your summer home is 'going upta camp'. It's always 'up' to camp, no matter what direction the camp lies from your original starting point.

However, you don't go camping at a camp. You go camping at a campground, like the one that Nic's family owns, on the west shore of the lake.

Anyway, that's the spiel that I give to people who aren't from Maine and then, if they are still interested, I explain that our family camp was bought by my great-grandfather, who was a Maine native, though he married a lady from Connecticut and raised his family there, which was where I mostly grew up. The camp has been in our family for years and we go there every summer. It's called Paradise because that's what Nic and I used to call it when we were kids, and eventually my dad got a painted sign that he hung on the side of the house, above the door.

This is how families work. You have your own language, your own names for things, based on history that no one else knows, and no matter how many places you travel to, whenever you come home, you start speaking that language again.

Dad drives even more slowly along the road that follows the shore of the lake. We pass the campground where Nic's mother still lives. I think.

Everything looks the same to me. But then again, little ever changes at Morocco Pond. It's not a tourist spot, really. There are a few year-round houses, but, other than that, it is all but abandoned between September and June, except for hunters and ice-fishing shacks on the frozen lake. Even the campground attracts the same people year after year – in some cases, generations of the same family. The lake is beautiful. The mountains surrounding it are pretty. The camps are modest. The store doesn't stock much except barbecue supplies, ice cream, beer, and T-shirts that say *EVERYTHING THAT HAPPENS AT THE POND, STAYS AT THE POND (but nothing ever happens at the pond)*. I have two.

As we near the turn-off to our unfinished drive I peer out the window, but there's no sign of where my accident occurred. Someone has taken away my bicycle and cleared up whatever debris there was. None of the trees appear to have a head-shaped dent in them, but I'd have to look closer to make sure.

Dad obviously knows what I'm thinking, so he says, 'The old Durham place is looking nice,' and nods to the small camp, the last before our drive. It used to belong to Lydia Durham, a battleaxe if ever there was one, who would regularly yell at us kids to get off her lawn and go get a summer job. Lydia died about five years ago – seven years ago, I guess – at the age of nine hundred or so. As I recall, her camp has been vacant ever since, slowly listing to one side, the paint peeling. But now someone has jacked it up so it's even, put new shingles on the roof, painted the clapboards white and put green shutters on all the windows. There are tomato plants growing by the side.

'When did that happen?' I ask. I know he's trying to distract me from thinking about the accident, but now I'm thinking about my amnesia instead.

'They did most of the work this spring. Had to dig out a whole new septic system. Tessa says the new lady who lives there is nice. A scientist, I think.'

Tessa thinks everyone is nice, so I'm none the wiser. But the Durham place is the first sign I've seen up here that I've lost a year and a half, and because of that I'm not inclined to think too kindly of its owner.

Dad and I pull up outside Paradise (there isn't a parking space – you park on the lawn). A couple of minutes later, Bryan pulls up beside us and my hiatus time with Dad is over. We all get out of the cars and stand there for a minute. Nobody seems to know what to say or do, so I look at the house and take it in.

It's two storeys, painted a soft weathered grey with white trim. A screened-in porch wraps around three sides, surrounded by day lilies and wild roses. The chimney is crooked and for years now we've been saying the roof will probably need replacing next year, depending on how heavy the winter is. The camp isn't winterised and it has no foundation; it balances on four large granite rocks, one underneath each corner. It's set in a clearing in the woods and it overlooks the lake, with a set of stone steps going down to the beach. Since the house is set apart from the other houses on this side of the lake, the beach is more or less private. A stream runs along one side of the property, from the forest to the lake.

According to family legend, my great-grandfather got this

place for cheap because, as a lawyer, he helped the owner with a complicated family will. He was canny enough to buy land on either side of it, too, so that no one could build close by. The house is furnished with things that were probably second-hand when my great-grandmother brought them here. The whole place creaks when you walk. If you drop a marble on one side of the kitchen, it will roll without stopping to the other side. There is a family of bats living under the eaves, which none of us have ever had the heart to get rid of. The pantry door only opens with the employment of a very specific set of pushes, pulls and twists.

Paradise is family and sunshine, and wood fires and listening to the rain while tucked up with a book. It's long dinners and morning swims, and the sun setting in different colours every night. It's leaving seeds out for the chipmunks and wading in the stream looking for frogs. The house in Connecticut that I grew up in was sold long ago, when Dad married Tessa, but that never bothered me because we had Paradise.

'Anybody want some coffee?' Bryan says finally.

'Sure,' says Dad.

'I think I want to go down to the beach and sit there for a little while,' I say, and before the two men in my life can start another contest over who can be more solicitous of me, I walk away from them, past the house and down the stone steps to the beach. Maybe if I can sit there for long enough, this place will work its magic and my memory will come creeping back, like a stealthy peace, like a secret happiness.

It's a beautiful day – sunny, warm but not hot, with a breeze coming off the lake as there always is in the afternoons. I kick off my tennis shoes, pull off my socks and sink my feet into the warm sand, and for the first time I gaze out over the lake.

The house looks the same. But Morocco Pond is different.

I remember it as a crystal-clear stretch of water, from the beach to the mountains, the shores dotted with wooden camps of all colours and sizes, pines rising behind them. But tall grass-like weeds have grown in the shallows where the stream that runs by Paradise empties into the pond. It looks almost like a floating field, swaying with the waves.

The beach is different too. I've never seen it so small, eaten away by the lake in nibbles and gulps. Usually you can fit a dozen lounge chairs down here; now it's a thin crescent, only about a metre wide, contained on one end by the rocky point and on the other end by the stream. The stream itself is wider than I've ever seen it, even after a big storm, and it's carved a deep channel through the sand that's left.

And for the first time it really hits me and I have to sit down on the sand. My new and unknown boyfriend, the talk of a pandemic, whatever's going on with Nic – all of that is shattering, but it's to a certain extent abstract. All I have to go on is what I've been told and the circumstantial evidence that dances around the real thing but doesn't denote it – the masks; Nic's strange behaviour.

But this. A lake doesn't change its entire nature and appearance overnight. Land doesn't wash away into water all at once. Something has happened here. Something real.

And I have lost seventeen months of my life.

Chapter Seven

There's a sound behind me and almost instantly, a small, cold and wet nose inserts itself between my arm and my body from behind. A tiny white creature climbs onto my lap. In colour, shape and texture, it resembles nothing so much as a cotton ball. It has black eyes and a tiny black nose. Its tail is wagging so hard that its entire body is vibrating with excitement, and this is the main reason that I can tell that it is a dog. It stands up on my lap and starts frantically licking my chin.

'Hey, hey.' I laugh, holding the creature away from my face in self-defence. 'Who are you? Are you a dog or a Q-tip?'

Unable to lick my face, he wriggles and wags and licks the air.

'That's Eebie,' says a voice behind me, and Bryan puts a cup of coffee on the sand beside me, a safe distance from the dog. 'He's happy to see you.'

'Nice to meet you, Eebie,' I say to the dog, who whines with happiness. 'Strange name for a dog.'

'Eebie, as in the initials E.B., which is short for "Existential Breakdown".' Bryan sits on the sand. 'Your dad decided to go home and check on Tessa.'

So it's just me and the man I don't remember dating.

'Existential Breakdown is a very strange name for a dog,' I say. 'Is he yours? I don't remember you having a pet.'

'He's yours. Well ... ours.'

I put down Eebie, who instantly scrambles back up.

'We have a dog together?'

'We do.'

The dog lies down in my lap, belly-up for a scratch. He definitely knows who I am, but I've never seen him in my life.

'I like dogs,' I say. 'But I can't have one. I travel too much.'

'That's exactly what you said when Eebie turned up.'

'I'm sorry, you're going to have to go back a little. You and I started dating, and then we adopted a dog together?'

'No, it was the other way round.'

'Can you fill me in?'

He frowns. Now that he's not wearing a mask, I'm reminded of how good-looking he is. He's got high cheekbones and a strong nose, dark-brown eyes with thick black lashes. He's wearing shorts, and his legs are lean and muscular. Runner's legs.

This is reassuring, I suppose. Everything else is completely upside down, but at least I have decent taste in men.

'OK,' he says. 'I'll try to fill you in. The thing is, that time gets a little vague after the pandemic starts, so I have to think about the dates.'

'A general gist is fine. Start in January 2020.'

'We didn't know each other then – just to say hi. I thought you were beautiful, obviously.'

'Obviously.' But this is nice to know.

'And we introduced ourselves that time when you got my pizza by mistake.'

'It had jalapenos on it. I looked before I gave it to you.'

'So … you do know me, a little.'

'I know your awful taste in pizza. So what happened?'

'Well. We were stuck indoors. When the lockdowns started—'

'*Lockdowns?*'

There is a pause here while Bryan, in very basic terms, tells me what it was like living through a global pandemic.

'Fuck,' I say.

'There's a lot,' he says. 'It was … a lot. Everyone will be able to tell you their experiences.'

'Because everyone remembers living through it. Except for me.'

'In some ways, I envy you a little,' he says, and I look out over the water and try to take it in. But I can't. It's too much.

'Wait. What about the election? Who's President?'

Then he fills me in on *that*, and the Capitol and the violence, and that's another whole thing.

Is nothing normal at all, any more?

'Back to ... how you and I got a dog,' I say.

He nods. 'Right, so in March, I think, when the lockdowns started, you and I were the only people living in the building. The Singhs went to stay with family in New Jersey and the Allens had moved out recently. I didn't even know the Singhs were gone at first. I was working on a pretty big project and I was trying to adjust to working from home and hit deadlines at the same time, because we thought the world was going to go back to normal in a few weeks or months. Nobody was really interacting with anyone in real life at that point. We were all scared of infection. I could hear you moving around sometimes, though. And I heard you playing music. Otherwise, it was ... eerie. It felt as if Philadelphia was completely deserted. There we were, right in the middle of the city and there was hardly any traffic. No sound from the trains. No airplanes. Just sirens. All the time. And then one afternoon in April, you knocked on my door and you had this dog.'

'*I* got the dog?' I look down at Eebie, who has closed his eyes and seems asleep, totally relaxed on my lap.

'You said you went out for some exercise and he was on the front step of the building. He didn't have a collar or tags, and he was dirty and hungry and thirsty, and seemed to want to come in. So you brought him inside and knocked on everyone's door to see if it was their dog, which is why you came to me.'

This does seem plausible. So does the next part, which is that I enlisted Bryan to put on a homemade mask and a pair of latex gloves, and help me go door to door in the neighbourhood, asking around about the dog. They're the actions of a good citizen, but also the actions of a person who has been saddled with responsibility and wants to get rid of it as soon as possible. I don't remember it, but all of this sounds like exactly what I would do.

But, Bryan goes on to tell me, very few people answered their doors and the ones who did didn't want to talk. We called animal shelters, but they weren't able to take any more dogs that day. Apparently they were working on skeleton crews, and there were a lot of abandoned animals in Philly. So we had to keep the dog until a space opened up or until we found the owner. Or, rather, *he* had to keep the dog, because he owned his apartment and my lease didn't allow pets. But I walked the dog and fed him, and frequently smuggled him into my apartment.

'And we kept the dog.' I conclude the story for him.

'We sort of fell into it. He's a great dog, but he's also the dumbest dog ever. He can't do any tricks, he can jump up on chairs but he's too small to jump off them, and most of the time he doesn't remember his name.'

'And what's the story of our relationship?'

He's been talking quite happily – more than I can recall ever hearing him speak before – and comfortably, while I absently scratch Eebie on my lap, but now he goes quiet.

'It's harder to talk about that,' he says, after a little while.

'You don't remember what happened either?' I immediately know my joke has fallen flat. 'Sorry.'

'I do remember,' he says. 'But you don't and that's ... hard.'

'I'm sorry,' I say. 'I didn't forget on purpose.'

'I know. It's OK. Well ... it's not. But you know.' He takes a deep breath. 'Katie, I know this is a lot for you, but I want you to know one thing. I love you. And I believe that before your accident, you loved me. We were happy together. But if ... if you need to take some time, if you need me to leave until you're feeling more yourself ... I can do that.'

His voice is a little rough. His hair is a little long. I like his hands.

I wish I remembered falling in love with him.

'I never thought I'd fall for someone called Bryan,' I say.

'You told me that, too.'

'I'm a terrible person.'

'You're a wonderful person.' He touches my arm, then takes his hand away. 'Do you want me to go? I can get a hotel.'

I can't make any decisions. I don't feel like I have the information to make the right one.

He waits for me to answer – not impatiently, but calmly, looking out over the water. He's doing his best not to put any pressure on me, and I appreciate that, but his presence is a pressure in itself. I have to think about how to act, what to say, how not to hurt him, how I am stunted and wrong.

'Can I decide this tomorrow?' I ask. 'I'm worn out and my head hurts.'

'Of course,' he says right away. 'I'll sleep in the guest room downstairs.'

I look at him. 'Are you angry with me?'

'I'm angry,' he says. 'But not at you.' He stands up and brushes sand off his legs. 'I'll move my things to the guest bedroom.'

Eebie wakes up and scampers after him. Bryan picks him up to carry him up the stairs. I watch the two of them go up to Paradise. I don't know either of them.

So why do I feel sad?

Chapter Eight

I wake up to the scent of something delicious, and, before I can think too much, I'm out of bed, into my robe and halfway down the stairs. My appetite has been sketchy at best since the accident and I'm starving.

Then I pause and recall last night when I went to bed early, exhausted by the day and unable to contemplate any more revelations or emotions. Despite my exhaustion, and the painkillers I'd taken, I lay awake until very late, intensely aware that I was sharing the house with a stranger. I heard Bryan walking around downstairs and talking to Eebie. I heard him getting ready for bed and then a door closing downstairs, the door that used to be to Shane's room, and is now a guest bedroom. And then it was quiet, but I could still feel him in the house.

I was borderline hysterical when I spoke to the doctor about my memory loss, but I wasn't lying – I am not a relationship person. I like going on dates and hooking up with people. I enjoy sex and the heady, fun part of getting to know someone. But I've never wanted to settle down or date anyone long term. The closest I've come, as far as I can recall, was Michel. He was a great guy: fun, handsome, solvent, adventurous, good in bed, Canadian. Basically he was a walking, talking wish list of the perfect man. I extended my stay in Montreal because of him. One night, after an evening of particularly satisfying sex, when I was glowing with perspiration and three orgasms, he wrapped his arms around me, kissed my neck and whispered, 'Do you think it's time we talked about moving in together?'

I split up with him a week later. I felt bad about it, but, after it was finished, I was mostly conscious of being relieved.

Nic told me I was an idiot. That was four years ago.

Or … five and a half.

I'm a financial services consultant, working medium- to short-term projects with international banks. Since my early twenties I've been perpetually on the move, seeing new places, living in rentals, adjusting to time zones, travelling light.

No one chooses that sort of lifestyle because they are prioritising compromise or companionship. I value freedom and flexibility, and autonomy. I have a father who adores me, a stepmother who treats me as her own, a brother whom I love, a best friend who's my rock. And I come back to Paradise every summer. That's everything I need right there.

And breakfast. I need breakfast, right now.

Bryan's in the kitchen, presiding over a skillet that is the source of these amazing scents. Eebie greets me exuberantly and Bryan looks up when I come in, and for a split second his smile is warm and unfettered. But then, like me, he seems to recall what's going on and though he keeps smiling, it's more guarded than before.

'What's in the pan?' I ask, squatting to scratch Eebie's ears.

'Huevos rancheros. It's your—'

'Favourite,' I say, at the same time that he does. 'Spicy?'

'Knock your socks off. How'd you sleep?'

I pour myself some coffee from the pot and lean against the counter to watch him cook. 'Are you making my favourite breakfast so I won't send you to a hotel?'

'No.' Bryan lifts a poached egg and puts it on a crisped tortilla, which he's already arranged on a plate next to some sliced avocado, and adds tomato and pepper sauce. 'I'm making your favourite breakfast because it's your favourite, and I like to do nice things for you because I love you. And also, I like huevos rancheros too.' He gives me the plate. My mouth is watering.

'Are you a chef?'

'I'm a software designer. Let's eat on the porch.'

I follow him to the porch, where the table is already set with cutlery, napkins, glasses and a jug of orange juice. From the way that Bryan takes his seat I can tell that he has already claimed this particular chair as his own, at other meals that I don't remember. Eebie sits at my feet, looking up expectantly.

The eggs are delicious – perfectly cooked so that the yolk runs into the chilli-rich tomato sauce and soaks into the crispy tortilla. 'You are a *good* cook,' I say.

'Thanks, but I have to admit that I'm not very good at things that are not egg-based.'

'Was this … did you make me breakfast every day? I mean … do you?'

'The verb tenses are tricky, aren't they?'

'Yeah.'

'I mostly cook breakfast on weekends. On the weekdays you like to do this overnight-oatmeal jar thing.'

'Do I? I've never heard of it.'

'It's a healthy thing that you started up last autumn.'

'How long have we … been dating?'

'We hooked up in June 2020. And it got more serious in the autumn. Though we didn't go on any actual dates until things started opening up more.'

'So over a year?' I have never dated anyone for that long. 'Have we moved in together? Do we have a joint bank account?'

'Not yet. Your lease is running out in September so you were going to move in with me until we found somewhere we both loved.'

'We were going to move in together? How was I planning to travel for work?'

'During the pandemic, almost everything shifted online.'

'Am I …' Oh God, I can't believe I only just thought of this. 'Are we going to have a baby?'

'We've been using birth control.'

'How's the sex? Can I ask that?'

'The sex is great.'

I can't say I'm surprised about that part. I used to see him sometimes in the hallway after he'd been for a run. He looks good sweaty.

'Whose idea was it to move in together?'

'It was mine, because it's my apartment. But you agreed it was a good idea.'

I let that sink in for a little while as I eat my breakfast. Bryan is eating, too, but he's also watching me.

'I don't recognise myself in this,' I say. 'I know it's insulting and I'm sorry. But ... I am not—'

'Not a relationship person,' he says. 'I know.'

'I said that to you?'

'It's one of the things that you say to define yourself, Katie. You said it to me a lot when we first started seeing each other. Like a shield, almost.'

'It's not a shield, it's the truth.'

He shrugs. 'Seems to me that if you're in a relationship, you are a relationship person.'

'Have I changed that much?'

'I think you're the one to answer that.'

But I can't. I don't have any inner sense of anything having changed.

'A little over a year is not that long,' I say eventually. 'It's hardly any time at all, in the scheme of things. You've still got your own place. You could – you could cut your losses, we could call it a day, no hard feelings on either side. Wouldn't that be easier?'

Bryan doesn't answer. He stands, picks up his plate and leaves the porch.

After a moment, I follow.

He's back in the kitchen, but he's leaning with his arms braced against the counter, head down, eyes closed.

'I'm sorry,' I say. 'That was insensitive of me.'

'You think? Telling me to cut my losses? I've never had anyone break up with me by forgetting me.'

'I wasn't breaking up … I just …'

'I know.' He lets out a long breath. 'It's everything that I've felt in the last year. Everything *you've* felt. All gone, like that.'

'I'm sorry.'

'It's as if you're a different person, but you look and speak and move in exactly the same way. And I can't touch you, or tell you how I feel, or share anything with you. And then you say, blithely, *we could call it a day*.'

'I'm sorry,' I say for the third time.

He doesn't look at me. He doesn't move.

'Maybe my memory will come back,' I say.

This is all I can offer him.

I pat foundation and concealer around my eyes with the tips of my fingers, to cover the bruises. Some of the swelling has gone down, but they're still not their correct shape so I put on sunglasses.

When I reach the end of the drive, there's a car outside the old Durham place and a woman kneeling as she digs next to the tomato plants. She looks up as I approach, and waves and calls out. 'Hi!'

This is normal up at the pond. You say hello to everyone.

I hesitate and she stands up, brushes dirt from the knees of her trousers, and walks across the lawn to me. She's older than me, late thirties or early forties, with long straight hair pulled back into a ponytail. She's wearing a big flannel shirt and jeans, both rolled up.

'How are you?' she asks.

I lie. 'Oh, I'm good. How are you?'

'Not bad. I'm going to try some marigolds in there. Apparently they help with pests.'

'The house looks great,' I say.

'Yeah, thanks. I'm pleased with it. It's a beautiful spot.'

I have never been a person who readily admits her problems. I don't even really like asking a question unless I know the answer already – and there have been too many of those questions lately.

But this is my reality now, for who knows how long, so I brace myself and say, 'Have we met before?'

'Not formally. I'm Audrey.' She holds out a hand, notices it's dirty, and laughs. 'Maybe we'll shake later.'

'Katie. But have we... have we talked at all?' Her surprise is evident, so I add, 'I got in an accident a few days ago and it's affected my memory.'

'Oh! You're the person who got knocked off her bike?'

'That's me. Local celebrity.'

'I saw your black eyes, but I didn't want to say anything.'

I guess the makeup and the sunglasses haven't worked so well.

'And it's given you actual amnesia, like in the movies?'

'Yes.' I now know that this is going to be spread all around Morocco Pond within hours. Everything always is. But it was going to be, sooner or later anyway.

'Sucks to be you,' she says.

This makes me snort a laugh. 'Yeah. It does.'

'So you're going around re-introducing yourself to all the neighbours?'

'Actually I wanted to ask if you'd seen the accident. Or if you'd seen me riding my bike, before it. I don't remember where I was going or anything about that day, so it's useful if I can try to put things together.'

'I think I was out in the canoe that morning, so I didn't see the accident, or even know anything had happened until later, when your partner – Byron?'

'Bryan.'

'Bryan, that's right. He knocked on the door, asking if I'd seen anything, and I helped him pull the bike out of the ditch. They were both in bad shape. The bike and Bryan, I mean. He was worried out of his mind. He had no idea what had happened. Is he OK?'

No. He really isn't.

'Yeah, he's fine. We're both fine. Just … my black eyes and I'm pretty sore. And my memory.'

'Well. Don't worry about forgetting me. We don't have any memories together.' She considers. 'Though I've been stupid, haven't I? I could have said that I loaned you money. Is it too late to change my answer?'

'Maybe you'll get lucky and I'll lose my memory again.'

'I'll keep my fingers crossed.' She nods at me in a friendly way and goes back to her digging.

I stand on the end of the drive and look either way. Some of the vision is obscured by trees, but it's difficult to believe I could have missed an ATV coming. They're noisy. I must have cycled out right in front of him if he didn't have any time to brake, or he must have been going way too fast. Or possibly both.

A familiar figure comes round the bend and I can't help but smile at the sight of Nic, in shorts, T-shirt and baseball cap, walking her mother's two dogs. Statler and Waldorf are two big basset hounds – Statler brown and white, and Waldorf black, brown and white – and they are pulling at the leashes. Nic says that you can't walk a hound – they walk you.

I wave to her and she stops, as if she's forgotten something and is about to turn back for it. But the dogs spot me and pull her forward, their ears and jowls flapping and their tails wagging.

'Hey,' I say, kneeling down and greeting the dogs like the long-lost friends they are. They immediately set to sniffing my legs to catch all traces of Eebie. 'If I'd known you were coming, I'd have brought some cheese.'

'You're feeling better,' Nic says, the length of the leashes apart from me.

'Yeah. More like a person.' I stand and wipe off my legs.

'Do you remember anything yet?'

I shake my head. 'I was hoping that the accident scene would prompt some memories. But I've got nothing.'

She looks at the road, where there's a set of skidmarks on the asphalt, presumably from the ATV. 'Which direction do you think you were headed?' she asks.

'I don't know. Bryan said he was at the cemetery. So maybe that way? Or I could have been heading to see you. Did I say anything to you that morning?'

'No.' She examines the skidmarks as if they contain the secrets of the universe. Then she straightens and points at the side of the road, a section where the ferns and brush have been flattened. 'That's where you went off after you were hit.'

'Can you tell which direction I would have been going?'

'No.' She nods at the way she's come. 'That's where the ATV was coming from. He was staying at the campground.'

Despite how weird I feel after my accident, with a big hole in my past, this sort of conversation is familiar and comforting to me. Nic and I spent most of our childhoods pretending to be sleuths and investigating mysteries, both real and imagined.

'Remember that summer we spent sneaking around the old hotel?' I ask her, just to anchor the two of us together in a memory. 'Before it got pulled down?'

'We're lucky we didn't get killed.' She's staring at the skidmarks again.

I wander to the side of the road. I have scrapes on my legs that were probably caused by these bushes. Behind them there are a few trees, but most of them are slender choke cherries and birches, so the obvious candidate for The Tree That Stole My Memory is the thick, tall spruce.

I go over and put my hand on the trunk. My head is evidently softer than this tree, because there are no marks on it at all, only rough bark. Fragrant sap leaks from it in places, solid droplets of amber. This tree is more than a hundred years old, older than most of the camps around here. If trees have memories, it has seen this road being built, it has seen cars going faster and faster, the shores slowly inhabited; it has seen generations of children and even more generations of deer.

'It's this one,' I say. 'This tree has the last year and a half of my life.'

'Too bad it can't talk,' says Nic.

'Yeah.'

'Or maybe it's a good thing.'

I've been studying the tree, but at this I glance at her. 'What do you mean by that?'

'I mean, you have a boyfriend you can't even remember. How embedded can he really be in your life?'

'He says we were going to move in together.'

'That doesn't sound like you.'

'I know.' I chew a nail. 'It's all very weird.'

'Whereas you remember *me* perfectly. Right?'

'Of course. Like I said in the hospital.' But that conversation was so strained and vague, like one of those dreams where no one seems to understand you. 'Why were you crying?'

She shrugs and bends to scratch Waldorf behind the ear. 'It was a shock seeing you hurt, I guess. I'm just saying, maybe this guy isn't so important to you if all it takes for you to forget him is a knock on the head.'

'I did forget an entire pandemic too.' I wade through the brush and back onto the road. 'And a dog. Did you know we had a dog?'

'I'd heard about that.'

'Come back to Paradise with me, Nic. I could use you there. I need someone familiar – someone who knows me.'

She hesitates, then straightens. 'I've got to give these guys breakfast.'

'But let's talk soon?'

'Sure, sure.' I watch her hurry off. Usually those dogs go crazy at the mention of food, but she has to pull them along behind her.

We haven't solved any mysteries at all.

Chapter Nine

I am one of these people who have their phone permanently glued to their person. My phone is literally my job. I also travel a lot, so my phone is also my diary, my memory, and my main link to home and people that I know. But I'll admit I take it to extremes. I put it on the table in restaurants. I keep it beside my bed and take it into the bathroom with me. I have it plugged into my Bluetooth earbuds when I'm driving or at the gym. I ignore all that well-meaning advice about not looking at a screen for an hour before you go to sleep. I've had to turn off the function that tracks my usage time because the shame is too great.

My phone addiction is more than a habit. It's a subconscious hormonal co-dependence between me and that small case of computer chips.

Now, my phone is an objective witness to months of memories that I have lost. And I can't find it.

It's taken me at least two hours of courage-building even to look for it. I don't really want to see the date on the screen, or see the likely frantic messages from people who have found out about the accident. And the likely sea of emails I don't remember, and photographs I have no recollection of taking, is a lot to deal with. In fact, if I don't look too closely at the lake or the beach, Paradise is so similar to how it always is, that I could probably indefinitely ignore that I have any problem.

If it weren't for Bryan. Who's giving me space, but who is indubitably here, along with his expectations and memories and emotions. And a small fluffy dog.

But my phone isn't on my bedside table or in my handbag. It's not in my jacket pocket or on the kitchen table, or in the car or anywhere else obvious. Did it get smashed in the accident?

I call downstairs. 'Bryan? Do you know where my phone is?'

It feels like an intimate thing to ask, somehow. He comes to the bottom of the stairs and looks up.

'Unless you moved it,' he says, 'it's in your underwear drawer.'

Well, that's one place I definitely didn't look. I do. It's there, under a pile of bras.

I call out to him again. 'Why is it in my underwear drawer?'

He comes upstairs. I close my underwear drawer, but he stays at the top of the stairs and talks to me from there.

'You put it there when we arrived.'

'Why?' It's also turned off. I turn it on.

'You said you wanted to forget about everything and live in the moment.'

'And you let me say that bullshit out loud?'

He leans on the wall. 'You said you wanted to be less connected to your phone, so you've been turning it off outside of working hours.'

I stare at him. 'Seriously? How long have I been doing this?'

'Pretty much as long as we've been dating.'

'Wow.' I glance at the screen. I have almost no battery left. 'Do you know where I put my charger?'

'You broke your charger,' he says. 'You've been using mine.' He disappears for a moment, then comes upstairs with it in hand.

'I'm sorry,' I say. 'I hate not remembering anything.'

'I know. It's OK. I'll give you some space.'

He goes downstairs and in a few minutes I hear the screen door close. From the upstairs window, I can see him heading to the beach with a folding chair and a book. I wait until he's settled, then I plug in his charger, connect my phone and power it up.

But I can't look at it. It's become something foreign, evidence of a person I don't remember becoming. Instead I leave it on the bedside table, go down to the beach and tell Bryan I'm going to take Eebie for a walk.

Nic is the only person who can really give me answers. And she hasn't yet.

Morocco Pond campground is about a mile from Paradise, following the main road that curves around the lake, and then down a small paved side-road through trees. It's marked with a large wooden sign with a hand-painted loon on one side (as you arrive) and a moose on the other (as you leave). While our side of the pond is quiet, it's high season here; as I approach the campground I'm passed by a group of six ATVs – the drivers all wave, which is how I know none of them are the one who hit me – and I can hear the sound of children in the playground, dogs barking, and the distant sound of splashing and laughter on the beach.

The campground itself is a wide, cleared area surrounded by pine trees, with a narrow path down to the lake. Right in the middle is a wooden platform that sometimes serves as a stage. All the pitches are occupied, either with RVs or with big family-style tents, grills and plastic chairs and tables in front of them. It all looks incredibly familiar and it smells familiar too – the scent of fresh pine, charcoal briquettes and hot dogs, with the faintest whiff of chemical toilets. But, then again, ninety per cent of the business is made up of regular customers who return year after year.

When we were growing up, Shane and I considered the campground to be the social high-point of the lake. There were always loads of kids, always a kickball game to join or water chicken to play. They were local kids with strong Maine accents, who knew how to ride an ATV or a jet ski, who used 'wicked' as an adverb, who ate red hot dogs and Humpty Dumpty chips. In the evening, there was always music – either blaring out of speakers, or – before Gene died – from the occasional folk-music jams featuring Gene Leblanc and his buddies.

Shane loved it even more than I did – when he got better, he wanted a taste of normal kid life – but I also spent plenty of time here. I had my first kiss at the campground, in the back of the equipment shed, with a boy from Lewiston who was down here visiting his cousins. I learnt how to play Marco Polo on this beach and I learnt how to make perfect s'mores at the fire pit, which was lit on every clear night in summer. Nic's mother, Jeannette, is the best cook I have ever known. Before my dad married Tessa, she was the closest thing to a mother that I had. And before he died, Nic's father, Gene, was always ready to play his fiddle for us or teach us how to play cards.

I loved their house, too, because it wasn't like any other house I knew. Apparently it started out as a mobile home back in the seventies, when there wasn't a permanent resident of the campground. But then Jeannette and Gene got married, and decided they wanted to live there year-round, and instead of building a house from scratch, Gene built the extra rooms they needed around the mobile home. Over the years, he added more and more, often with salvaged materials, so the house is a bit of a hodgepodge, one room leading off another, all on one level and sprawling over the side of the campground. The kernel of the house is the original trailer, but with most of the fixtures stripped out so that became the living room.

When I was a kid, Nic's house felt so different to the suburban houses I was used to, that were all basically the same. I liked how the floors of the rooms were on different levels and how none of the windows were quite alike. It felt like a ramshackle fairytale cottage, something that didn't follow any of the normal rules.

Nic always acted shy about it – she usually asked to come to Paradise instead and we always had sleepovers at my camp instead of her house. I only noticed once we were older, around thirteen or fourteen. When I asked her why, she said, 'Because it's a trailer.'

'It's only a trailer on the inside,' I said. 'You'd never be able to tell from the outside.'

'It's a trailer all the way through,' she replied, and didn't want to discuss it any more.

I pause at the entrance to the campground and look around. I'm relieved to see that here at least, nothing has changed. I could be myself at age nine. I could be myself as the adult that I remember.

As I'm walking across to the house, it suddenly occurs to me that Nic might not be here. She lives in Portland for most of the year and helps her mother with the campground in the summer. She might have only been visiting for the morning.

A woman sitting in a lawn chair next to one of the RVs calls out to me. 'Who you after, dear?'

'I'm looking for Nic.'

'She's not in. Jeannette is, though, if you want to visit.'

There's a muffled woof from inside the house and Eebie strains on the leash. I let him pull me over to the house, where I knock on the door. A torrent of barking and scuffling erupts within, followed by a sharp call. 'Pipe down, you hounds.' A moment later, Jeannette opens the door.

Relief washes over me. She looks exactly as I remember her. She hasn't even aged and I'm pretty sure that's the same flannel shirt she has had for as long as I've known her. Her freckled, weatherbeaten face lights up at the sight of me and she opens the door wide.

'Come in! Come in,' she says. 'These hounds will only be noisy a minute.'

Eebie can't wait to get inside to his new friends. He goes ahead of me into the house, where Statler and Waldorf immediately engage in an elaborate greeting ritual of sniffing and tail-wagging.

'You got a dog!' says Jeannette. 'Cute little thing. Like a puffball mushroom.'

'I had to carry him half of the way here.'

'What's his name?'

'Eebie.' Eebie glances up at his name and then goes back to

investigating the hounds. Jeannette has always had hounds – beagles or bassets or foxhounds, or a mixture of all three. The current pair are brothers and I remember when she adopted them, when her last beagle, Kermit, was about eleven years old and starting to fail. She didn't want to be without a dog for even a day.

'It feels like an age since I've seen you,' Jeannette says, leading me to her kitchen. This, too, is completely unchanged – pine cupboards, an oilcloth-covered table with mismatched chairs, an old gas cooker.

'I don't believe you've still got that fridge,' I say, delighted.

'Oh, ayuh, they built things to last in those days. Coffee?'

I accept and take a seat at the table. 'I was looking for Nic, but I'm glad I've found you.'

'She's around here somewhere.' Jeannette stands in the middle of the kitchen, peering around as if looking for her daughter, and I laugh.

'I'm glad to visit with you,' I say.

'I thought I had some cookies, but I must have eaten them.' She opens a cupboard and looks in.

'That's OK, I had a big breakfast. Coffee is great.' Though, truthfully, Jeannette makes the best cookies I have ever eaten and I wouldn't have said no to one, or maybe four. She sits across from me with her coffee. Eebie is sniffing around the kitchen linoleum looking for fallen and forgotten titbits, with the bassets following his every move like benevolent, saggy-faced shadows.

'What's wrong with your eyes, dear?'

'I got in an accident. Did you hear about it?'

'No, what happened?'

Nic hasn't told her mom, which is strange, but maybe she didn't want to worry her.

I give Jeannette a rundown of what's happened: the bike, the ATV. 'And now I've got a bit of a memory problem.'

'Oh, ayuh, don't we all,' says Jeannette, and I laugh and decide, in that moment, that I'm not going to ask her lots of questions about Nic or the lake, or the pandemic or anything that's changed. I'm going to sit here in her kitchen and talk about dogs, the weather and pie, like we have a million times before, and pretend that everything in my world is exactly the way it is meant to be.

An hour later, I've had two cups of coffee and Jeannette has taught Eebie how to do a high five, and I'm feeling sane and comfortable for the first time in days. 'Thank you.' I get up and hug her. 'It's good to see you.'

'Always glad to visit,' says Jeannette, hugging me back. She smells of coffee and my childhood.

'Tell Nic I came by, OK?'

'I will.'

She walks me to the door and I say goodbye to the dogs. I'm going to be covered in dog hair and basset slobber, but that's comforting too.

'Come by any time – I'll have cookies for you.'

'Thanks, Jeannette.'

'Bye, Cynthia!'

By then I'm already down the porch steps and Eebie is pulling me on to the next big adventure, so I just wave and don't correct her, but the mistake gives me a little twist of pain in my gut.

Cynthia is my mother's name.

Chapter Ten

I was seven when our mother left. Shane was undergoing leukemia treatment and it went on for what seemed like for ever, but in
reality was maybe six months. He hadn't started kindergarten yet.

I was young, but I have a few memories of our mother. I
remember that she was pretty, with auburn hair that neither of
her children inherited. I remember her laugh and I remember
one time when she yelled at me for giving a chocolate bar to the
neighbours' dog. (Shane did it, but I kept the secret.) I remember
she wore a vanilla-scented perfume. My strongest memory is
probably her teaching me how to swim in the lake, with one hand
under my tummy to keep me afloat.

I felt so safe. That's why it's my best memory, and also my
worst.

She left the day after Shane's fifth birthday, or maybe technically two days. That year, he had to have his birthday in the
hospital in Connecticut. Even though he was sick for what felt
like most of his childhood (and therefore mine), I only remember
him having his birthday in the hospital once. I remember we
bought a big chocolate cake with Oreo frosting, because that was
his favourite, and we brought chocolate ice cream in a cooler. My
grandparents brought balloons and the nurses surprised us by all
turning up in silly pirate costumes. Shane was too sick to have
friends outside the hospital, but three of the other leukemia kids
were there and they all piled on Shane's bed and played video
games. I remember two of them were bald, which frightened me

a little bit. Shane still had all his hair at that point, though he wouldn't for much longer.

Shane's present was a Hot Wheels set, so Dad set it up around his bed and Shane and the other three kids all took turns whizzing cars down a ramp and seeing who could get them the farthest. Everyone had cake, including all the hospital staff. I remember all of us, together as a family, cleaning up the wrapping paper and the food. Mom made it a game, to see who could throw a paper cup into the garbage can from the farthest away. She used to be good at making boring things fun.

I really loved her.

Then it was time to go home and leave Shane behind. After the party, the car felt very quiet. When Shane was sick, it seemed like most things were quiet and that we were always waiting for bad news. Mom and Dad talked in low voices in the front and I sat in the back, trying to rub a bit of chocolate frosting off my tights.

And then, the night of the day after his birthday, I woke up in bed, suddenly. It was dark out and there was some kind of a sound outside. I didn't know what it was, but it was in the front of the house. In Connecticut we lived in the suburbs and a couple of weeks before, Dad had said that a raccoon turned over our garbage cans. So, excited to see a raccoon, I crept to the window and looked out.

It wasn't a raccoon. There was a car on the road, engine running, lights on, and my mom was opening the passenger door. I guess the sound I heard was the house door closing or the sound of the trunk being shut. I watched as she got in the car and it drove away.

The car was red, and our car was blue, so I didn't think that Dad was driving, and I knew that my parents would never leave me alone at night, but I thought maybe she was going to the hospital. I went downstairs to check. Dad was sitting on the couch in the living room. The couch was this flowered thing that was sort of itchy when you sat on it in shorts. My dad was looking ahead of him, at the wall or something.

'Is Shane OK?' I asked him. We asked that question a lot.

'He's fine, Kittycat.'

I remember quite clearly that he wasn't crying, so I knew he was telling the truth. He always told the truth. He did look sad, though, and lonely, so I climbed onto the couch with him and lay down with my head in his lap. I was wearing pyjamas and the couch didn't itch me. He put his hand on my hair and stroked it, and I fell asleep. I don't think we said anything to each other.

I woke up in my own bed, so he must have carried me upstairs. It was light outside but I didn't hear anyone moving around. But the house was often quiet, when Shane was in the hospital. I was used to it.

I went into my parents' bedroom to see if Mom was asleep. Dad wasn't in bed and the bed was made. Something made me open the door to their closet and I saw that all of my mother's clothes and shoes were gone. Every single thing.

My dad made me toast when I came downstairs. He put two pieces on my plate and said I could spread as much jam on them as I wanted. He did this pretty often, because Mom usually slept late on weekends and sometimes didn't emerge until lunch. After I finished, he told me we were going to see Shane.

I didn't ask why Mom wasn't with us. I didn't ask why her clothes had gone or where she was. I think even at that age, I could tell that these were dangerous questions and I wouldn't like the answers.

In Shane's hospital room, the walls painted all over with Winnie-the-Pooh, Dad told me to sit on Shane's bed and he stood near it and said, 'Kitty, Shaney, I have to tell you something. Your mother has gone to live somewhere else. She's not going to live with us any more.'

'Where did she go?' said Shane.

'I don't know.'

'Why?' I asked.

'She doesn't love me any more,' Dad said. 'But she loves the two of you. She'll always love the two of you.'

'Why doesn't she love you any more?' I asked. I couldn't imagine not loving my dad, who was tall and handsome, and kind and smart, and who was a lawyer, like I was going to be one day.

'Because she's fallen in love with someone else. But that doesn't matter, Kitty. What matters is that it's not your fault and that she loves the two of you very, very much.'

'Who did she fall in love with?' Shane demanded.

'It's no one you know,' Dad said. 'What's important is, that I'm still here and I'm always going to be here. The three of us are still a family and I'm going to take care of you. I'm not going anywhere.'

'Mommy's not coming back to see me?' said Shane. He started to cry.

'She'll come back to see you. I know she will.' He bent over to hug Shane, and held out his arm for me to come and join them in a family hug.

But I didn't. I stayed frozen on the end of the bed. I said, 'If she loves me and Shane, then she shouldn't have left.'

Dad didn't say anything in reply to this. I guess he couldn't, because he was trying not to poison us against our mother. But it left me with a question that was never answered, not fully.

I found out later, from my Gramma Stone, that Mom went to live in Canada with a man she'd met as a teenager and who she'd been writing to for a while, unknown to my dad. Gramma didn't know where she was in Canada, and she said the name of the country with scorn; it was as if the entire country was a vast, unknown, shadowy state, the place where errant mothers disappeared.

A couple of years later, around Christmas, two letters came in the mail. One for Shane and one for me. They had Canadian stamps with maple leaves on them and they were addressed to

Miss Katherine Jane Stone and *Master Shane Joseph Stone*. Dad gave them to us without saying anything and he let us decide what to do with them.

I never asked Shane what he did with his letter, addressed so formally, as if it were from a stranger. Maybe he read it. But I brought mine up to my bedroom, and, carefully and slowly, I used a pair of scissors to cut the unopened letter into long shreds. Then I cut each shred crosswise into tiny, and then tinier, squares. I saw edges of my mother's handwriting, but I did not see any of her words. Then I gathered up all the squares and I put them into my shiny pink wastepaper bin. I remember how they looked, tiny pieces like confetti, that didn't mean anything.

See? I remember a lot of things that matter.

Chapter Eleven

By the time I get back to Paradise, my phone is charged up. I curl up on my bed, take a deep breath, and unlock the screen.

The new messages pop up first. They are all from Bryan – texts, missed calls and voicemails, all on the day of the accident. I listen to one of the voicemails: 'Katie, where are you? What's happening? Are you OK? Get in touch as soon as you can, sweetheart, please.'

He sounds breathless, terrified, desperate. I delete it right away.

My phone tells me that he called me six times after leaving that message. Before that, I made a call to my dad when I arrived in Maine. Before that, a tally of frequent calls, some with names I recognise, a few I don't.

Am I going to have to call all of these people to try to put together the pieces of the last year and a half?

I open my calendar app and scroll through the months. I see dentist appointments, I see birthdays, meetings, work deadlines, nights out with friends, flight details.

'Fuck, fuck, fuck, fuck,' I mutter, because this is not merely the small matter of my personal life, but also the millions of daily interactions, personal and business, that have disappeared. Am I even going to be able to work again?

I call Nic, but she doesn't pick up. 'Call me,' I say to her voicemail, and then I stare at my phone screen again with dread.

I check my photo library.

My last photo was taken five days ago. It's a selfie of me and

Bryan in a car. We're both smiling. He looks happy. Do I look happy? Do I look calm?

It's a normal selfie, albeit one that I don't remember taking. I'm doing my normal selfie smile.

I scroll back further. Here is me wearing a yellow dress that I've never seen before. It's cute. I'm cute. Bryan is standing beside me, holding my hand. In another, he's kissing my cheek and I'm grinning directly at the camera. There are a lot of photos of Eebie, a ridiculous amount of them, and nearly as many of Bryan and me. Eating cheesesteaks in Reading Terminal. Striking a pose in front of the art museum. Hiking on a trail surrounded by trees.

These photos are all of me. It's undeniable. My eyes, my hair, my clothes, my smile. I recognise myself in that faintly out-of-body way you have when you look at photos of yourself, and think: *is that really how I look to everyone else?* Yes. This is what I look like to everyone else. This is what I look like to me, even though I don't remember being the person in these photos. Which brings me back to that question again.

This person who is me and yet who isn't: is she happy?

I can't think too deeply about this, so I automatically open my texts to send a message to Nic, or at this rate maybe an essay, but when I see the last text in our conversation, one that I don't remember, I freeze.

Nic has written:

I made a mistake. Can we go back to how it was before?

I haven't replied to her.

It is dated 13 June, 2020. Over a year ago.

And when I check my call log, I haven't called her since the day before that.

What has happened, that I haven't spoken to my best friend in just over a year?

Chapter Twelve

Bryan and I are lying on our backs on floats on the lake. We're far enough out so that we're not close to the weeds and when I look up, all I can see is blue sky and fluffy clouds. In the distance, a bird circles on the air currents. It might be an eagle – it's too far away to tell.

'Tell me about yourself,' I say, trailing my fingers in the water.

He laughs. 'Is this a first-date situation?'

'Is that what we did on our first date?'

'We didn't really have a first date, in a getting-to-know-you sense. We couldn't go out anywhere for months, so when we did go on a real date, we already knew each other.'

'So tell me what I need to know.'

He turns his head on his float so he's looking at me. 'Did you Google me?'

'Yeah. You're a software engineer, like you said. You grew up in Michigan. Tell me the stuff I can't find on Facebook. Favourite colour, family history, first kiss, all of the normal stuff that I couldn't find on Google.'

'Blue. I'm the third of five kids. My dad is a high-school biology teacher and before my mom took early retirement, she was an administrator at the school he teaches in, which is how they met. I have my oldest sister, Rebecca, who's also a teacher and is married with one kid and another on the way; then there's Polly who's a lawyer and we never stop torturing her about that; then there's me and then there's Ed, who dropped out of college to give juggling workshops, and Isaac, who's eighteen years younger than

Rebecca and the baby of the family. He wants to be a tattoo artist and it's a measure of how chilled out my mother has grown that she is not freaking out about that.'

'Why do you torture your sister for being a lawyer?'

'She's the most conservative of all of us and she works as a patent lawyer. We call her "Better Call Poll".'

'I'm guessing you had a happy childhood,' I say.

'Most of the time. We're a big, loud Jewish family. There was the normal sibling rivalry. My parents went through a rough patch when I was a teenager, but they got through it.'

'Have I met your family?'

'No,' he says, and paddles his arms so his float spins around in a circle. 'Not yet.'

I gaze up at the sky. That is definitely an eagle up there; it's big, with a splay of feathers at the end of each wing. I imagine what Bryan and I look like to him, lying on our backs in the water instead of soaring high above.

I dreamt about this. Before I woke up in hospital. Or was it a dream? Was it more like a clue?

I think about Nic's final message on my phone, from last summer.

'What did I tell you about Nic?' I ask Bryan. 'Have I talked about her?'

'You said that you'd been best friends with her since you were nine and that she was dating your brother.'

'What else?'

'You said I'd love her. Why are you asking about that?'

'Not important.' I don't feel like explaining it to him when I can't explain it to myself. I kick my feet in the water and change the subject. 'Did I tell you that I had a little bit of a crush on you?'

'You sure did.' He smiles over at me and I have a flicker of something – memory? Desire?

A feeling that I know his smile. The way the corners of his eyes crinkle up. This is familiar to me – lying next to him, with him smiling.

'What's the matter?' he asks.

'Nothing,' I say, because I don't want to get either of our hopes up. 'Why did we name our dog "Existential Breakdown"?'

'I insisted. You wanted to call him Ringo.'

'Why did you insist?'

He paddles his float a little closer to me before he responds.

'Because we'd spent two days trying to find the dog's owner and no one would take him. We walked for what felt like miles and it was hot. And the city felt like a ghost town and we were supposed to stay in our apartments all alone. There was nothing but bad news on television. And we sat six feet apart on your balcony, drinking beer, complete strangers to each other, and you said that if you had to stay in this place for one more minute you were going to have an existential breakdown. And I pointed to Eebie and said, "You've got him instead." And so we called him E.B.'

I try to imagine it. It is not that difficult. I hate feeling weak, and trapped, and powerless. And then I imagine taking all that fear and frustration, and naming a little fluffy dog after it so it was something that I could contain. Bryan, somehow, even when we were strangers – like we are again, now – understood me well enough to know that it would help.

'I like you,' I say to Bryan.

'Yes,' he says. 'I like you too.'

Chapter Thirteen

I am at the hospital, being tested again. Counting my accident, this is only the second time I have ever been at Casablanca hospital as a patient. I spent quite a few hours here as a visitor, though, when Shane had leukemia. At the time I took it for granted that he would continue his treatments up in Maine while we were at Paradise, but it occurs to me now how much organising our dad would have done to take leave from work for the whole summer, and arrange for Shane's chemotherapy to take place here instead of Connecticut, and find childcare for me while he was in the hospital with Shane – all so that his children would be able to spend their summers at the same place where he had spent all of the summers of his life.

Still, though, Casablanca hospital is not a place of happy memories for me so I perch on the edge of my chair, ready to bolt as soon as the doctor is finished. Bryan is outside in the waiting room; I'm not allowed to drive yet.

'Have any memories started to come back?' asks the doctor, who has ascertained that my head hurts much less, I'm not feeling dizzy and I haven't had any seizures.

'Not really. I get déjà vu sometimes. But it's difficult to tell whether that's normal déjà vu, or genuine recollections.'

He nods. 'I'm confident it will come back. It might be slowly. You don't live up here, do you? It might be easier when you're in familiar surroundings.'

'I've been here every summer of my life. It's the most familiar place I know.'

'Well, that's good.' He starts typing into his computer.

'The thing is, it's not just memories. It's ... I don't know who I am.'

He looks up. 'You have a sense of dissociation?'

'I'm not sure what that means.'

'You feel separate from yourself. Almost as if you're watching yourself from a distance.'

I think about that. 'Not exactly. It's more that I've always had a good sense of where I fit in, you know? I can usually understand how people relate to me and I can predict my own behaviour. But now it feels as if everything and everyone have changed in some way, and they don't quite make sense any more.'

'You're describing what I've heard is a common feeling, post-pandemic.'

'But I don't remember the pandemic. I'm missing vital pieces of myself. And I'm missing vital pieces of other people, too. And a lot of how you define yourself is by how other people perceive you, right? So how do I know who I am, when I don't know who other people are?'

The doctor smiles. 'This is more philosophy than medicine, I'm afraid.'

'Great. Now I've got to read Descartes.'

'We all change,' says the doctor, sounding a little impatient this time. 'This could be a chance for a fresh start.'

Chapter Fourteen

My stepmother, Tessa, is feeling better, so Dad has arranged for the family to come up to the lake for the afternoon. He's promised to bring ribs for the grill and Tessa is making coleslaw and a chocolate cake. I have zero choice in this; they informed me this morning.

'I'll make potato salad,' says Bryan, but I shake my head.

'No. You go buy beer. I'll make the potato salad.'

I need something to do with my hands.

By the time my dad and stepmom arrive at Paradise, I've made the most perfect bowl of potato salad ever – a delicate shade of mustard, studded with green onions, with bright-red paprika sprinkled over the top. It's covered in plastic wrap and resting in the fridge. In contrast, I am not restful at all. I tidy the house and I pick some wildflowers to put in a glass jar. I change my outfit twice.

I'm not usually nervous about seeing my family, but this is different. There are too many relationships to deal with at once. Too much that I might have forgotten.

Bryan, wisely, stocks the fridge and cooler with beer and spends a long time cleaning the grill, out of my way.

I go out to greet my parents. Tessa gets out first. She's dyed her hair red. She rushes over to me and hugs me close to her substantial and magnificent bosom. 'Oh, my God, baby girl, I've been so worried about you!'

I close my eyes and hug her back. My father didn't start dating again until I was nearly grown up, but Tessa has never restrained herself from mothering me and, to be honest, I love it. Both Shane and I lapped it up, and we still do. Tessa didn't have any biological children, and we hadn't seen our mother for years. It was a match made in heaven.

'How are you feeling?' I ask her chest. Tessa is several inches shorter than me but she hugs from the bosom – it's just the way she is.

'Oh, I'm fine. I had a little bug. You, though!' She steps back, holding my shoulders still, and clucks over my bruises.

'I'm sure it will all be OK,' I say, lying.

'Actually, we stopped by Walmart and picked you up something.' My dad holds out a Barbie-themed bicycle helmet, in pink.

'Ha ha,' I say, and put it on as Shane drives up in his pickup truck. I go over to help him unload the food he's brought and it's only when we're safely inside the kitchen that I reveal my true purpose: to get him alone so I can ask him some questions.

'What is going on with Nic?'

'You tell me.' He cracks open a beer and offers me one.

'Is she coming later?'

'Don't think so.'

'Why didn't she come with you?'

'This is a family thing.'

'Nic is family.'

He shrugs and drinks his beer. As usual, I am going to have to drag everything out of him, so I prepare myself for the long haul, and ask, 'Are the two of you having problems?'

'How is that any of your business?'

'You're my brother. She's my best friend.'

'Don't I know it.'

'What does that mean?'

'Nothing.'

'Why is everyone acting so weird?'

'Look who's talking. Can we drop this and just have a family barbecue?'

'I just want to understand why Nic isn't here. Did you have a fight?'

He gazes out the screen door. 'If I'd known I was going to be interrogated, I would've stayed home and watched the game.'

I huff impatiently. 'Can you get her to call me, at least?'

'Sure. Now aren't you supposed to be resting, instead of acting like the Spanish Inquisition?'

He picks up his beer and walks out the door.

We eat at the picnic table, which has been moved to the other side of the house because the stream has eroded away part of the yard. Shane, the coward, sits as far away from me as he can, on one end next to Tessa and across from Bryan. I'm on the other end next to Tessa and across from my dad. It's as if I've been located on purpose next to the two people who haven't changed at all, and who are oblivious to the tension all around us.

I'm wishing I asked Shane more questions, like whether he knows about what happened between me and Nic, and why she sent me that text about making a mistake. Though it's unlikely he would tell me anything anyway. He has always been like this, ever since he was a little kid. He never used to talk about being in the hospital, or being sick, or about how he felt about our mother abandoning us. As if talking about it would make it all the more real. And I know it's a man thing, being strong and silent, but it's not an *every* man thing.

But, frustratingly, the conversation has split itself along gender lines. Dad, Bryan and Shane are all talking about sports, while Tessa is more interested in asking me about my recipe for potato salad and about how she went to a cookout where one of the ladies put raisins in hers and caused a huge controversy. Every time Shane speaks, I bristle, because why is it OK to talk about the Phillies with a guy he barely knows and not with his sister about his girlfriend?

Listening with half an ear to their conversation, I hear Shane telling Dad that the camp at Howard Pond should be ready to have the water turned on tomorrow.

I interrupt them. 'Whose camp on Howard Pond?'

'You know, my uncle Frank's,' says Tessa.

'You probably don't remember,' Dad says. 'Frank passed away in February and he left the camp to her. We've been going up there and doing some renovations. Shane's project-managing it, doing a lot of it himself.'

'Oh, that's nice. What's the market like? Do you think you'll be able to sell it quickly?'

The table goes quiet.

'What?' I ask.

'Well,' says Dad. 'We were talking about winterising it and moving in there year-round.'

'Why would you do that? You've got a house and this place.'

'The camp is on one level,' says Tessa. 'Which isn't a consideration now, but it might be in a few years.'

'Why?'

A chickadee is going nuts in the tree above us. Across the road, there's a cacophony of crows. My family don't say a single thing.

'What's going on?' I demand.

'Nothing, Kitty,' says Dad. 'We can talk about it later. It'll keep.'

'Today is about *you*,' says Tessa. 'You've just had a terrible accident. We could so easily have lost you! Let's concentrate on spending time together.'

'They're not telling me something.' I'm drying dishes and putting them away in a fashion that makes the maximum noise. Bryan is elbow-deep in soapy water. Everyone else has gone home. After I asked my awkward questions, the party atmosphere never really recovered.

'They're trying to protect you. It's better that you remember things organically, rather than being hit with eighteen months of memories all at once.'

'Am I that fragile?'

'It's like Tessa said. We almost lost you. Right now, we just want to celebrate that we didn't. And besides, we're getting used to being back to normal.'

'I'm not normal.'

'None of us are normal. But most of us remember spending more than a year inside the house.'

'It's not my fault that I don't remember.'

'That's not what I meant. It's good to spend time with people.'

'They're ageing,' I say. 'They're thinking about getting older, which is why they want a house without stairs. It makes sense. But I don't like to think about things changing.'

'During the pandemic, a lot of people reassessed their priorities.'

'Including me.'

'Including *us*.'

Right. There is an us.

I twist the towel between my hands, as if I can wring out my emotions and be rid of them.

'Dad and Tessa are getting older,' I say. 'And I'm missing a whole eighteen months of their lives.'

He glances at me, frowning. 'I missed out on months of my family's lives, too. You're not the only person who feels like a big chunk of their life is missing. Memories we should have. Things we should have done, but didn't.'

'I know, but—'

'But what?'

Bryan stops doing dishes, his hands dripping into the sink. I see when he notices that I'm close to tears, because his face softens.

'What is it?' he says.

'It feels as if everything's turning around and around, spinning like one of those playground rides, and I can't focus on any one thing. It feels like everything's changing, or it's already changed, and I don't have anything to hold on to.'

'You can hold on to me,' he says.

And he's looking at me like that and I don't know anything any more, and I don't know what to do, but I need to do something concrete, to make the world stop spinning.

So I drop the towel and I step across the room, and I kiss him.

His lips are warm. His chin is a little rough. He doesn't move, doesn't touch me, but he kisses me back, right away, as if he's been waiting for this.

And he feels ... familiar. A snatch of music – Ella Fitzgerald's honey voice. It's almost a memory.

Then Bryan puts his hands on my upper arms and, gently, pushes me away from him.

'That's not what I meant,' he says.

I don't want to stop. I feel as if I'm on the verge of something coming back to me. That song ... what is it?

'Why not?' I say.

'Because I deserve to be more than a distraction to you when you're upset. And because if you have feelings about something, even if they're awful, you should feel them.'

I back away. 'Right. Yes. Sorry.'

I've made everything about me. I wipe my mouth, where I can still feel the sensation of his lips. He winces, and I can see how much I've hurt him.

'Sorry,' I say again, and flee upstairs to my room.

Chapter Fifteen

At Paradise, when I wake up in the morning, it's always the same. Some days it's sunny and warm, and I wake to the sound of the waves lapping against the beach and birds singing in the trees, the scent of water and green. Some days it's rainy, the drops pattering on the roof, and I nestle under my blankets, safe, warm and dry. On overcast days, the calls of loons float across the water. When the house is full of family and friends, there's the scent of coffee, the murmur of conversation downstairs; when the house is empty, it's peace and timelessness.

I have woken up here, in this house, on summer mornings since I was born, and, yes, time moves on and I get older; the scents and sounds change with the weather. But, still, it's always the same. Exactly the same. I wake up and I think, *Oh, I'm here.* And I know I'm home.

Today, it's sunny. I can tell even before opening my eyes. A frog squeaks outside. I think, *Oh, I'm here.* Then I stretch my arms and legs, yawn, and remember all the ways that things are different.

I owe Bryan an apology. A proper apology, not the anguished 'sorry' that I threw at him last night. I should do it right now. I should've done it last night.

But when I put on my robe and go downstairs, he's not there, and he hasn't left a note to say where he's gone. I glance into the guest room, and the bed is made and the room is neat. I'm dating a person who makes his bed when he wakes up. Does this mean I have also become a person who makes the bed when she wakes up?

I don't know.

I go back upstairs to my unmade bed, my mystery novels and, more crucially, my phone. As soon as I've picked it up I'm on Google, searching. Because I can't remember everything, but I can learn more.

Every web page leads to six other web pages. Quarantines, death counts, Ivermectin, protests, curfews, lockdowns, PPE, vaccines, ventilators, graves. I tap and scroll and tap, and the information rolls into my head like a fog, like a black cloud, like a storm that's about to strike but you're not sure when. More and more and more of it, pressure rising, the words and graphics blurring. But I keep on tapping and scrolling and tapping, and, when I look up, Bryan is standing in my doorway with a mug in his hand.

'What is it?' he asks, coming closer, putting the mug down on the bedside table. Eebie, who has come up behind him, barks his high-pitched bark. Bryan picks him up and puts him on the bed, where he immediately flops down next to my leg and rolls onto his back, little legs in the air.

'I'm ... I'm looking up ...' My voice feels as clogged as my brain.

'What are you looking up?'

I turn my phone to show him.

'The pandemic?'

'Yes. It's ...' I can't finish the sentence.

'How long have you been searching? All morning?'

I nod, and I realise that my cheeks are wet. 'I can't believe I forgot all of this.'

He takes my phone from my hand. I don't resist.

'This isn't going to help you,' he says.

'But I need to know.'

'No, you don't. This is just torturing yourself.'

'How else am I supposed to find out what I've missed?'

Bryan turns off my phone. He opens my underwear drawer and puts the phone inside. 'You talk. We talk.'

'Every time I talk, I seem to say something wrong.'

He sits beside me on the bed. Eebie is still belly-up, and Bryan scratches him.

'My uncle died,' Bryan tells me. 'My dad's brother. Quite early in the pandemic. And later, his son, my cousin, died too. He was only thirty-six. I couldn't get back for their funerals. We had my cousin's over Zoom.'

'What's Zoom?'

'It's an online video conferencing platform. It became very popular. It means you can sit in your living room across the entire country and watch everyone you love have the worst day of their lives. The rabbi called in from his own living room. Everyone was on their own little screen. We couldn't see my cousin's body. We couldn't hug each other. We couldn't properly say goodbye.'

'That sounds horrifying.'

'It was after Joshua died that you and I really talked for the first time. My aunt Leah – I had never seen so much pain on a human face. All I wanted to do was to reach out through the laptop screen and touch her. But I couldn't. She had lost the two people who meant the most to her and she was all alone in a room.'

'I'm so sorry.'

'Last night, when we were doing the dishes, I actually *envied* you. I wished I could forget that pain. And all the fear, and the loneliness.'

'But I've forgotten all the good things, too.'

'Yeah. I know.' He stands up. 'No more Googling. You need to talk with your dad. I'm going to drive you over there so you can spend the day with him.'

'But I need—'

'You'll always have Google. But you won't always have him.'

I swallow and wipe my eyes with the back of my hand.

'OK. You're right. Thanks.' I get up. 'Listen. I'm sorry about last night. I know it was … a confusing thing to do. I felt like I wanted some human connection. But it wasn't fair on you.'

He nods. 'Don't worry about it. I'll drive you over whenever you're ready.'

I pull on some clothes, help Eebie off the bed and the two of us go downstairs. Bryan's in the guest room and when I bring him his phone charger, his suitcase is open on the bed.

'Are you packing?' I ask. 'Are you going home?' I feel a stab of panic. I know I suggested it -- but if Bryan leaves, somehow that means I've failed.

'I'm unpacking,' he says, taking a pile of T-shirts from his case. 'Last night, I was looking for flights to Philadelphia. But today I've changed my mind.'

'Because I'm a wreck and you don't want to leave me?'

'No. And it's not because you apologised for kissing me, either. Which felt terrible, by the way. Please don't do that.'

'Kiss you?'

'Apologise.'

'Sorry. I mean ... OK.'

He puts the shirts in a drawer, then digs in his pocket for his car keys. 'You ready to go?'

I follow him outside.

'Why are you so nice to me?' I ask him. 'And don't say it's because you love me.'

'What other reason is there?'

'I mean, why aren't you getting angry at *me*?'

'Because you've got a brain injury. It would be like punching a kitten.' The car beeps and he gets in the driver's side. I grab the door, though, and don't let him close it.

'But I'm awful to you,' I say. 'I don't know you and I keep on asking you stupid questions, and doing stupid things and then apologising, which is even more stupid. I know I keep on hurting you, over and over and over.'

'You're not doing it on purpose.'

'Yes, and you're not yelling at me because you're a kind person.

And you said you were angry at the world. But aren't you angry at me?'

'Are you angry, Katie?'

The question hits me like a ton of bricks.

'I'm furious,' I tell him, only realising it as I say it.

He puts his hands on the wheel and sighs. 'I'm furious too.'

'What are we supposed to do about it? I don't want to keep hurting you. I don't want to keep being hurt. And you said I should feel my feelings, but ... I don't *do* that. I hate feeling my feelings. I don't want to be angry. I just want to run and escape. That's what I do. But I can't escape from myself.'

'It's harder to stay,' he says, and I get the feeling he's talking to himself instead of me.

'But how's it possible to stay when there's so much pain?'

He doesn't answer. Instead he gets out of the car, closes the door and walks across the lawn by the side of the camp.

'What are you doing?'

'Come over here.' As I do, he takes his phone, wallet and keys out of his pockets and puts them on the grass.

'Are you challenging me to a fist fight?' I ask. 'Because I think I could take you, but I do have a brain injury, so.'

'I don't want to fight you. Take off your sunglasses and take out whatever's in your pockets. And then I'll tell you what we're going to do.'

I put my sunglasses and my keys to the camp on the ground next to his belongings.

'OK, I'm ready, I guess?'

'First, we're going to face the lake,' he says. 'Then we'll close our eyes. And then we're going to take a deep breath, as deep as we possibly can, and we're going to let ourselves get as angry as we want – even more angry, in your case – and then we're going to scream really loud.'

'Scream.'

'And preferably swear a lot.'

I shake my head. 'This is nuts.'

'Close your eyes, take a deep breath and feel angry. Do you want me to kick you in the shin to get you started?'

I huff a laugh. 'No.'

'You can get mad, Katie. It's OK.'

'You need to do it, too.'

'Oh, believe me, I'm going to.'

I stand next to him, facing the lake, my hands on my hips.

'At the count of three,' he says. 'Yell bloody murder. Go.'

I close my eyes. The sunshine reflects off the lake and shines directly at my face, so that with my eyes closed all I can see is red. I hear Bryan taking a deep breath and I take one too. I peek at him – he's got his eyes shut tight and he's frowning.

So I go back to my own anger and I think about … everything. All of it. My mother leaving and my brother not talking to me and my best friend not calling me and the climate warming and the world changing and the politicians lying and the children starving and the animals suffering and me, who has never really been in love before and yet who somehow fell in love, and now that's been completely taken away from me.

Oh, I'm angry all right. I'm angry enough to power a planet.

My hands fist, my teeth clench, my eyes screw up tight. 'One … two … three,' Bryan says, and I scream. Next to me, Bryan yells. 'FUCK! SHIT! DAMN!'

'FUCK!' I yell back to him.

'FUCK!'

'FUUUCK!'

'FUUUUUUUUUUUUUCK!'

The last 'fuck' is a good one. Full of rage. When it's finished, emptied out into the air, Bryan grabs my hand.

'Now run,' he says.

He doesn't give me a chance to ask where. He tugs on my hand and we run together, across the lawn, down the stairs to the beach, onto the dock and straight out to the end, where we both jump into the lake with an enormous splash. Heads under, shoes weighing us down.

The water is cold, immediate, displaces everything else: breath, words, anger, thought. I open my eyes, but all I can see is green water and the bubbles of our descent. A whole other world, where nothing else exists and we can sink and sink.

And then, under the water, emptied out by the cold, I remember.

Chapter Sixteen

First, I remember Dad – a cold, bleak day in February when I sat on Tessa's cream-coloured sofa and heard the words that made everything crumble. I remember how the lamplight reflected off his glasses and how, when I couldn't bear looking at his face, I gazed out the window where grey sleet fell on the stark black trees. I remember getting up, leaving my plate with its half-eaten cake on the side table. I was desperate to leave. I wanted to run.

I kick my feet under the water, my arms flailing, and I remember Nic. A flickering fire, stars above us, the set of her chin. How I looked at that last message from her again and again, and then made myself stop looking.

I remember everything.

Every single thing that happened and every single thing I've done comes back to my world in a rush.

Dad. Shane. Nic. Bryan. Eebie.

All those emotions: grief, despair, betrayal, panic, falling in love.

And before I've hit the bottom, pushed myself, and emerged into the air, I know something else.

If I want to hold on to my own personal paradise, I can't tell anyone that I've got my memory back.

Chapter Seventeen

Nic

The morning of the accident

Nic got up early, as always, and walked her mother's dogs. Although 'walked' was a euphemism when it came to these particular hounds – Statler and Waldorf dawdled and sniffed, and then lurched and tried to bolt when they caught a scent or saw a friend. She walked under a sky of pink and orange, and to the sound of peepers and a morning chickadee.

Yesterday, Nic had said words that she should not have said. They had escaped her mouth and sucked everything into themselves. They had made a void that could never be breached or undone. And last night, as she'd been unable to sleep, she'd listened to the cackling of the loon on the lake and had thought about millions of other words she could have said instead, which would not have ruined everything.

But none of those words would have been the truth. So what else was she supposed to do?

Still, this morning she was a trembling shadow, a walking regret.

Even if something new began today, her past life had finished. So she noticed the colour of the sky and the scent of last night's rain; the snuffle of the dogs and the conversation of the birds; the precise shade of green in the birches. It would never be like this again.

When she returned to the campground, she could hear a radio

from one RV and smell coffee from another. Inside the house, her mother was still fast asleep in bed.

She fed the dogs their breakfast and then put on a pot of coffee. She took down Ma's favourite mug and put the creamer next to it along with a spoon. She put an apple muffin on a plate and covered it with plastic wrap. The toaster was in the cupboard above the fridge, out of reach. In a fit of optimism, she got the orange juice out of the fridge and left it on the counter, next to a little paper cup with Ma's pills. The pills were a bone of contention, but Nic kept trying.

She took as much time as she could over these daily tasks, but when she checked the kitchen clock it wasn't yet eight. She poured herself a cup of coffee, but the scent made her queasy so she went to the bathroom and made herself look at her face. She looked plain, though that was nothing new. There were dark circles under her eyes, and her cheeks were hollow and pale.

Why would anyone want her? Why bother thinking of a life other than the cracked kitchen linoleum and trying to get her mother to take the goddamn pills?

Nic let out a short, sharp sigh in front of the mirror, a noise familiar to her from her own childhood. Then she pushed her hair back from her face, checked on her mother again (still asleep) and went outside.

The campground was busy now. Kids yelled at each other on the swings and slide; Doreen and Dale were making pancakes on the communal grill; Archie was already asleep on his beach chair under his awning with a Dan Brown book splayed on his chest. It would take him all summer to read that damn thing. Last night's arrivals from New Jersey had emerged from their tents and were unloading their ATVs from the trailer, calling instructions and swear words at each other. Any minute Rhiannon would go over, cigarette dangling, and tell them to watch their language in front of children.

Doreen waved to Nic and she went over. 'Can you keep an eye on the house?' Nic asked her. 'I've got to go out for a little while.'

'Sure thing, honey.'

'Thanks,' Nic said, and for a split second she wondered what would happen if she walked out of the campground right now and never came back. Who Doreen would call. How long it would take for her mother to notice. What kind of hole she would leave behind.

A guy had turned up last autumn with nothing but a tiny RV hitched to his truck, and had stayed until the first snow, playing a sad country-music playlist through his little windows.

Katie and Shane's mother had left one night with a garbage bag full of shoes and clothes. And Katie herself, too, moved from place to place in an echo of what her own mother had done. It wouldn't be difficult for Katie to leave it all behind. But Nic didn't walk lightfooted through this world. She couldn't kick dirt off her shoes so easily.

She stuffed her hands into the pockets of her shorts as she walked up the dusty track from the campground. As she reached the main road, she heard a roar up behind her and stepped to the side to let the Jersey boys through on their ATVs.

She checked her watch – chunky, leather-strapped, once belonging to her father, a man who had treated time as elastic. Nic couldn't do that, either.

It was 8.47. Within a quarter of an hour, she'd know the shape of the rest of her life.

Chapter Eighteen

Many years ago

It was Nic who named the house Paradise. She remembered the first time she'd seen the inside of it, though of course she'd seen the outside of it before, from the water when she was riding in her dad's boat. It was the summer she was eight – high summer, when the campground was full and noisy, and her parents were too busy to spend time with her. Of course there were always kids to play with at the campground, but, this year, Renée Whitehouse had come back again, and Renée Whitehouse was mean.

At the end of last summer Nic had got a particularly bad blister on one of her feet and had to wear a sock with her sandals, and Renée had started calling her 'Ick'. During the year, Renée went to a different school than Nic, but, in the summer, her parents parked their RV on the biggest space and kept it there. She'd started up again with the evil nickname as soon as she'd arrived, and some of the other kids had started, too. Not in front of Nic's parents, of course, because they owned the campground. But on the beach, or when passing, in whispers or choosing sides for ball. Games of tag would devolve into 'stay-away-from-Ick'. They'd get bored with it eventually, but for now she was spending most of her time in the house.

Today, though, it was hot, and the only fan in the house was broken. She put on a bathing suit and a Red Sox cap, and found their old hound dog, Grover, lying stretched out and panting on the kitchen floor. 'Wanna go for a boat ride?' she asked him, but he just looked up at her with sad eyes and flopped his tail once.

She checked that the coast was clear before she scurried to the shed where they kept all the boat stuff. It was also full of spiders, so she ran in as fast as she could, grabbed a life jacket and paddle, and got out of there. She still had to shake out her hat and brush her shoulders off to make sure nothing had landed on them in those thirty seconds. Then she went the long way down to the beach, the way through the trees, to where they kept a canoe upside down on the sand. The other kids were playing Marco Polo in the lake so they didn't even notice her as she turned the canoe over, pushed it out into the water, stepped into it and paddled away.

Strictly, she wasn't supposed to go in the canoe by herself. But she had been paddling since she was born, practically. Plus she was wearing a life jacket and she wasn't going to go where the water was over her head. All she wanted to do was to get out on the lake a little bit to cool down, and then, if the Richardsons were down on the beach, maybe she could get out and swim there in front of their camp. Mr Richardson was a friend of her dad's and they let her do that sometimes. Even though the water in front of the Richardsons' was weedy and the bottom was mucky.

Still, it was better than being called 'Ick'.

She paddled along the shoreline, making sure to stay where it was shallow. She liked this view of the houses on the lake; they showed their best faces to the water, with wide-eyed windows and screened-in porches. A lot of people were out in the water, swimming and floating on inner tubes. One lady in a skirted bathing suit, who was standing in the water up to her knees, smoking a cigarette and watching toddlers in water wings, called, 'Be careful there, young lady.'

'I will,' she said, and kept on going. It felt good to paddle this canoe by herself. It didn't go as fast as when her dad was in the back, but she got to steer it and decide her own course. No one was on the beach at the Richardsons', so she kept going a little further. She'd never been this far before. She paddled around a little point, over some submerged rocks that looked like the backs of turtles, and on the other side there was a crescent-shaped beach with a pink umbrella and a single folding chair, in which a girl with bobbed brown hair was sitting, her legs crossed, reading a book.

She looked up as Nic came round the corner and watched her as she got closer. She looked about Nic's age. She called out. 'Hi.'

Nic called back. 'Whatcha reading?'

'*Harriet the Spy*.' She held up the book and Nic squinted at the cover.

'Is it good?'

'Yes, I've read it before. Is that your canoe?'

'Yeah,' Nic said, and honesty compelled her to add, 'It's my dad's.'

'Where are you going?'

'I'm looking for somewhere to swim.'

'You can swim here, if you want. My grandmother will come down and watch us.'

Nic figured, why not, and landed the canoe on the beach. She hopped out and pulled it up onto the sand while the girl watched her.

'You're good at that,' said the girl.

'I've been paddling it since I was a baby, practically,' said Nic, pleased. 'I used to have a little paddle, but now I can use a full-sized one because I'm tall for my age.'

'How old are you?'

'I'm eight.'

'I'm nine. My name is Katie.' Katie stood up from her chair. She wore a two-piece bathing suit, red with little white polka dots. Nic was still wearing her same one-piece blue suit from last year and she would have felt more self-conscious about it if the other girl hadn't complimented her boatsmanship.

'I'm Nic.'

'Do you want a Coke before we go swimming?'

This was too good to turn down, but she kept it cool. 'Sure.'

A series of stone steps led up from the beach. On their way up, they established that Nic lived at the campground but Katie had never been there, that Katie was from Connecticut but had been coming here since she was a baby, that Katie's grandmother was here staying with them because Katie's little brother was sick and was getting treatment at the hospital in Casablanca, and her dad was staying with him, but they would both be back tonight, and usually they brought pizza back from the store in town and Katie's favourite pizza was black olive.

'What about your mom?' asked Nic, impressed. She'd never had an olive, let alone on a pizza. She'd never had a pizza from a store. She didn't have a little brother, even a sick one.

'I don't have a mom.'

Nic was still taking this in as Katie opened up the door to the screened-in porch and they walked into an actual alternate world.

Here, there were cane-backed rocking chairs with colourful cushions. There were pots overflowing with pink and white geraniums, and side tables with thick white candles on them. There was a ceiling fan that made lazy circles above. Katie led her into the main part of the camp and this was more of the same – a squashy sofa with bright pillows on it, another ceiling fan, wooden chairs that looked old but fancy-old instead of old-old. Like they were old on purpose, instead of being something that you kept on using because new ones were expensive.

When she was more mature, Nic would understand the simple reason that made the Stone family camp different from her house: generations of money. This was a house for people who expected to take pleasure in their houses, instead of just eating and sleeping and living in them.

But at eight years old, it seemed like an entirely different way of living, something she had only seen on TV and hadn't thought was real. Everything was in order, like it had been made to be specifically where it stood now. There was a stone fireplace with gleaming brass tools beside it, and dried flowers in a vase on the mantelpiece next to a gold-framed painting of the lake.

And books, stacked on the coffee table, on shelves on the wall, glossy hardbacks and worn paperbacks, heavy books of photographs and slender books for children – more books than Nic had ever seen in a house before.

'This is paradise,' she burst out, and then she was embarrassed.

'Yup, we love it here,' Katie said. 'Do you come to the pond every summer?'

'I live up here.'

'Year round?'

'Yeah.'

'Wow, you're so lucky! Wanna see my room?'

Katie's room was upstairs and it had a slanted ceiling where the roof came down, and a sweet window overlooking the lake. She had a double bed with a pink quilt, piles of stuffed animals, and two white-painted bookcases that were also stuffed with books. So many books. Nic squatted to look at them. 'I've read this one and this one, from the library,' she said, and Katie squatted down next to her and started taking them off the shelves to share them.

Hours later, Nic was wearing a pair of Katie's shorts and one of her T-shirts, their wet bathing suits drying outside on the line, side by side. They were on matching chairs under the pink umbrella, finally drinking the Cokes that Katie had offered at first. Nic was reading *Harriet the Spy*, which was about a girl sneaking into people's houses to see how they lived and writing down everything she saw. She and Katie had already made plans to keep their own diaries about people they saw, though neither one of them was sure about sneaking into actual houses, and they agreed that they would never let anyone find their secret diaries, like Harriet had, but they would share them with each other.

'This looks like a good way to spend an afternoon,' said a voice behind them, and Katie jumped out of her chair to run over and hug a man standing on the steps to the beach. Katie's dad was tall and thin, with round wire-rimmed glasses. He wore long pants and a shirt with buttons, like a doctor or a teacher. Nic was instantly shy.

'This is my new best friend, Nic,' Katie told him. 'Her family own the campground and they live here all year, isn't that cool?'

'It's very cool. Nice to meet you, Nic. I'm Bill Stone.' He walked over and held out his hand. Nic had never shaken a grown-up's hand before, but she liked it. It was like pretending to be an adult.

'Nic and I decided that we're going to call the lake house Paradise from now on,' Katie said.

'That sounds perfect,' said Katie's dad, and, although the two girls hadn't actually discussed this – although 'paradise' had been Nic's word, not Katie's, and she'd been embarrassed about it before – she felt proud and happy. They were in Paradise and she had a new best friend, and she didn't have to be lonely any more.

Chapter Nineteen

For most of Nic's life, summer only started when Katie arrived from Connecticut. The rest of the year felt like a pause. In school, she hung on the periphery. An only child, she was used to being alone. She played several instruments but she didn't like to perform, so she didn't join a band, where she might have found a place to belong. She didn't want to belong; it felt as if that would be a betrayal of her summertime. She had people she was friendly with, but not any friends.

Late May and early June were bug season, waiting for the school bus by the side of the road, swatting black flies. Time passed slowly. When school let out, when most kids her age were looking forward to endless days of doing nothing, Nic had to help get the campground ready for the season – repainting the toilet block, cutting back the brush, rebuilding the barbecues, repairing the stage. Winter's snow and ice, and the mud of spring, made everything crack and slip; warmer weather brought wasps nesting under eaves and groundhogs digging up mounds, and waves of detritus on the beach that had to be raked up and hauled into the woods, so it could rot and wash back down next year. Nic's special job was touching up the campground sign – the moose on one side, the loon on the other.

There was a calendar hanging in what they called the campground office, but was really just a utility-and-junk room off the kitchen, home to endless boots, much-read paperbacks and a desk shoved in the corner. The calendar contained the summer's bookings with each one written in a shorthand that only Jeannette

Leblanc understood, but Nic would put a tiny red dot in the corner of the day when the Stones were going to arrive up at Morocco Pond. She would count down to those days. And the day when she knew the Stone family were coming to Paradise, Nic was in a frenzy of anticipation. She would drop things, not pay attention to her mother, forget to brush her teeth and then brush them three times. It felt as if her limbs were too long and her T-shirts were all too short, her sneakers too dirty, her hair too unkempt, with mud under her fingernails and bug bites on sunburned skin.

And she would wonder: would this be the year that Katie was too grown-up for her? The year that Katie compared her to all of her Connecticut friends, with their real houses and their effortless clothes, and found Nic lacking? Or the year that she just forgot? Katie was sunshine, and Nic was mud and dirty fingernails.

Every year Nic wanted to go down to Paradise and wait for Katie, to be there as soon as they drove up in their car (a new one every two years). And every year she would hang around the campground instead, getting in her parents' way, clumsily avoiding the other kids' kickball games or knots of gossip, until her mother would get fed up and say, 'Why don't you just go down there?'

But she didn't.

Then Katie would turn up, running down the dirt road to the campground, and she would yell, 'Nic!' in her loud voice that was never ashamed and Nic would jump up from whatever she was pretending to do, eaten by relief and joy, and the two of them would hug each other, and in Katie's arms everything would be in colour, sharp and full of light.

Summer could begin and with it, her real life.

Chapter Twenty

Nearly eighteen months before the accident

It had been snowing for about an hour, but inside the Le Passereux clubhouse it was steamy and warm, lit by neon beer signs and heated by a woodstove in the corner. The place was populated entirely by men. Shane stamped the snow from his boots and ordered coffee, and when the bartender looked at Nic, she said, 'I'll have a glass of water please. We're actually looking for someone – Pierre Robichaud? I heard he comes here on Saturday afternoons?'

The bartender leant on the bar. 'Now that depends – are you looking for money?'

'I just want to talk with him about music.'

'Ayuh, that should be fine.' He nodded at an elderly man in plaid flannel and a baseball cap, who was sitting by himself at a table in the corner near the woodstove.

'What does he drink?' asked Nic, and bought a bottle of Coors Light to match the one in front of the old man.

Shane stayed at the bar to talk weather and the Bruins with the bartender, and Nic brought the beer over to the corner. The man raised his head at her approach. He had watery blue eyes and grey stubble, his calloused hands curling around his beer.

'Mr Robichaud?' she said. Her voice sounded nervous even to herself. She rarely initiated conversations with strangers.

'That's Pépère to you.' His Québécois accent was strong and

blunt, and familiar as a favourite pair of mittens. 'What's your name, dear?'

'Nicole Leblanc.'

'Which Leblancs?'

'My father was Eugène, my grandfather was Roland.'

Robichaud's face, which had been mildly cordial, lit up. 'Rollie Leblanc's girl. Sit down, sit down.'

She sat across from him and slid over the beer, which he accepted with a nod. 'You knew my grandfather?'

'Play with him once or twice. Your family have that place up Oxford County – what was it?'

'Morocco Pond. The campground. I'm running it now.'

'Your father play the fiddle too. You?'

'He passed away twenty years ago. I don't play much, a little.'

'Now, *petite*, you know this is a men's club, yes?' A twinkle in his eye showed he was teasing.

'Yes, sir, but I was specifically looking for you. I'm actually ...' She had rehearsed this, so she wouldn't sound as much like an impostor as she felt. 'I'm doing a PhD with the University of Maine in music ethnography. That's the study of—'

'The folk music. You interested in the Acadian music?'

'That's right. I'm gathering resources right now. I wrote to you before Christmas. Did you get it?'

'I don't read, *petite*. Blind since eighty-six. I throw all them letters away. They're all bills.'

She hadn't realised he was blind. Still, at least that meant he couldn't see her blushing.

'I wondered if I could talk to you about your music and maybe ... maybe record some songs?'

'You want to make a record with me, *petite*? You a big music producer?'

'Not for commercial use – for research. I wouldn't be selling your recording at all. It's to document the existence of songs and their variations. I have release forms here with all the details. I'll read them to you.'

'You a student, eh? That pay good money?'

'I give music lessons during the school year.'

'So you can't pay me?'

She shook her head, and then remembered and said, 'Sorry, no. But I'll pay for your beers.'

'You make many of these records?'

'You're my first,' Nic admitted. 'There are archives belonging to the Maine Folklore Society and the university, and that's how I did my master's degree, but for my doctorate I have to do original research, which means trying to find material that hasn't been studied yet. I've only just started.'

'I make some recording twenty year ago. My niece says it's on that thing now, on the computer. Somebody put it there. I don't know who.'

'That's how I found you, sir. YouTube.'

'That your husband at the bar, come in with you?'

'He's my boyfriend.'

'You going to marry?'

'He hasn't asked me. We don't have to record anything now, sir. I can come back another time, when you're prepared.'

He laughed, a raspy bark. 'I'm always prepared.'

He used a borrowed guitar that Nic suspected the bartender kept here just for Pierre. His voice was hoarse but tuneful, his accent smoothing out the French words of the songs. He sang 'Partons, La Mer Est Belle', and everyone in the club gathered around the woodstove to hear him sing. Aside from the beer lights and the muted TV over the bar, aside from Nic's own iPhone connected to a microphone, they could have been in a similar room a hundred years ago. Or four hundred years ago, when French settlers came to the land they called Acadie. The Acadians settled in the Maritimes of Canada, the valleys of Maine, bringing their music with them. In the French and Indian War they were driven off their land to Louisiana, to France, to death. The ones who survived, the ones who returned, preserved their songs. Nic's father had taught her some of them.

No one applauded between songs, this audience of men and Nic the only woman. They listened and acknowledged this old music with silence. He sang 'Angélique' and he stopped, holding his guitar, and he said, 'This what you want, *petite*?'

'It's wonderful,' she said. 'Thank you.'

But Robichaud chuckled. 'No, you want something else. You hear all these songs already.'

'I have,' she said. 'Do you have anything I might not have heard before?'

He thought, his rough hands draped over the guitar. She didn't know what his job had been, but she knew it had been manual labour. The Acadians had come to Maine to saw and mill, fish and build. The music had been woven around that hard life. It had been something to sing while working, to play when resting, to lull children to sleep and give consolation to those who suffered.

And then, later, the descendants of these people, like Nick, treated these songs as artifacts, something to be separated out and studied.

'"Le Moineau et le Martinet",' said Robichaud. He began to sing. No guitar this time – just slow notes, lilting, not as suited to his gravelly voice as the livelier songs he'd been singing. Nic caught a few words: le moineau, le martinet, chanté ensemble. The sparrow and the swift sang together. She had never heard this song before, she realised as she listened, hardly daring to breathe. He sang two verses and a chorus, and then he stopped.

'That's all I remember,' he said. 'You speak French, *petite*?'

'Not very well.'

'The song is about two birds who fly together all summer. But when autumn comes, one of the birds has to fly away and the other bird, he die.' He paused, thinking. 'There are more verses, three, four – I don't remember.'

'How do you know the song?'

'My mémère.'

'Your grandmother sang it to you.'

'Maybe she make it up – I don't know.' He shrugged and put down the guitar. 'Come back another time. Maybe I remember more.'

In the parking lot, the snow was inches deeper and it was still coming down fast. Nic practically danced to the truck and helped Shane wipe the snow off the windows.

'That was amazing,' she said, climbing in and rubbing her gloved hands together to warm them while they waited for the cab to heat up. 'Wasn't that incredible?'

'Yeah,' said Shane.

'And he said to come back next month. Maybe he'll remember the whole song. A new song! I could do half my thesis on this. Philippa is going to go nuts. I can't believe this – he just came up with it like that. The first person I interviewed.'

Shane drove carefully out of the lot and onto the road. 'Looks like the plough has been, but there's been a lot of snowfall since then.'

'And the atmosphere in the room! All those hoary old men looked stunned as children. What else do you think he'll remember? We need to come back. And he knew my pépère. He told me to call him Pépère.'

'If we'd been smart, we would have been on the road half an hour ago.'

'But I wouldn't have gotten "Le Moineau et le Martinet".'

'Right.' Shane gripped the wheel and squinted through the snow. 'I'm glad you're happy.'

'Didn't you love it?'

'I don't know much about music, babe.'

'And about two birds who aren't meant to flock together. Sparrows and swifts don't mix, do they?'

'I know even less about birds.'

Her hands had warmed up a little, so she took her phone out of her coat pocket and played back the recording of that last song. Two verses and a chorus. Just a scrap. But so beautiful and sad... She played it again and again.

'My dad would be freaking out,' she said. 'A new song. And Mr Robichaud can probably introduce me to more sources, too. And he was talking about his grandmother's notebook. There might be even more in there. We *need* to come back.'

'Babe,' said Shane. 'Can you turn it down for a minute? It's going to take us a couple of hours at this rate; the weather is terrible and it'll be worse in the mountains.'

'We could go back home instead. The weather won't be as bad near the coast, maybe.'

'You want me to give up your mom's chicken pie?'

'Fair point.'

'But I need to concentrate on the road, here.'

'Oh. Yeah, of course. I was going to call Katie.' Katie would be as excited as she was. Maybe even more so – Katie was good at being excited about things and she'd encouraged Nic to go for this PhD place, giving her pep talks and shoring up her confidence about the undergraduate seminars she'd be teaching and the strangers she'd have to approach for research.

'Wait till we get to your mom's,' said Shane.

'OK,' she said, tucking her phone back into her pocket while Shane drove slowly and in silence.

Darkness fell winter-early and though it wasn't dinner time when they reached Morocco Pond, it was full night. The roads here had been ploughed, but not the drive to the campground and even with the four-wheel-drive on Shane's truck, they skidded twice before pulling up in front of the house. Inside, all the lights were on. As Shane turned off the ignition with a sigh of relief, Statler and Waldorf came bounding out through the open front door and were immediately engulfed up to the jowls in snow.

'We're back!' Nic called, climbing out of the truck, but her mother didn't appear in the doorway. She shepherded the dogs up onto the porch, knocked snow off her boots and called, 'Ma? Where are you?'

No reply, though she could hear the TV. She wiped her feet but didn't take off her boots before walking into the kitchen. If her mother didn't want wet footprints on her floor, she shouldn't leave the front door open. There was a glass of milk on the kitchen table. Her mother's cast-iron skillet sat on the stove, the burner turned on underneath it. Nic shut it off. 'Ma! You left the burner on!'

'Why'd she leave the door open?' Shane came into the kitchen, unwinding his scarf.

'I don't know.' Nic felt the heated air above the skillet, then licked her finger and touched the handle, which sizzled. She checked the living room, where the TV was on but Ma's chair was empty. Her room – bed made, overhead light on. The dogs followed Nic, sticking close to her ankles.

'Did she go out?' Shane asked behind her.

'Her car's in front.'

'For a walk?'

'Where? And why?' She hurried to the office, which served as a boot room in the winter, and there were her mother's LL Bean boots, sitting neatly in their usual place. Her winter Parka hung from its peg.

'Double-check the house,' Shane told her. 'I'll check the campground.'

But five minutes of calling and looking in every room, and even behind the shower curtain and under the bed, revealed nothing. It was as if she'd vanished, leaving a pan on the stove, her half-finished cross stitch on the coffee table. Nic tried calling her mobile phone, but it rang in the bedroom.

Dogs trailing behind her, Nic went out to the porch. She saw several sets of footprints in the snow – hers and Shane's from the car, scuffled up with dog prints, and then Shane's heading off around the perimeter of the campsite. Whatever footprints her mother left had been covered up by the fast-falling snow. How long had she been out in this weather?

There were four plausible places she could be: somewhere in the campground, along the main road, towards the beach or in the woods. That was the worst option. If she were in the woods, Nic didn't know how they would find her. Ma had no reason to walk into the woods – but then she had no reason to walk anywhere, in her house shoes and no coat.

She could hear Shane calling. 'Jeannette!' He was somewhere in back of the stage area. She couldn't see him though – visibility was that bad, in the darkness and the storm. She shooed the dogs back into the house – they would be more of a liability than a help in snow this deep – and then hesitated before striking off towards the frozen lake.

Fleetingly, she remembered how, as a child, she'd read Laura Ingalls Wilder and pretended that she was also lost in a blizzard in the deep woods. That was only enjoyable when it wasn't really happening. 'Ma!' she yelled out and heard only the distant wind.

The path went between trees that were only stark black shadows, and here the snow was less. She saw indentations in it, which could be from an animal, or could be her mother. Calling out again, she hurried forward and now she wasn't thinking about Laura Ingalls Wilder. She was thinking about her father, blue from the lake, the laughter gone from his face for ever.

She emerged from the trees to an expanse of white blankness – the lake, frozen over and coated with snow. This time of year, the ice was thick enough to drive a truck on. She didn't have to worry about her mother falling through. But you could walk and walk out here, and reach nothing. She paused to listen.

Snow has a sound, a whisper as it falls. So does a frozen lake, which cracks and grinds on itself. Wind keens, but it does not sound like a sobbing woman. Nic ran as best she could through the snow, slipping and wading, towards the grey shape in the distance. When she got close enough, she yelled again. 'Ma!' Jeannette turned towards her. She was wearing a sweater and jeans, and was shaking violently as she sobbed.

Nic threw her arms around her mother. 'Ma, what are you doing out here? You'll freeze to death!'

'Do you know where he's gone?'

'Who? The dogs are inside – they're safe. Shane is with me. We're both looking for you – we've been frightened! Come inside.' She took off her scarf and coat, and wrapped them around her mother. Snow instantly began falling down the back of her neck. 'You're not even wearing boots!'

'I need to find him.' Her mother pulled away from her and gazed out at the lake.

'Did you find her?' Shane from behind them.

'Yes, she's here!' Nic turned back to her mother, who had started to walk away, further out onto the lake. 'Ma, where are you going? Who are you looking for?'

Her mother looked over her shoulder and in that moment, Nic's panic curdled into horror. Jeannette's face was pale, her lips nearly blue. Her teeth were chattering. Tears had frozen her eyelashes together.

But she looked at Nic as if she did not know her.

'I have to find Gene,' said her mother. 'I need to find my husband. Do you know where he's gone?'

Chapter Twenty-one

February 2020

She was doing laundry, hers and her mother's, when Katie called. 'Do you know what all of this is about with my dad and Tessa?'

Their conversations often started like this, as if they had kept on talking continuously without any interruptions – one long conversation that spanned years.

'Go back a few steps and catch me up on what you're talking about,' Nic said.

'I'm literally at the airport right now. My flight is about to board. Didn't Shane tell you anything about it?'

'He's at the lake for the weekend, but he's taken Ma to get her car serviced.'

'I thought your mom had to stop driving.'

'We hide her keys. But she likes it when Shane drives her in her own car.'

Vascular dementia, the doctor had said. She'd had a mini stroke and this was most likely combined with early-onset Alzheimer's. No treatment for what had already been lost – all the years and memories. A slow death sentence. Otherwise, Jeannette Leblanc's body was healthy.

They'd only had a few weeks to get used to the new normal. The main blessing was that as long as Ma stuck with her routine and she had near-constant supervision, she wasn't too bad yet. She could follow her well-rehearsed tracks from bedroom to bathroom, to kitchen to living room, do chores, interact with the dogs, enjoy her TV programmes. She didn't realise what she was losing – what she had already lost.

Jeannette could stay at home for now, the occupational health therapist had told Nic, acting as if it were good news that Nic would have to give up her own apartment in Portland close to the university and become a part-time student from home, so she could look after her mother.

Which it was. It was good news. It could be worse.

It would get worse.

'What's going on?' Nic asked, bringing it back to the present question.

'Fucked if I know. Dad called this morning to ask if I could visit this weekend, because he wanted to talk to me about something in person.'

'Huh.'

'Right? Good thing I happen to be on the east coast. So of course I cancelled everything and got a flight. I'm assuming that he spoke with Shane, but he hasn't returned my calls or messages. I thought you'd know what was happening.'

'I haven't heard anything. I'm just here folding underwear.'

'I'm going to rent a car and go straight to Dad's. If I don't see you there, I'll come by after. OK, they're boarding my flight. I'll see you soonest. Kisses.'

Bill had told Shane that he wanted to talk to the kids in person and it might as well be this weekend because Shane was close by at the lake. Tessa had baked a cake and if on their way over they wanted to pick up ice cream to go with it, that would be great.

Shane and Nic dropped Jeannette at her friend Natalie's house for a visit, and drove the rest of the way in silence. The roads were slushy with grey sleet.

Nic knew when bad news was coming. It was a pinching in the gut.

When her father drowned, when her mother was diagnosed

with dementia, and everything in between, she felt that pinching, like her insides were being squeezed by an invisible hand. It was almost worse than the news itself.

'You OK?' she asked Shane. He shrugged.

They picked up a gallon of Gifford's Moose Tracks ice cream. When they got to Bill and Tessa's house in Casablanca – a big, brick Victorian with bay windows and white gingerbread trim – a rental car was parked out front and Katie was in the kitchen, drinking coffee and pacing. Of course, Bill, Shane and Tessa acted as if nothing was happening and this was a regular family reunion. This was the Stone family all over. When she was younger, she'd thought that it was impossibly glamorous to have a family who didn't argue over dinner or slam doors, or yell at each other across the house.

Stoicism equals sophistication. Subtext equals depth.

Everything remained unspoken.

Nic hugged Katie, who was too distracted to hug her back properly. Tessa made more coffee. 'When are you and Shane going to tie the knot and give us some grandbabies?' she asked Nic.

She asked this every time. As always, Nic shrugged and put on a smile, hoping the conversation would move on quickly.

'Who wants cake?' Bill started getting out plates.

'What's going on?' asked Katie. 'You are driving me nuts. Just tell us!'

'Let's enjoy this cake and ice cream first,' said Bill.

They ate cake in the living room on their laps and Tessa kept up a running commentary, talking about her icing recipe and asking about Nic's mom and all of her friends. Shane ate his cake in silence. Katie, sitting beside Nic, ate a bite of cake and then put it aside. 'Can you stop torturing us now?' demanded Katie.

'Well,' said Bill. 'We need to tell you some news.' He reached for Tessa's hand.

*

Katie had come back to Nic's and the three of them were drinking Jack Daniel's in the kitchen. Katie was crying, not loudly but continuously; Shane was looking up mobility aids on his phone.

Nic sat close to Katie, her hand on her leg. Heartbreak, she had learnt, could be slow, and tangled up with the relentlessly practical.

'He's never going to finish the Appalachian Trail,' Katie was saying now. 'He could be in a wheelchair by next spring.'

'The drugs are helping, though,' said Nic. 'They'll give him a lot more time and there are breakthroughs every day.'

'But being active is so important to him. It's so unfair.'

'I know. It's the same for my mom.' Except there were no drugs to slow her own mother's descent. At least, to a certain extent, Jeannette didn't notice.

'How can he be so calm?'

'That's Dad,' said Shane. 'He's always been like that.'

'What do we need to do?' Katie said. 'Do we need to look at assisted-living places? Do we need to hire someone? Tessa won't be able to do it all herself.'

'I'm not going anywhere,' said Shane. 'I'm perfectly capable of it.'

'OK,' said Katie, but Nic could hear the 'but' in her tone and so could Shane.

'What can't I do?' said Shane. 'I only live half an hour away. I can drive him to his appointments and help him get around. I can adjust the house for him so he can get around easier. I can check in on him every day, if he needs me to.'

'And I'm here too,' said Nic. 'I can help Tessa.'

'Yeah,' said Katie. 'But what if there's a storm and you can't get out for a couple of days? And you've got Jeannette to worry about.'

'It's not really the time to make any big decisions,' said Nic. 'There will be plenty of time for that. And like he said, he's fine now. If I know him and Tessa, they're going to make the most of the time they've got.'

'It's not as if you're going to come back to Maine,' said Shane.

'I can't do my job here,' said Katie. 'You know that.'

'There are banks in Maine. Anyway, we can handle it.'

'We're going to need a second opinion, at least,' said Katie. 'I'll make some calls tomorrow.'

'The doctors are pretty good at CMMC, though,' said Shane.

'Yes, but what have they got? One specialist maybe? It's got to be worth checking out Boston and New York.'

'You're not a doctor, Katie.'

'Maybe they need to start looking at places further south, where it's warmer and they're closer to a major hospital. We can look for live-in assistance.'

'Or maybe you can trust me, for once!' Shane burst out. He shoved his phone into his pocket and left the kitchen. Nic heard the front door slam.

Katie sighed and wiped her eyes.

'He'll cool down after a walk,' Nic said.

'Getting angry isn't going to help.'

'I was plenty angry when my mom was diagnosed,' Nic said.

'How did you deal with it? It hurts too much to think.'

'I just got through it, I guess. I'm still getting through it.'

Katie started crying again. Nic rubbed her back. This was another thing they had in common, another thing that bound them together.

'I can't,' Katie said. 'I can't think about it, it hurts so much. My dad was always the strong one. And now...'

'Give it some time,' said Nic, which she knew was a stupid and useless thing to say, because time didn't make things better, especially when time was going to steal away the person you loved. Not like how autumn always stole Katie from her – with Bill and with Jeannette, it was going to be permanent.

But what else could you say?

Katie tore off a paper towel to blow her nose. Nic poured them both another drink.

'Is he supporting you?' Katie asked.

'I'm doing just fine.'

'I meant with taking care of your mom.'

'He's really good with her. Anything practical she needs, he sorts it out.'

'Strong and silent. The fucking men in my fucking family, am I right?'

But the men, at least, did stick around. Bill had moved to Maine when he'd retired. Shane had got his degree at Bowdoin and had got a job in a civil engineering firm in Portland. They were here.

This was only one of a million things that she did not say. Instead she allowed herself to open her arms to Katie, who leant into them.

'Would you consider moving to Maine?' she asked.

'I can't,' Katie said. 'Not with my work. So I don't know why I'm arguing with him. It's not as if I can do it myself. I just hate feeling helpless.'

'Shh,' said Nic. She held Katie and stroked her hair. Felt Katie's heartbeat against her breast and her breath on her neck.

She closed her eyes and tried to hold this moment close. Painful and precious. To keep it for ever, even though that was impossible.

Chapter Twenty-two

It was hard to pinpoint when she'd fallen in love with Katie Stone. It was difficult to remember a time when she hadn't caught her breath at Katie's voice, when she hadn't felt dizzy from a glance of her eyes. Had it been when they were children, when they'd been everything to each other and hadn't yet learnt that there were different types of love? Had it been when they were teenagers, when Shane had tagged along behind them like a loyal puppy and Katie had gone off to make out with Tommy Pfaff behind the stage, leaving Nic, standing guard, burning with a jealousy she'd not been able to name?

Or had it been somewhere between these moments, in the times when they'd been hundreds or thousands of miles apart, and Nic could think and dream and wish, create a reality in her head that had had nothing to do with the reality of life?

Whenever it had started, by the time they had both grown up, it had become as inescapable a fact of Nic's being as her brown eyes or freckled skin. But it was also hopeless. Katie was as far out of her reach as heaven itself.

Katie never stopped moving. As a child, she'd been only present for eight weeks a year, and the rest of the time she'd been a voice on the telephone. Katie had gone to Yale, like her dad, while Nic had taken out loans to study at the University of Southern Maine, often studying part time while she'd worked full time to pay bills and tuition. Katie had always had a new boyfriend, all of them temporary. Katie had moved from job to job and city to city, restless and full of adventure.

'You're my only constant,' Katie had told Nic, along with, 'You're my true home.'

But she was only at that home in the summertime. The rest of her life was lived elsewhere.

When he was alive, Nic's father used to sit outside in the evenings playing his fiddle, and Nic would sit beside him and play too, on the fiddle or guitar or harmonica – all of the Acadian music he'd grown up with and learnt from his own dad, mixed with bluegrass and sometimes, just for fun, a little Bon Jovi. When they'd finished playing, her father would lower his instrument and tell her, 'This is where we belong, Nicole. This patch of land. We came here temporary, but we'll die here permanent.'

That was how Nic had been taught that the trees and the mountains and the lake were part of this music, and part of her, too. She could never leave.

Sometimes, she lay awake and thought about telling Katie how she felt. What possible outcome there could be. She pictured Katie's eyes filling with surprise and dismay. Katie's stumbled apology – 'No, I didn't mean that.' Or even worse, Katie laughing, brushing it off, pretending the words had never been spoken.

Sometimes she pictured the opposite. Katie smiling, opening her arms. Kissing her under a summer-blue sky.

But the dreams could never end there, because what happened next? Katie came to live in Maine? Nic travelled with her? And then how long before they resented each other?

So she never said anything. She wondered if Katie knew already. Sometimes it felt as if she did, that the two of them had forged this silent pact with each other over years of not saying, and that breaking that pact would be the end of everything.

In college, Nic had kissed a woman for the first time – a flute player with long hair, who'd worn silver rings on every finger and had swayed when she was playing, delicate and strong as a willow. The next morning, Nic had called Katie.

'What was it like?' Katie had asked.

Nic thought about it. *It wasn't you.* She said, 'It was nice.'

'I mean, was it different than kissing a man?'

Nic had not kissed many men.

'I could kiss you some time and show you,' Nic said.

Katie laughed, as Nic knew she would. 'Just describe it.'

'It was ... softer. We're the same height so there was none of that stooping or standing on tiptoes, or bending backwards. It was comfortable. She had really smooth lips. And I could play with her hair.'

'That sounds really nice.'

'That's what I said.'

'So, are you gay now? Does Shane not have a chance any more?'

Nic realised, for the first time in a life of yearning, how action changed everything. A simple kiss, a moment between two human beings, a connection after a gig in a student bar, meant that she now had to start defining herself. She, a private person, had to wear this most private thing openly or forever risk being misunderstood.

'I don't really want to label myself, you know,' she said.

'But you still like boys?'

'I guess so.'

'But also girls?'

'Some girls.'

'Would you say that you're attracted to people of different genders or that you're attracted to people regardless of their gender?'

'Are you reading a definition off your screen? Did you just do a Google search?'

'I want to make sure I get it right.'

'There's nothing to get right, Katie – I am just me. Same as always.'

'Are you going to ask her out?'

'I got her number. So maybe.'

'Are you going to sleep with her?'

'I don't know.' She paused, thinking about all the boyfriends Katie had dated over the years. 'Why? Are you jealous?'

'A little, maybe. If you fell in love with a man, that would be OK. If you fell in love with a woman, I'd sort of worry that she'd take my place.'

'She wouldn't.'

'OK, good.'

Katie's unaccustomed and unexpected vulnerability was what made Nic brave enough to ask, 'Would you ever want to be with a woman?'

It went quiet on the other end. Nic wished she could see Katie's face and also she didn't want to.

'I guess it depends,' Katie said.

'Depends on what?'

'Who it is.'

'What do you mean?'

'I'd be worried, with a woman, that things would get too... intense. Like men, they're different, you know? But with a woman, I might understand her too well. It might be too difficult.'

'You mean that you might fall in love?'

'God forbid, me? Fall in love?' And Katie laughed, and Nic laughed too, and that was the end of that conversation.

Later, she went through that conversation in her mind and wondered if she could have changed its direction somehow, if she had been braver. If she could have changed everything.

But as it was, regardless of the nature of their relationship, she would always be the most important person in Katie's world.

Nic dated Maya for a year, on and off, keeping it casual. A couple of years later, when Shane finally asked her out – Shane who had had a crush on her for years, Shane who had Katie's eyes – she said yes.

Chapter Twenty-three

April 2020

'Damn!' The screen froze and Nic slapped her hand against the desk that was crammed in the makeshift office, underneath the collection of hanging winter coats.

'What's up, babe?' Shane appeared in the doorway.

'The internet's down again. I was in the middle of an undergraduate seminar.'

'I'll have a look.' He went to check the router. Nic pushed her hair back and sighed. It probably didn't matter much anyway. In January, in person, this seminar had started out with eighteen students; now, a few weeks into lockdown, only four had turned up to her online session and two of them had their cameras off. She didn't know what had happened to the rest of the students. Maybe they'd gone home, or given up, maybe they were glued to their phones scrolling bad news and conspiracy theories. Maybe they found the idea of online education so dispiriting that they hadn't bothered to get out of bed.

She didn't blame them. She could understand the appeal of lying with the blankets over your head, listening to music and ignoring the fact of a global pandemic rampaging outside the walls of your bedroom.

Shane had moved in when everything had shut down. To help out, he said. Because he didn't want Nic and Jeannette alone in the woods. And he'd be only a short drive from his dad, even if they had to talk through a closed door. It would only be for a little while. Until the pandemic was over. Until the worst had passed.

But who knew how long it would really be? Every day, the news seemed to be worse.

At the pond, April was a dull and wet month. The snow lingered in dirty patches, exposing the layers of dogshit that had lain frozen all winter. Trees were still bare and the streams rushed with snowmelt, pouring themselves into the pond that had only recently opened up from ice. Eventually, crocuses would poke their purple and white heads into the world. Nic hadn't seen any yet.

There was nowhere to go and nothing to do, and within these four walls, no privacy for doing it in. Before Shane had moved in, she'd had a small desk in her bedroom, but they'd had to move that to make space for a double bed. The campground office had always been crowded and unfit for purpose, but it was terrible for academic work – the windows were draughty, the heating came from a rickety electric heater that emitted a strange, mousy smell, and there was no room, among the coats and boots and general detritus, for her to spread out her papers.

Her research had stalled. It was so difficult to concentrate on anything. With the internet cutting out, she couldn't reliably access the university databases to do any more research, and, of course, research in person was out of the question, especially with elderly subjects who were vulnerable and unused to technology. She'd tried calling Pépère Robichaud, thinking maybe he'd sing to her over the phone, but no one ever answered. She hoped it was because he was still dodging bill collectors, or maybe he'd moved in with his family.

Through the window, she glimpsed Shane tramping around the side of the house – a wire must have gone down somewhere. She shut her laptop. She missed her tiny apartment above a laundromat in Portland, where you could glimpse Back Cove from the top of the living-room window. She did not want to live in the middle of nowhere, a pond that was abandoned every winter. She had thought that by this age, she would no longer be living here with her mother, cowering from a disease in this patchwork house that her father had built from a trailer.

Blinking back tears, she gave herself a talking to. *You have it good. You're safe, you're healthy, you have fresh air, water, heating and enough to eat. Your boyfriend helps out, your mom is relatively cheerful, you have a room where you can close the door and get a little bit of work done.*

But this work was finished for the day. She got up and went into the living room, where a cooking show was playing loudly on the TV. At least cable TV still worked. It was playing to an empty armchair. Ma was across the room, rummaging through the drawers of the large, battered dresser.

For most of Nic's childhood and early adulthood, she could barely recall her mother sitting down at all, except at Sunday during Mass. She'd always been doing something. Cooking, cleaning, gardening, decorating, shopping, walking a dog. For several years, she'd kept chickens for the eggs. She'd sat down to eat meals or balance the checkbook, but only for minutes at a time.

The younger Jeannette Leblanc had not lounged on the beach, or built sandcastles with her daughter. She hadn't watched TV or played cards. She'd never read anything except for cookbooks, standing up at the kitchen counter. Her only real hobby had been visiting with the guests at her campground, but even then she'd usually be standing up, holding her ever-present cup of coffee and her cigarette, chatting in doorways and next to plastic chairs.

She'd hated it when Nic had sat still, too. 'Go outside and play!' she'd command if she'd found Nic curled up with a book, or if it were winter and there'd been too much snow, 'Come help me with this laundry.' Even when Nic had been doing homework or practising the fiddle, she'd feel a lingering guilt that she wasn't up on her feet doing something to help her mother, because there'd always been something to be done. Or, more usually, a dozen somethings.

After her husband had died, Ma had done twice as many jobs. She was lean and busy, in practical hard-wearing clothes and her hair cut short. She'd bought birthday cards in advance and had written detailed notes on every recipe she'd tried. She'd loved it when mobile phones had been invented, because then she could make all her phone calls and keep up with her friends while doing something else.

Nic thought now that it was probably because her mother was so active and so good at multitasking that they'd all missed the signs of dementia for so long. That activity was what had kept the campground and her family going for years. But now her mother had to be watched constantly, for her own safety.

'What are you looking for, Ma?' She turned down the volume a bit.

'Your father hid my cigarettes again.' Her mom shut one drawer and opened another.

'You quit smoking ten years ago.'

'I can never find them.'

'Come sit down and watch Iron Chef with me and the dogs.'

Her mother kept rummaging.

'Ma! Come sit down for a minute.'

'Those people are so silly.' But her mother came and perched on the edge of her armchair for about four minutes before she was up again and looking.

'Ma, you don't smoke any more. You said you'd decided you'd rather not die.'

'Your father hid my cigarettes again. I guess I'll have to go get some more.'

She left the room. Nic followed her and found her putting on her jacket in the kitchen.

'Ma, it's a lockdown. We're in a pandemic. You can't just go to the store four times a day.'

'Where are my keys?'

'You can't drive now.' How she would like to drive and drive and drive, far and never-ending and alone, until she didn't have to deal with any of this any more.

'Of course I can drive.'

'Listen, we'll go later, OK?' She tried to take her mother by the arm, but she pulled away.

'Gene!' Ma started hollering. 'Where are you?'

'Ma! You don't smoke! If you go to the store, you might catch the virus and get sick!'

'Let go of me!'

'Ma, you need to stay inside.'

'Gene!' She pushed Nic's hand away and went out the door. Nic followed.

'*Dad is dead!*'

She shouted it, louder than her mother had been shouting. Ma turned around and her face was shocked, distraught, fearful.

Shane came running up. 'Hey! What's going on?'

'She keeps asking for Dad and I can't…'

He took Ma's arm. She didn't fight him. 'Come on inside, Jeannette. I need you to make me some lunch.'

Shane led her mother, completely docile now, into the house. Nic walked as fast as she could away from the house, down the campground drive to the main road. She walked right in the middle of the road, her arms spread out on either side of her. The road was empty and all the summer homes that lined it were empty, and so were the sky and the mountains and the lake. No planes, no cars, no people. It was the perfect place to weather out a pandemic. In the cities, millions of people were dreaming about the isolation of a house in the woods. Almost every day, Katie texted her that she wished she was in Paradise instead of stuck in Philadelphia.

She was lucky. She was in the most beautiful place in the world, she was safe and she was with people she loved. And if

Shane wasn't the person she really wanted, she cared about him. He was a good man, a kind man, and he adored her.

She was the most unhappy she had ever been.

She came back to a kitchen strewn with pots and flour, and Shane alone on the sofa, typing on his phone with the TV on. 'Where is she?' she asked.

He put down his phone. 'She went for a nap.'

'A nap? My mom?'

'I guess you tired her out arguing.' At her stricken face, he added, 'She doesn't remember it.'

'I do.'

He moved aside on the sofa and held out his arm along the back, to give her space to slip in beside him. When she did, he held her. He was big and warm.

'I feel terrible,' she said. 'I don't want to get angry at her. It's not her fault.'

'I know.'

'Doesn't it make you angry? What's happening to our parents? What's happening to everybody?'

He shrugged. 'I don't get angry, I guess.'

This was untrue. She saw him sometimes, outside when he thought no one was watching him, taking out his anger on the snowbanks or woodpile.

The news came on and Nic wrenched her attention back to the present. How many cases, state by state. How many people had died. Global shortages. Hot spots. Doors shut, walls built, people gasping for breath. She was trapped here with her disappearing mother and a man she only tried to love enough, and Katie was hundreds of miles away, stuck in her own box.

'It's all falling apart,' she said.

'It's all right,' he said. 'Whatever happens, we'll be together.'

Shane held her tighter and God help her, she held him tighter, too.

Chapter Twenty-four

June 2020

Summer was coming, but it was a summer unlike any she'd lived through before. She went for a run along the main road as the sun came up, and then returned to the house and walked the dogs in her exercise clothes. It was her new routine to get up before anyone else. It was her only way of grabbing some time to herself. She knew her mother was still asleep and didn't need her, and since Shane had been on furlough, he'd become more and more nocturnal, staying up late on his computer, coming to bed after she was asleep and staying there until late morning.

She could run and run and walk and not see anyone, not have to pretend that things were OK. She could windmill her arms, take up space, spend an hour or two not having to keep herself small. She hadn't played her guitar for months – she didn't have enough privacy. Sometimes she sang to the empty road and the empty camps on either side of it, belting out her thin and untrained voice, answered only by the crows in the pines.

Sweaty, bitten by black flies, she felt looser and restored, and was able to face the long day in front of her, where everything was the same as the day before and the future was so uncertain.

When she returned to the campground, her mother was outside digging in a flower bed. She'd learnt that when her mom was absorbed in a task, it was best to leave her, or else she'd lose the thread and it would remain unfinished. Once an effortless multitasker, Jeannette Leblanc was now only really herself when she was carried by the flow of doing a single thing. Nic cleaned Statler and Waldorf's paws with the old towel they kept on the porch for this purpose and went inside, wiping perspiration from her forehead. It was going to be a hot one.

To her surprise, when she went through to the bedroom to get a change of clothes before she showered, Shane was standing near the bed, showered and dressed. Even more of a surprise, there was a bouquet of bee balm, dog roses, and marguerties in his hand. Lilac, pink roses, marguerites – hand-picked and tied together with a bit of yellow yarn.

'What's this?' she asked.

'They're for you.' He held them out and she took them. The scent was strong and too sweet.

'Thank you.'

'I took off the thorns, but be careful.'

'What brought this on?'

'Things haven't been great,' he said. 'I know they haven't.'

'Well. It's a difficult time. We'll get through it.'

'I moved in here so we could get closer, but we seem to be drifting apart. Sometimes it feels like whenever I come in a room, you're leaving it.'

'It's OK,' she said. To herself, she admitted it was easier for them to do their own thing. It was a simulacrum of a bit of freedom. 'We can't spend every waking moment together. We're both doing our best.'

'I want to be a better person. You know?' He was a big man – tall, muscular, with broad shoulders and calloused hands – but his eyes were soft, like those of a child.

Her heart broke a little. It was a struggle for Shane to talk about emotions, she knew. He showed love through actions. But now he was trying as best he could.

She knew he was forcing himself out of his comfort zone because she pulled back all the time. Looked for space. Left a room when he entered it, because it was easier than confronting his needs. With everything that her mother required from her, with everything going on in the world, with everything she was lacking herself, she had nothing left to spare for him.

'You are a good person,' she said, and put her hand on his shoulder. He took it and held it.

'I want to be here for you. I love you.'

'I love you too,' she said, as she always did, because it was true. How couldn't you love Shane? He was steady, he was kind, he was smart, he was handsome. She would do better, she promised herself. She would try to share more with him.

'Good,' he said. 'I have to ask you something. Finally.'

He let go of her hand. He got down on one knee. He reached into his pocket.

'What are you doing?' she asked, though she knew.

He took out a small box. Opened it. A diamond ring.

She couldn't move. Couldn't speak. He was looking at her. All she could think was, *I am supposed to be happy.*

Years, decades, minutes later, Shane stood up. He put the ring on the bedside table and left the house. She heard his car starting up outside, crunching on the dirt road.

She sat on the bed. After a moment or two her mother came into her bedroom. 'Who was that?' Jeannette asked, then reached for the bouquet in Nic's hand. 'Oh, that's pretty. I'll put it in a vase.'

Chapter Twenty-five

I'm here, said the text, and Nic, running shoes laced, flew out the door into the night. Above the trees, the moon was fat and she glimpsed its reflection on the lake between camps as she ran. Even with all the jogging she'd been doing, she was out of breath by the time she reached Paradise. The car was parked outside, but none of the camp windows were lit up, and for a moment she stood on the lawn, confused, until she smelled the sharp hint of wood smoke and saw an orange glow coming from the direction of the beach.

Katie sat in a lawn chair facing a little driftwood fire. A second lawn chair was placed six feet away. She jumped up as soon as she heard Nic coming down the stairs to the beach.

'Harriet!' she said. 'I don't know if I'm allowed to hug you. I did take a negative test before I got in the car.'

'Probably better not hug,' Nic said. 'Just in case.'

'Twelve hours on the road and I feel like a criminal. My car has Pennsylvania plates. I was tempted to try to hide it.'

'No one'll be coming down here.' Nic flopped into the second lawn chair. There was a six-pack of beer beside it. Nic cracked one open. 'Thanks for this. I needed it. And thank you for dropping everything and driving up here.'

'I literally have nothing else to do.' Katie had another six-pack next to her chair. She picked up her own beer, already open, and added, 'Actually, that is not true. I have been doing my neighbour.'

'Your hot neighbour who helped you with the dog?'

'His name is Bryan.'

'You're sleeping with him?'

'We can't go anywhere so basically we're spending the whole time having sex.'

'For how long?'

'Week or two. I have to do *something* to keep from going mad.'

Nic downed half her beer in one and wiped her lips. 'He lives next door to you. Don't shit where you live.'

'It'll be fine. This'll end eventually and I'll move somewhere else.'

'Do you know that you're being a complete cliché of yourself.'

'Yes, yes, it's all good. I didn't drive all day without a pee break to talk about my sex life, though. What's going on?'

'Shane didn't tell you?'

'Shane never tells me anything. I have to learn it all from you.'

Nic finished her first beer, dropped the can in the sand and reached for another. 'Shane asked me to marry him.'

An outrush of breath from Katie. 'Whoa. Finally. Good for Shane.'

'I didn't say yes.'

'You said no?'

'I didn't say anything.'

'What do you mean?'

'I couldn't answer. Which was an answer in itself, I guess. Shane took it as one. He drove off and a couple of hours later I got a text saying he was back at his house in Bethel.'

'Left all his stuff behind at your mom's?'

'There wasn't a lot of it, but, yeah.'

'Shit,' said Katie.

Nic nodded. She watched the flames dance on the driftwood. 'Why...'

This question, which Katie didn't finish, was exactly why Nic had asked her to come up to Maine.

'I was standing in my bedroom,' she said. 'And he knelt down, actually got down on one knee to ask properly, though he didn't ask – he pulled out a ring and it was lovely. He'd picked me flowers. And I know how much he loves me, Katie. I know he would move the moon for me. But I saw him kneeling and I saw the ring, and all I could think was, I can't live like this for ever.'

'So you couldn't answer.'

'If I said no, it would have hurt him so much.'

'Why did you stay with him, if you didn't want to marry him?'

'I do love him. I didn't want to hurt him. That's why I let it go on for so long.'

'But that makes it *worse*, Nic.'

'I know.'

The fire crackled. Katie sighed. 'This will really fuck him up,' she said. She sounded sad, not angry.

'I know. I feel terrible.'

'It's what he's always wanted, since we were kids. I don't mean to twist the knife. I'm not taking sides, I'm just saying what's true.'

'I know.'

'I think he fell in love with you at first sight, when he came out of the hospital that summer.'

'All bald and skinny.'

'You do love him, though, don't you?'

'Of course I do,' Nic said, knee-jerk reaction, both defence and denial, and then she took a breath and thought. 'I do love him. All the years we've spent dating haven't been wasted. I care about him and he's always been wonderful to me. But I don't want to marry him. The thought of waking up with him every day makes me feel … suffocated. Like I'm in a box and I can't escape. I've tried and tried to make things equal, because he deserves it, but he loves me more than I love him. That sounds terrible to say, but it's the truth. Every day makes me feel like I'm living a lie. Sometimes I can't even make myself look at him. And the crazy thing is that he said that was *why* he was asking me to marry him. As if a ring would fix everything, and make it more equal. But it would only make everything worse.'

'So ... it's over?' asked Katie.

'I don't see how we can get past this. Will you talk with him?'

'I can try, but he never tells me anything. Sometimes I think that I know you much better than I know him.' Katie swept her arm out. 'I should be pissed off with you for breaking my brother's heart. But I can't take sides. You know that, right?'

'Yeah.'

They drank their beer in silence, the sort of silence between intimates that Nic had heard other people describe as 'comfortable' but that for her, with Katie, had always been in some way electric.

Nic leant her head back on the chair and looked up at the inky sky. Found Orion, the little dipper, Cassiopeia, the north star.

When Katie spoke again, her voice was tired, a little dreamy. 'Is it Shane specifically who you don't want to marry? Or is it marriage in general?'

'I'm not meant to be with Shane. I tried, but it's not right.'

'Who are you meant to be with?'

Nic, suddenly aware of every part of her body sprawled in this chair, beer can resting on her belly, feet in the sand, moved her head the slightest bit so she could see Katie. Lit by fire, six feet apart, her face turned to the stars.

Had Katie just asked what she thought she had?

All of those conversations over all of those years. The glances, the brush of their hands. Whispers on the telephone, letters written on flowered stationery, the two of them crowded into the single bed in Katie's room in Paradise, warming each other's bare feet. That one time, those thousands of times, when Nic had been too afraid to dare to change everything.

'I'm meant to be with you,' Nic said.

'Nancy and Harriet, solving mysteries,' said Katie with a smile.

It was an old joke, said lightly. Nic could do it too. Step back, let everything stay the same. Or say nothing, as she had with Shane, and let it all slip away.

Was it too much, after everything she had lost, to *try* for once?

'No,' Nic said. 'Not that. I meant that I love you. I can't marry Shane, because I'm in love with you.'

Such thin words, to mean so much.

The stars shifted. Moon wobbled.

Katie sat up and carefully put her beer down in the sand.

'What?' she said.

'You knew, didn't you?' Nic said, desperate now, too late to turn back. 'You must know. It's always been you.'

'My brother,' said Katie, slowly, 'just asked you to marry him.'

'And I couldn't. Because—'

'No.' Katie stood up. 'No, I can't listen to this.'

This was not the way it was supposed to go.

'Because you never want to commit to anyone,' Nic said. 'And you've been running away from it your whole life because of your mother, but, Katie, we know each other, better than we know anyone else. You were just saying that. All our faults, all our best things. We share everything, we always have. Of course I love you. That's what love *is*.'

'No,' Katie said. 'This isn't right. You can't break up with my brother, and then say you love me.'

Nic was standing now, though she didn't notice doing it. 'How would you even know what love is? You're fucking your neighbour because you're bored. You never allow anyone in. You keep everything superficial, so temporary. With every single person except for *me*.'

'I'm not going to talk about this.' Katie walked away, up the steps, towards the camp.

'You can't run away from me, too!' Nic shouted after her.

She heard the camp door shut.

Nic swore. She kicked sand over the fire, then kicked the wood, scattering embers that glowed for a brief moment, and died.

Chapter Twenty-six

The next morning, Nic could see that Jeannette knew that something was wrong but could not name it. She moved from room to room, looking for her cigarettes, then looking for her glasses.

'It's Shane who's gone, Ma,' Nic told her, again and again. 'We've split up. He moved back to Portland.' She supposed he would turn up, eventually, to collect the stuff he'd left here. There wasn't much of it. He had always been visiting, she realised. Maybe unconsciously, he'd known they were temporary. His proposal had been a last-ditch attempt to change that.

But he'd known. Just as Katie had known how Nic really felt about her.

Last night, Katie had said no again and again. But none of it had been a denial of knowledge or truth, or feeling. She had said, 'No, this isn't right,' and, 'No, I'm not going to listen.'

She had never said, 'No, you don't love me,' or, 'No, I never knew,' or, 'No, I've never felt the same way.'

Katie had to know. How could you know everything about another person and not know *that*?

And deep inside, Nic herself had also known all along how this was going to end. Why else had she kept her feelings quiet for so long, a lifetime almost?

There was the waking mind, the thinking mind, the part that hoped and reasoned. And then there was the heart, which understood the truth, the great howling emptiness of it. All those mouldering, irrecoverable rooms. The heart understood loss and was afraid.

Her mother, with her ravaged mind, felt the loss in her heart and thought it was her missing cigarettes.

To occupy Ma's restless feet, they went for a walk with the dogs. Statler and Waldorf were happy to go in any direction, but Nic steered them towards Paradise. With every step, something mounted in her: fear, despair, self-recrimination, hope. But when they got there, Katie's car was gone. The camp was locked-up and empty.

That afternoon, she called Katie, without much hope of a response. Unless she'd gone to her dad's house, she was probably driving. It went straight to voicemail. She didn't leave a message.

At night, though, she was weaker. She texted.

Call me.
Please, call me.
I can see you're getting these. Just let me know you got home OK.
We need to talk.

And finally, after hours of silence, when the sun was rising and Nic sat, sleepless and despairing, in her bed:

I made a mistake. Can we go back to how it was before?

But Katie never replied.

After a while, Nic stopped trying.

Months passed, while she did her best to feel nothing at all.

Chapter Twenty-seven

Many years ago

One summer, they explored the old hotel on the south shore. They'd talked about it for weeks beforehand, gaining the courage, and then they told Katie's dad that they were at the campground, and told Nic's mom that they were at Paradise, and then they went in the morning before Shane woke up so he couldn't follow them. It was the summer before Nic's father died, the summer after Shane had gone officially into remission, when they felt invulnerable.

The hotel was called the Miramac; the sign still hung from the lakeside frontage, but the *mac* had fallen down so it only said *The Mira* in big white letters against the greying siding. It was a big wooden building with wide porches and two wings of bedrooms, with a ballroom in the centre structure. Back in her grandparents' time, it had been grand and full all summer long. Not that Nic's grandparents had ever gone there, or her parents either. The Miramac had been for out-of staters and wealthy people, people who had cocktails before dinner. It had closed before Nic was born and had been falling to pieces ever since. As long as she could remember, it had been a place where the kids were told never to go because it was too dangerous.

Nic and Katie brought a hammer and a crowbar – their hearts fluttering at the thought of doing anything illegal like breaking something – but, in the end, the main door only hung from a single hinge and all they had to do was walk through. The east wing was more or less flattened and the main building was a shell. All the furniture had been taken away or stolen long ago. Floorboards rotting, the roof leaking sunlight and rain, a maple tree growing where the reception desk used to be.

They took it methodically, room by room, day by day. While other kids at the campground were playing kickball or Marco Polo, while Shane was catching up on lost time and learning how to swim, Nic and Katie kept returning to the Miramac. They crept through that empty building full of moss and splinters and bugs. They found a few old newspapers, tin cans and empty beer bottles. They startled a family of wild turkeys, who ran through a hole in a wall. Someone had lit a bonfire in the remains of the ballroom. The old kitchen smelled strongly of a skunk family; the girls steered clear, though once they glimpsed the mother and a baby strolling through the ruins. Their fur was stark black and white against murky brown and grey.

When they were in the hotel, they said almost nothing. They were quiet and reverent, as if the ruins were the Catholic church that Nic had been made to attend every Sunday of her life, where she was taught what was sin. There was something about the hotel that made them stay quiet even on their walk back through the woods to the road. Then, when they got back to Paradise, they talked about other things, as if their exploration had never happened.

And yet they kept coming back.

Nic had thought there would be some signs of what the hotel used to be – some traces of glamour, a scrap of wallpaper, a whiff of perfume. An echo of all of the passions and conversations that must have been housed here, words spoken over cards or whispered over pillows. She'd hoped to find some sort of secret or a story. A grand adventure or a lost love, something she could get lost in. Something she could share with Katie, only the two of them.

But this was just an empty old building, crumbling back into the forest, and all she heard was insects and crows.

Chapter Twenty-eight

April 2021

Nine months after Nic ruined everything

They said there were four seasons in Maine: summer, fall, winter and mud. By the end of April, the snow was mostly gone. Snowbanks taller than their house had melted down to forlorn heaps of dirty snow. It lingered in patches in places where the sun rarely shone – under trees, along the side of the house. It dripped and mixed with the sand and salt from the roads, and made everything gritty and brown. On the lake, the ice was turning to slush.

They might have more summer business at the campground this year. If the vaccine worked; if people were less frightened. Nic had taken some tentative bookings. She hoped so – they needed the money. She wasn't sure how she was going to run the campground and look after Ma at the same time. Her own research felt too heavy to do; she hadn't looked at it in months and it was guilty static in her brain. Pierre Robichaud had never called her back. She had never found any trace of 'Le Moineau et le Martinet' anywhere else. Sometimes she found herself humming the tune, singing the lyrics under her breath:

> O, le moineau et le martinet
> Dans le même ciel ils ont volé
> Ils ont chanté ensemble tout l'été
> Puis trop tôt l'automne est arrivé ...

Whenever she realised she was doing this, singing words in a language that was in her blood but she didn't speak, she immediately stopped herself.

She tried her best to feel nothing at all.

She ran when she could, and every day she walked Statler and Waldorf. It wasn't exactly brisk exercise. The bassets' normal pace was slightly slower than that of a couple of tortoises. They sniffed every single clump of dead grass, pile of mud and scrap of snow, and then carefully, one basset at a time, they lifted their stubby legs and pissed on it. The ambling, sniffing and pissing was their way of savouring the spring weather.

She took off her wool beanie and stuffed it in the pocket of her coat. She and the dogs passed empty cottage after empty cottage, many of them with the windows still boarded up.

Up ahead on the road, she could hear machinery and clanking, raised male voices. Although she'd planned to turn around soon – she avoided Paradise – she and the dogs followed the tracks of heavy vehicles on the muddy road. Something new would be a distraction.

She was rewarded by the sight of a crane, several trucks, a skidder and the Durham cottage dangling in the air. The largely decrepit, long-unloved building had been jacked up off the ground. Men in hard hats and high-vis vests clustered around the four corners of it, debating something.

A woman stood by herself on the lawn. She wore a black woollen coat, a red scarf, jeans and ankle boots. Her hands were in the pockets of her coat and she was watching the men from a distance. Waldorf pulled Nic over to the woman.

'Well, hello, handsome,' the woman said. Waldorf wagged his tail and slobbered on her shin, leaving a silvery trail of drool on her jeans.

'Sorry,' said Nic. 'He's too friendly for his own good.'

'No such thing,' said the woman. Statler wagged his way up to her too and she bent over to give them each a scratch behind the ears. 'Beautiful dogs.'

'Thank you.' Nic nodded at the cottage. A couple of the workmen recognised her and waved, so she waved back. 'Are they putting in a foundation?'

'Yes. The place was going to fall down in a year or two. I should have done this last year, but... Covid.' The woman straightened and squinted at the cottage. 'Does that roof look crooked to you?'

'Yeah.'

'I thought so. Another item for the list.'

'Is it yours now? The cottage? I didn't see that it was for sale.'

'I inherited it. It belonged to my aunt Lydia.'

Lydia Durham had been a terrible human being – mean, stingy, a bully who hated kids and dogs, and who always complained about noise from the campground even though her camp was nearly a mile away. She'd picked a fight with Nic's parents every chance she'd got.

Nic said, 'I'm sorry for your loss.'

'Thanks.'

'Did she die of...?'

'Well, it was pancreatic cancer, but I'm convinced it was a build-up of spite. My mom loved Aunt Lydia for some reason, but I thought she was a bigot. She never liked me and every chance she got, she told me that I was going to hell. And then she died and we all thought she'd leave the cottage to my brother, but she left it to me instead.'

'Did she like your brother any better?'

'No, but he was a boy. I'm Audrey.' The woman had long hands, short nails, chunky silver rings on several of her fingers. Closer up, she had hazel eyes, strong eyebrows and dark hair with a little bit of grey threaded through it.

'Nic. My family owns the Morocco Pond campground.'

'I passed the sign when I came in,' said Audrey. 'It's beautiful around here.'

'Well, it's not looking its best right now. Wait till the mud subsides a little.'

'It's going to be muddy here for a while. After this, we've got to dig a new septic tank. We had to wait until the ground thawed.'

'Will you be here for the summer?'

'Hope to, if it's habitable by then.'

'Well, I know most of those contractors and they're reliable. They did our tank. Do you need electrical work done?'

'I need everything done.'

'OK, well, Donny, who's the guy over by the backhoe, is going to recommend his brother George Junior, but you don't want to hire him. Donny does good work but George Junior is a lawsuit waiting to happen. We use a guy from Andover. I can drop you his card later today if you want.'

Audrey nodded. 'Thanks for the tip.'

'Sure. Are you up from Massachusetts?' She pointed at the car with Massachusetts plates, parked among the trucks.

'From Boston. I'm up here for a few days over spring break. We're mostly back on campus now, thank God.'

'What do you do?'

'Lecturer. Chemical engineering. You?'

'I'm meant to be doing a PhD in music. Part time.'

They watched as the workmen jacked up a corner of the cottage a little bit more. It was nice that there was something new going on up here. At least someone was getting a fresh start, among the grit and the greyness and the melting snow.

'Do you want my number?' Nic asked abruptly.

Audrey raised her eyebrows. 'Well, that was fast, but sure.'

Heat flushed down Nic's body, taking her by surprise. 'I meant – you know, with the work going on here, while you're in Boston. Or if you needed more recommendations.'

'Of course. That would be great, thank you.'

They exchanged numbers and Nic headed back with the dogs, wishing that the bassets would move a little more quickly.

Had that woman been flirting with her? Why would anyone flirt with her when she looked this terrible, with uncombed hair and wrinkled tracksuit bottoms, muddy boots and bitten nails, a non-existent skincare regime, and never enough sleep?

Waldorf stopped to sniff something and she stopped too. She was being ridiculous. She was over-thinking a simple conversation because . . .

Because she'd felt something. Something other than grey.

Her phone pinged. Audrey had texted.

Nice to meet you.

She looked over her shoulder. In the distance, Audrey waved. Nic texted back.

Nice to meet you too.

Chapter Twenty-nine

20 June, 2021

The day before the accident

She was doing the weekly grocery shop at the big Hannaford in Casablanca when she saw Katie again. Well, heard her first. Nic was in the produce section choosing a head of lettuce, enjoying the air conditioning, leaning a little forward so that the mist that was spraying over the cool green leaves could touch her face. A peal of laughter sent ice and heat right into her heart. She looked over and there was Katie, standing next to the deli counter, wearing shorts and a sleeveless tee, her hair pulled up into a ponytail, sunglasses on the top of her head. She had a box of baked goods in her hand and she was not looking in Nic's direction.

Nic turned around and pushed her cart out of sight, into the World Foods aisle.

She was back. Of course she would be. She always came to Maine in June, every year. Even last year during the pandemic, for that one night. Nic's inner clock was set to June. She'd just been trying to ignore it.

Nic tried to work out what to do. *I love you*, she could scream. Right here in the supermarket. *I love you and I should have told you years ago, but you broke my heart and now you're laughing.*

That was not an option.

She could carry on her shopping, trying to avoid Katie. If she ran into her, she could pretend that Katie didn't exist. She could abandon her cart and leave, hide in the car and wait for Katie to finish shopping and then go back in. That seemed like the most sensible thing to do. She bundled her reusable bags under her arm and pushed the cart to the side. Then Katie rounded the corner of the aisle in front of her, saw Nic and stopped.

Nic could not move or speak. Katie stared, also frozen, but only for a split second, and then she smiled.

'Nic!' she said. 'Hey, I didn't know you were in here!'

Nic could only stare. Katie's shopping cart was between them; it might as well be a wall. Katie looked exactly the same as she always did, hair artfully streaked with blonde, so beautiful Nic could hardly bear to look at her, and she was smiling and acting happy to see Nic as if nothing had ever happened, as if they had been sending cheerful messages only yesterday.

'Yeah,' Nic managed to say, her mind racing. What the hell was going on? Did Katie not want to cause a scene in public? Was she just doing what her family always did, pretending nothing was wrong, never talking about the bad stuff, going on as normal?

'We just got here,' Katie continued. 'We drove up from Philly. Haven't been to Paradise yet – we're picking up some supplies first, then going to stop by Dad's.'

We?

For the first time, Nic noticed that Katie was not standing by herself. There was a man next to her. He was clean-shaven with dark curly hair, tall and lean, wearing jeans and a blue T-shirt. He was smiling and looking delighted. She'd never seen him before.

'You're the famous Nic,' he said. 'It's great to meet you!'

Who the fuck was this guy?

'This is Bryan,' said Katie.

'Bryan.' Who the hell was … 'The hot neighbour?' she asked, with some incredulity.

Katie laughed. 'Yeah, that's what I used to call him.' She put her arm around his waist and the two of them smiled at each other in an intimate, sickening way.

Holy Mary Mother of God.

Katie had a boyfriend? An actual boyfriend, not a fuckbuddy? She'd brought a boyfriend *here*?

Everything hurt. She couldn't breathe.

Bryan was speaking. 'I'm so glad to meet you finally. I've heard lots about you.'

'Have you.'

'Only good things,' said Katie, and was she imagining the panic in Katie's eyes? The way her smile was a tiny bit stiff? How her gaze met Nic's for a little too long? Was there a message there, like: *please don't blow this for me by airing your messy emotions?*

Nic opened her mouth to air her messy emotions and Katie interrupted her by saying, 'We've got to go – Dad's expecting us, but can I drop by the campground tonight for a quick chat, just you and me? To catch up?'

No. Yes. Please, please yes. All those messages she had sent to Katie, all the times she'd wanted to take back what she'd said, wanted to work things out, but Katie had met her with blankness, left her with nothing to do and nothing to feel. And meanwhile, Katie had been getting herself a boyfriend.

This was not something that could be resolved with a 'quick chat'. *No.*

Yes.

'Nine o'clock, on the campground beach,' she said, and hated herself for accepting so little, now and for all those years before.

Chapter Thirty

It was chillier than that night last year in June and clouds covered the moon. Nic wore jeans and a sweatshirt, the sleeves pulled down over her hands. She wanted to pace, but she forced herself to sit on the weathered driftwood tree trunk that people used for a bench during beach cookouts, or to sit out and watch the stars. She drank coffee laced liberally with Jack Daniel's. She'd been drinking it since dinner time. By nine o'clock, she had more bourbon than coffee in her Thermos cup.

The liquor sat burning in her stomach and she started at every noise – faint wind in the trees, a loon calling, someone laughing loudly at the campsite. Despite that, she identified Katie's footsteps on the path down to the lake long before she appeared through the trees.

'Hey,' said Katie. She came up to the tree trunk but she didn't sit down. She was a silhouette in leggings and an oversized sweater.

'Thanks for interrupting your honeymoon,' said Nic.

'I told Bryan that you and I needed to catch up.'

'Well. That was big of him.'

'Nic.'

'You're surprised that I'm angry?'

'No. I'm . . . no. I should have answered your messages. I'm sorry.'

'Who the hell is this guy? Why him?'

'He's a really wonderful person. You'd love—'

'Do not *dare* tell me that I would love him.'

Katie sat down. 'I get it. I'm sorry, Nic.'

'Sorry doesn't cut it.'

'I wanted to talk to you, to explain everything. I've missed you.'

'Whose fault is that?'

'Yes, it's mine. But it's complicated, because you also hurt my brother.'

'I didn't want to hurt him, but I couldn't marry him either. You know why.'

'I don't want to fight with you. I never want to fight with you. I just want to talk.'

'Then talk.' She crossed her arms. 'Why'd you bring a boyfriend up here? Was it to send me a message? Or to slap me in the face?'

'I didn't invite Bryan so that you'd be hurt.'

'Why did you?'

'I fell in love with him. And I wanted to show him Paradise.'

'And you told him that you and I were still friends.'

'We are ... aren't we?'

'I told you I loved you and you walked away. You've ghosted me for a year.'

It was dark, but Nic knew everything about Katie. She knew Katie was chewing her lip.

'I didn't know how to reply. I wanted to, but I couldn't think of the right words to say. I kept on writing replies and deleting them. And then time passed and it was harder. So eventually I thought I'd wait until June. I knew if we saw each other, in person, we would sort it out.'

'Here's what I think,' said Nic. The booze was making her reckless. Or maybe it was her whole life that was making her reckless. 'I think when I told you I loved you, it scared you to death. You knew that having feelings for me in any way made you too vulnerable, because we know each other too well and care about each other too much. And then you didn't want to think about it, or feel bad that you'd broken my heart. And you didn't want to feel responsible for Shane being hurt. And when you don't want to feel bad, you look for an escape, like travelling the country, or starting a new job, or having a fling, or coming back to Maine to see me. But this time, you were stuck in one place. So the only thing you could do, to make yourself feel better, was jump into a relationship with a stranger.'

'Bryan's not a stranger,' Katie said. 'And there's more to it than that.'

'Oh? Do tell.'

'You didn't just tell me that you loved me that night. You told me that I was scared of commitment because of my mother and that's why I keep everything superficial.'

'And you deny that?'

'No. You were right. You're right about me travelling to escape, too. That was a lot of truth bombs for one night, and I shouldn't have run away and ghosted you – I'm sorry for that. I really am, Nic. It was shit. But you made me think. So I made a conscious decision to change. Because of you.'

Nic let that sink in.

'You're saying that your relationship with Bryan is because of me?'

'Because you made me realise that I can't keep running away from loving someone.'

'So you chose the first guy who was halfway decent and happened to live across the hallway.'

'No! Bryan is amazing. I love him.'

'Like you love me. Like you've always loved me.'

'Nic, you weren't an option. You and I could never happen.'

'We did happen. We've been happening since the day we met. You've just been too chickenshit to acknowledge it and I've been too chickenshit to say anything.' Nic stood up, knocking over her flask. Her head spun with alcohol and emotion. 'Did you ever think about what we would be like together?'

'You were with Shane—'

'No, no buts. Did you ever imagine us together? Living together, loving each other?'

'It couldn't happen!'

'Why, because I'm a woman?'

'No. I've been with women.'

This was news to Nic. She took a step back, her hands flailing for a moment, sand insecure under her feet. Then she swallowed hard.

'Then what is it?' she asked. 'Shane and I aren't together anymore.'

'We're friends,' said Katie. 'You're my only friend, my only real friend. I can't lose that.'

'Tell me one thing. Just one thing. No excuses, no reasons. You owe me the truth. Have you ever imagined us together?'

'Of course I have,' said Katie.

A pain in Nic's chest doubled her over. Her hands braced on her thighs. How could knowing this, finally knowing this, hurt so much?

Slowly, she straightened up. Steadied herself. Looked Katie in the face. 'Here's the thing,' she said. 'You say you love me. And you say you've changed because of me. So prove it.'

'How?'

'Make a choice. No running, no avoiding things. Make a commitment. Either you stay with Bryan, and you and I aren't friends any more. It hurts me too much and I have to put myself first for once.'

Katie was standing now, too. They faced each other next to the driftwood tree, the fallen giant.

'I can't lose you,' Katie said. 'You're one of the most important people in my life.'

'You've done great for the past year.'

'I haven't. I've thought of you every day and missed you. Nothing's been the same. I hoped we could start again.'

'It's too late to start again. But you can take the other option.

Tomorrow morning, ten o'clock, I'll be waiting at the campground. If you turn up, then I know that you've chosen me.'

'Chosen you for what?'

'To start a new life together. You and me.'

'Where would we go?'

'It doesn't matter. We love each other, we always have. We'll figure it out.'

Katie raised both of her hands, empty. 'I can't do that either. I can't just run away.'

'Why not? It's what you've always done.'

The coffee and bourbon were bitter in the back of her throat. She turned and trudged up the sand towards the shadowy path.

'Harry, wait!'

She paused. Behind her, the lake glowed faintly, a grey darkness, and Katie was a silhouette against it.

'Whatever I choose, I'm going to lose someone,' Katie said. 'I'll lose you, or I'll lose Bryan and Shane. Everything's going to change for ever.'

'I know. I'm sorry. But I can't live like this any more. It's like walking around without a heart.'

'Please don't do this,' Katie said.

Nic walked away, heartless.

Chapter Thirty-one

The morning of the accident, 10.12 a.m.

Nic stood on the side of the road near the turnoff for the campground.

Katie wasn't coming. She had her answer.

And now, leaden and sick, she also knew she'd been wrong.

She shouldn't have given Katie that ultimatum. She should have allowed her time to think about it, more than twelve hours. She knew, full well, that Katie ran away from conflict. That was the whole reason they were in this situation. They should have talked about it without anger.

Maybe she would have been able to persuade Katie, to remind her how good they were together. Maybe even if Katie chose to stay with that man, that stranger, she and Nic could have salvaged something. Over twenty years of friendship deserved more than this.

But it was too late. And she'd been stupid and half drunk and desperate and reckless. She shouldn't have handed her heart over to Katie to break all over again.

She'd lost her for ever.

More dazed than hopeful, she walked a few hundred yards down the road towards Paradise, looking for Katie. But she wasn't there.

As she was walking back, an ambulance came speeding towards her from the direction of town, its lights flashing. She stood and watched it pass. Probably a heart attack or a fall – quite a few of the summer residents were elderly. Or one of those idiots on an ATV, or an accident with a barbecue.

Or a drowning. Like her father.

She stuck her hands in her shorts pockets and walked briskly back to the campground. Inside the house, her mom was out of bed and was kneeling on the floor, scratching Waldorf's belly. She looked up when Nic entered and smiled, and for a split second it all felt so normal that Nic knew she couldn't bear another instant of it.

'Hey, Ma, want to go on an adventure?'

In the shade of an umbrella, Nic and her mother lay on a blanket with the dogs drowsing by their side. Behind her, the ferris wheel spun, the roller coaster creaked and screamed.

This was a good idea – putting up a sign in the campground office and coming to Old Orchard for the day. The change of scenery, the excitement of a day's vacation and the crowds around them revived her mom, made her forget the constant nagging sensation of an unknown loss. They had eaten pizza and pier fries. They had tried the beanbag toss, and lost. Ma had stood with her feet in the surf, letting the waves foam around her legs and watching the horizon with an unaccustomed contentment. Statler had had a minor dispute with a seagull who wanted his dog treat. Nic had gone in the ocean, cold enough to make her heart feel as if it had stopped. She let herself relax into the motion of the water.

Old Orchard was as unlike Morocco Pond as possible for two places that were beside the water. It had one of the only sandy beaches on Maine's normally rocky coast, with a pleasure pier and an explosion of hotels, all flashing lights and greasy food, amusement rides and water slides, crafty seagulls and prizes to be won, and soon, after the sun set, bars blaring music. It was the noisy, vulgar cousin of the rich people's coastal resorts of Boothbay or Bar Harbor.

Her dad had loved Old Orchard. He loved the sand and the surf, and the shouting, lively fun of it. He loved shooting toy ducks and pitching the toss, winning plastic toy guns and giant stuffed animals for her. They had even, once in the off-season, stayed in one of those motor courts with the tiny cabins, like miniature camps, and an aquamarine swimming pool. She remembered getting a sunburn and eating the biggest piece of pepperoni pizza she had ever seen. She must have been about six. They'd never got to stay there again, because of course the summer was too busy for them, and in the winter Old Orchard was nearly as quiet as Morocco Pond.

Maybe that's why she came here when she didn't know where to go. Maybe that's what 'adventure' meant to her: a seaside pleasure town, ninety minutes from home.

Her dreams were so small, in the scale of things.

Beside her, Ma was snoozing. Nic reached over and brushed a bit of sand off her cheek.

Ma probably wouldn't remember this day, but Nic would for the rest of her life and the memory of a good day would always be ruined by the reason why they were here – because Katie had rejected her, and because Nic, in making her choose, had made a terrible mistake.

She would never have another friend like Katie. And she would never love anyone like she loved Katie, either. She'd ruined both of those loves. She'd broken Shane's heart. Her father was dead. Her mother was being taken from her piece by piece.

All that she had left was this present moment, here on this blanket in the shade of an umbrella.

One of the dogs snuffled and woofed in his sleep. A gull swooped and hollered. Another landed next to them and eyed a crust of pizza.

This was enough. She'd make it enough. She would dwell in her mother's shrinking memory and in the smallness of her own dreams.

She didn't know how yet, but she would figure it out.

Her phone rang in her beach bag. Carefully, without disturbing Ma, she pulled it out, hoping against plausibility that it would be Katie. But it was Shane – who she had not heard from in nearly a year.

'Hey,' she said into the phone, surprised. 'How are you doing?'

'I'm OK. Listen, have you heard about Katie?'

'Heard what?'

'Katie's in the hospital. She's had an accident.'

She sat up straight. 'When?'

Later, in the car, she would be ashamed of this – that she had asked when the accident happened, instead of whether Katie was OK.

'This morning. She got knocked off her bike.'

'Oh my God. I saw an ambulance up at the pond. Was that for her?'

'She was taken here in an ambulance, yeah.'

'I didn't know it was her.'

'She's not really conscious yet,' said Shane. 'Dad and I are at the hospital.'

'Oh no. OK. I'll head back now.'

'Head back?'

'We're at Old Orchard Beach. Has she broken anything? What are her injuries?'

'It's basically just her head. I don't know if it's a concussion or something worse. She's going to have a bunch of tests.'

'We'll leave now. Thanks for letting me know.'

Of course it took an age to wake her mother, explain where they were, persuade her that they were leaving, and gather all their stuff, even though she didn't bother to shake the sand out of anything and jumbled it all together into one bag. And then they needed the toilet before the drive, and there was a line for the public bathrooms. And of course it was heading for high season, so there was a long line to get out of the parking lot, and traffic on the way to 95 was at a crawl. The dogs were hot, even with the air conditioning on and the windows open, and they started howling.

All this meant that she couldn't think at all, until she was on the turnpike and the dogs had fallen asleep, and her mother had stopped talking and was gazing out the window.

Then she was hit by the fear. What if Katie was badly hurt? What if she had a brain injury or a broken neck? What if she wasn't going to wake up? Why had Nic given her that stupid ultimatum? Was it her fault that Katie was in hospital?

She called Shane from the road, but he didn't answer. She put her foot down. With every mile, her fear got worse.

What if she'd really lost her?

She had to go back to the pond to drop the dogs. To her surprise, when she got there, Shane's truck was parked outside and he was sitting on her porch.

'Hello!' cried Jeannette, getting out of the car and waving to him. 'Oh, it's good to see you!' She went right up to him and gave him a hug and a kiss on the cheek.

'Good to see you too, Jeannette.' He hugged her back.

Nic had not seen him since he'd picked up his stuff last summer. She did not hug and kiss him, though she sort of wanted to.

'Oh, God,' said Nic. 'Why are you here? Did she die?'

'Who died?' asked Jeannette, who was quite energetic after dozing most of the way home.

'I told you, Katie got into an accident.'

'She's awake,' Shane said. 'She seems OK. But it's complicated. I'll tell you about it in a minute.'

'Come inside,' said Jeannette. 'I'm going to make dinner. Come sit with me in the kitchen.'

While she made a meatloaf, her mother chatted with Shane in her vague but cheerful way, mixing up events from the past with what she was doing right that very minute. But Shane chatted right back, and her mom had made so many meatloaves that she could do it on autopilot (even when it was sticky hot outside, and even when she'd made meatloaf twice already this week and they still had leftovers in the fridge). This left Nic with a little time to feel how weird it was to have Shane at the kitchen table, as if they'd travelled back in time to a whole year ago.

Even for someone who didn't talk about emotions, he was acting too calm for someone whose sister was on the brink of death, so that was reassuring. And Katie was awake. So that meant ...

Nic went into the next room and called Katie's number. Usually it was right at the top of her contacts list but now she had to scroll to find it, because they hadn't talked in so long. Katie didn't answer. She called the hospital and found out that visiting hours were over for the day and visitors wouldn't be allowed until noon tomorrow. She considered calling Bill, but that would raise more questions than she wanted to deal with. She went back into the kitchen and poured a large glass of wine instead.

'Oh, that's a good idea,' said her mother, so Nic poured her a small one. Nic held the bottle up to Shane and he shrugged.

'Sure.'

'Let's talk outside,' she said, and they took their glasses to the porch.

'How was Old Orchard?' he asked. 'It's not like your mom to take a day off during the season.'

'We wanted pier fries. Why did you come up here?'

'Your mom's meatloaf.'

She looked at him.

'You needed to know about Katie,' he said. 'And it's easier to explain in person than on the phone.'

'What happened, exactly?'

'An idiot from New Jersey hit her with an ATV.'

'Wait.' She pointed at the cluster of tents and ATVs at the far end of the campground. '*Those* idiots from New Jersey?'

'Could be.'

'Where did she get hit?'

'It looks like the ATV hit the front of her bike and she went over the handlebars and hit a tree.'

'No, I mean ... where did the accident happen?'

'Oh. She was at the end of the drive to Paradise, turning onto the main road. And the Jersey boys were barrelling along. My dad hasn't stopped talking about ATV speed limits.'

She calculated backwards in time. She'd seen the Jersey boys just before ten, and the ambulance at probably quarter past. It could mean that Katie had been on her way to the campground when she was hit.

This might mean that Katie had chosen her.

Or was she grasping at straws?

'Why did you say it's complicated?' she asked.

'She's got amnesia.'

'Amnesia? Seriously?'

'She doesn't remember the accident.'

'So ... she doesn't remember what she was doing when she got hit?'

'And lots of other things. She doesn't remember that Bryan is her boyfriend. It's weird.'

'It's weirder than weird.'

'You should have seen it. It was like one of those soap operas. *Where am I? Who are you?* Doctor says it happens sometimes.'

'This is very ...'

Convenient, she was going to say. Very convenient that Katie had forgotten what she was doing right at the very moment when Nic's entire life was at stake. Very convenient that she claimed not to remember who her boyfriend was.

'Did she know who you were?' she asked.

'Yeah, she knew me and Dad.'

'Did she ask for me?'

'If she didn't forget me and Dad, she wasn't going to forget you.'

But did she ask for me specifically? She kept herself from scream-ing the question at him. *Did she say no, this all a horrible mistake – I'm supposed to be starting a new life with Nic?*

Of course Katie hadn't said that. She had amnesia. And fairly selective amnesia, at that.

Katie always ran away from her fucking problems. And Nic had created a problem, by falling in love with her and giving her an ultimatum.

Was this all a lie?

Where was Nic's loyalty, that she was able to think this about a person she loved?

'What's the last thing Katie says she remembers?' she asked.

'Early 2020, before the pandemic. She's wiped out most of the last eighteen months.'

Nic knocked back her wine and stood up.

'Where you going?' asked Shane.

She didn't know. All her fear had turned to fury, and all that fury was white hot in her chest, and she had no way of getting rid of it. It was balled up inside her like all her other emotions, with no place to go.

'I'm going to get rid of those assholes.' She strode out of the porch to the other side of the campground, where the Jersey boys had set up their tents.

Their ATVs were parked next to the trailer and the boys them-selves were sitting around on lawn chairs, distinctly less noisy than they had been the night before. At least two of them were holding beer cans. She marched up to them.

'Which one of you was in the accident this morning?'

'It was Troy,' said the one nearest to her.

'Which one is Troy?'

The bearded man in the red baseball cap and sleeveless tee, with tattoos all up one arm, raised his beer.

'Get the hell out,' she told him.

'What?'

'You can't stay here. That was my best friend who you mowed down today. You put her in hospital, and now you've got to leave.'

'But ... where'm I gonna go?' He sounded half cut.

'Not my problem.'

'Hey,' said one of his friends, a more sober one, standing up. 'We paid to be here. In advance. You can't kick us out.'

'I can and I will. I'll give you back your money. And I'm not kicking you all out. Just him.' She jerked her head at Troy. 'Though from the looks of it, he'll need someone to drive him.'

'It was an accident,' said the sober friend. 'You can't punish him for an accident. The police didn't even arrest him.'

'Yet,' said Nic.

'I'm sorry I hit your friend,' Troy mumbled. 'Scariest fucking moment of my life. I'm going to dream about it.'

'How do you think she feels?' Nic demanded. 'She's the one with the head injury. You've only got a dent in the fender of your death-trap vehicle, and some bad dreams.' She turned to the sober one. 'He has half an hour to pack up. You can try calling Moosehead or Ranger campground and see if they have space. Google the numbers. I'll get your refund in cash.'

She went back to the porch, where Shane was watching her.

'That was pretty badass,' said Shane.

'Thanks. And thank you for coming up here to talk to me.' She hesitated, then said, 'It's good to see you, Shane. I'm ... sorry it ended so badly. It was my fault.'

He ducked his head and nodded.

'Good to see you getting along better with your mom,' he said.

'How do you mean?'

'Oh, you know. You kept on fighting her when I was here. Fighting her illness. It's like trying to fight the ocean, you know?'

'Dinner!' called Jeannette from the kitchen.

Chapter Thirty-two

Shane left after dinner and her mom went to bed early. Nic sat on the porch, finishing the bottle of wine. All the boys from New Jersey had left the campground, considerably more quietly than they'd arrived, and she looked up at the stars and thought.

Was this a lie? Was it real? What was Katie playing at? Why had she asked for Nic? Was she pretending to have forgotten that Bryan was her boyfriend because she'd been on her way to meet Nic before the accident, and this was her weird way of letting him down gently? Was she pretending to have forgotten what had happened with Nic because she wanted to sidestep the whole declaration of love and then the ultimatum? Did she actually have brain damage? What if she were changed for ever?

In the morning, exhausted and still finding sand in her hair, she called Bill for an update. Though she hadn't spoken with Shane for the past year, she did see Bill every now and then, and he was always friendly, as was his nature.

Today, he was putting a brave face on, talking about how strong Katie was and how amazing it was that she'd escaped without any broken bones or major injuries, but he was distressed. Especially, it seemed, on behalf of Bryan.

'She doesn't remember her boyfriend,' he said, more than once. 'Imagine how that must feel, to be wiped right out of someone's life.'

Oh, I know exactly how it feels.

She replied, keeping her voice even. 'Yes, it's terrible.'

Would she be backing down on her ultimatum by visiting? Or would it be cruel not to visit? Would it hurt too much?

In the end, she decided that anything was better than torturing herself with questions she didn't know the answers to.

Katie was on her own in a corner of the small ward. She was sitting up in bed with a tray in front of her. Her hair was unbrushed, she wore a hospital nightgown, she had an angry-looking bruise on her forehead and both her eyes were swollen nearly shut. She looked brittle and vulnerable and afraid, and Nic's stomach rolled over with fear and yearning.

No. Anger was better. She clenched her teeth.

But when Katie saw Nic, her face lit up. 'Thank God you're here,' she said. 'What took you so long?'

She looked awful. Like she'd been hit by a two-by-four. Nic wanted to kiss her anyway. She'd missed her so much. Under her mask, she bit her lip.

'Are you OK?' Katie asked.

'Are *you* OK?'

'I'm having an existential meltdown, but, yeah, aside from that. Can I have a hug, please?'

If she hugged Katie, she would cry and rage and want to punch something. Or at least that would be the most appropriate reaction – better than kissing her on the mouth.

'Shane says that you've forgotten everything since like January 2020,' Nic said, not getting any closer.

'Apparently.'

'Is that real, or is it bullshit you've made up so you don't have to deal with stuff?'

Katie laughed shakily. 'It's real. Does it sound like something I'd make up?'

Yes, frankly.

They had spent their childhoods making up stories together.

Nancy Drew and Harriet the Spy. Amnesia would have been the least outlandish of their plot points.

'It seems ... very convenient,' Nic said.

'It's not convenient.' Incredibly, Katie didn't seem to be picking up on her sarcasm. 'Did Shane tell you I've forgotten I have a boyfriend?'

'I've met him.'

'What's wrong?'

'What do you mean?'

'This conversation feels slippery,' said Katie. 'Not normal. Are you not telling me something?'

This wasn't acting. Katie was close to tears. Her bruised face was still pale.

What the fuck. Was this ... real?

Had Katie really forgotten everything that had happened between them?

'Are you and I ...' She stopped and began again. 'What do you remember about me?'

She hated how insecure and needy her voice sounded.

'You? You're my best friend. We've known each other since we were nine. We spent every summer together growing up. We know everything about each other.'

'Do we?'

'Well, I seem to have forgotten the last year and a half, but aside from that, yes.'

'Hmm.'

'And you're dating my brother.'

To her dismay, Nic felt tears rising in her eyes. The mask couldn't hide them. Katie had lost her memory, but Nic had lost everything, even all of her mistakes.

'Harriet?' said Katie, trying to get up.

'Don't call me that.' She backed away, wanted to leave before she burst out sobbing, but she needed to know something first.

'Do they think you're ever going to get your memory back?' she asks.

'The doctor says I probably will, eventually.'

'Like, tomorrow? Or ten years from now?'

'Nobody knows. Nic, tell me what's wrong.'

'Do you remember what happened before the accident?'

'No. Did something happen?'

'I can't deal with this.'

'I need you, though, Nic. I can't remember any of this by myself. I need you to help me.'

'I can't.'

'You know everything about me. Right now, you know more than I do myself. Why can't you help me?'

'This is too much,' Nic said. 'I have to go.' She couldn't hold the tears back any more. She ran from the room, and out of the hospital, and to her car.

But on the way home, she thought, *Katie doesn't remember Bryan, but she does remember me. If I play my cards right, I could get her back.*

The force of it made her swerve the car a little. Fortunately the road was empty. She slowed down to a near-crawl.

Where had that come from?

It was her father's phrase. *If I play my cards right, I'll be driving a new truck next spring. If I play my cards right, we'll go to Disneyland for your birthday. If I play my cards right, we can replace that couch with the spring that sticks up your butt every time you sit down.*

Except in her father's case, he was talking about literal cards. Poker, usually, in backroom games, or when he could get to the casino in Oxford, but also blackjack, and also slot machines.

He wasn't fussy with his risk. But everything depended on it. What they ate, what they wore, how long a shower Nic could take. The mood in the whole house – not from her father so much as her mother, who'd sometimes be prone to dark mutterings that she was glad the campground was in her name, who'd sometimes glowered over their mealtimes while her father joked and tickled.

Nic hadn't understood this dynamic until she'd been much older. She'd thought her mother took life too seriously and prayed too much. Only later had she realised that her father was the only one who'd had the privilege of taking everything with a sense of humour, because he'd been the one who'd lost all of their money.

She loved her father and she missed him every day. But the phrase wasn't the only thing that reminded her of him. It was the selfishness of it. The sense that a person could do exactly what they wanted without putting anyone else first.

Nic had taken her biggest gamble a year ago, and she'd lost. And then she'd tried again, two nights ago.

Only a fool – or her father – made the same mistake twice and expected it to turn out differently. Like Shane had said – it was like trying to fight the ocean.

Part Two

———

Paradise Regained

Chapter Thirty-three

In their childhood games, Katie was Nancy Drew and Nic was Harriet the Spy. Their characters suited them, which was maybe why they used these nicknames for each other all the way to adulthood.

Like the girl detective in the books they loved, Katie was pretty, popular and her father was a lawyer. And though her light brown hair stubbornly refused to be strawberry blonde, Katie said, 'As soon as I'm old enough, I'm going to dye it.'

Like Harriet the Spy, Nic was a loner, an observer, someone who had one loyal friend and no more, someone who kept her feelings close to her chest. Nic tore out the used pages in her math notebook and used it as a journal; Katie found a magnifying glass that was part of an old stamp collection.

They had characters and unlimited time while Nic's mom ran the campground and Katie's dad was at the hospital with Shane. All they needed was a mystery to solve.

At first, they made the mysteries up. Who was the mysterious man who lived alone in the camp at the end of North Shore Road? (They never found out, but after a week's worth of surveillance, when he did nothing but drink coffee on his porch and go fishing every morning and evening, they got bored.) Who had pulled the garbage out of the campground dumpster and was the thief looking for a hidden secret? (It was raccoons.)

Their first success was The Case of the Purloined Pickup. Nic noticed that Mr Poirier, who had no money and whose camp was falling to pieces, was suddenly driving a brand-new Ford pickup in a brilliant cherry red. What was the reason? Theft? A bank robbery? Maybe even murder? They hid behind a woodpile and watched him coming and going, Nic taking extensive notes. Disappointingly, he never appeared carrying large sacks with dollar signs on the sides of them, and there were no traces of his burying treasure in his yard, though, when he was gone, they did check his lawn carefully to look for disturbed earth. They peeped in his windows, too, but saw little but empty beer cans and a collection of broken televisions.

It seemed as if the mystery had been solved, in yet another anticlimactic fashion, when they overheard Mr Poirier's neighbour shout over to him one afternoon. 'Where'd you get the fancy wheels?'

'My truck's in the shop so my brother-in-law lent me his,' Mr Poirier replied.

This was a letdown. Behind the woodpile, Nic and Katie regarded each other with dismay in their eyes. 'Maybe it's too boring around here,' said Katie with a sigh, and Nic was going to agree when suddenly a car drove up, parked beside the pickup, and a man jumped out and started yelling at Mr Poirier about borrowing his truck without permission while he was away on vacation. This was, apparently, the brother-in-law, and the whole thing came to a satisfying conclusion with the angry man threatening to call the cops and driving off in the cherry-red truck.

Their sleuthing instincts had been correct!

Buoyed by this success, Katie came up with the idea to knock on the doors of the camps along the lake, and ask the residents if they had any missing items or puzzling occurrences. The mere thought of this made Nic squirm with discomfort but Katie insisted, so she tagged along, standing behind her friend and trying at the same time to be supportive and brave and also to melt into the ground without a trace.

But it worked. They investigated misplaced bicycles, water floats that had been taken by the waves, and, in one case, a missing cat. Nothing as spectacular as the Purloined Pickup, but satisfying.

Until they knocked on Lydia Durham's door.

'I don't think this is a good idea,' Nic was whispering when Miss Durham opened the door, scowling.

'What do you want?'

Katie smiled, confident and professional. 'Hello, Miss Durham, I'm Katherine Stone and this is my friend, Nicole Leblanc. We're detectives and we wondered if you had any mysteries you would like us to inves—'

'Get off my porch, you filthy children. I don't have any money to give you.'

And she slammed the door in their faces.

'See?' Nic said, tugging Katie away, wanting to escape before Miss Durham came back with a gun or something. Katie went with her, but she was furious.

'She thought we wanted money,' she said, seething. 'As if we were begging. When we were only trying to help her!'

'She's mean. My mother hates her.'

'She's trying to hide something. She's got a secret.'

'Her secret is that she's a terrible old bat. We should stay away from her.'

But Katie had the idea in her head now, and the next day she told Nic, 'We need to do a Harriet the Spy.'

And how could she resist that?

The first stage was for Miss Durham to leave her camp. As she never spoke to the neighbours except to berate them, eavesdropping couldn't help them determine what her plans were in advance. They just had to wait, and wait, and one day when Nic was going to Paradise, she noticed that the witch's old Chevrolet was gone. She ran to get Katie.

They approached from the water. For one thing, Katie's dad had informed them that the water and the first five feet of shoreline were a public right of way, so it wasn't trespassing to stand on someone's beach. For another, who was going to be suspicious of two girls in bathing suits in the lake? For a third thing, Nic had noticed when paddling her canoe past that Miss Durham's porch door didn't quite shut all the way. When they reached the camp, they dried off their feet with the towel that Katie had draped around her neck and carefully removed all traces of sand. Then they tested the porch door, which swung open.

The camp was dark inside and smelled of mildew and old cigarette smoke. All of the curtains were drawn and no lights had been left on. 'She's too stingy to use sunlight,' whispered Katie. Nic, heart pounding with fear and excitement, and a sort of ecstasy that she and Katie were doing this very secret, very forbidden thing together, made a mental note to write this phrase down when she had her notebook. *Too stingy to use sunlight.*

'What are we looking for?' she whispered.

'Anything. Just keep your ears open for the car coming back.'

Like some of the more basic camps, this one was only three rooms: a single living area, with a cramped kitchen on the road-facing side and an even more cramped bathroom tacked on. Nic had no desire to go into a witch's bathroom and even without entering it she could smell curdled milk in the kitchen, so she busied herself in the main living area, which served as living room and bedroom. A hard-cushioned sofa and a scratched coffee table sat on one side, and on the other was a single bed. The coffee table was stacked with multiple copies of *TV Guide* and newspapers folded to the crossword section. Nic stared at these for a moment until she realised what was wrong. 'She doesn't have a TV,' she whispered to Katie, who nodded and went to investigate the sleeping area.

That's when Nic noticed that the coffee table had a drawer in it. She opened it. It was full of photographs, and even in the dim light she could see that something was strange about them.

'Psst!' She waved Katie over and the two of them gazed at the photographs. Katie actually reached into the drawer and took them out so they could get a better look.

'They're all of the same woman,' said Katie.

More than that – they spanned years. Black-and-white high-school-graduation photos; brown-tinged Polaroids from the seventies; glossy prints that had soft edges and fingerprints. The woman could be anyone. She had straight hair and wore glasses. Her clothes changed, her hairstyle changed, sometimes she was smiling, sometimes she was not. In one photo, the woman was standing by a man and his head had been ripped off. In a couple of the photos, there was someone else with her, someone with a shirt buttoned up to her throat and a smile that Katie and Nic had never seen on Miss Durham's face in real life.

But mostly they were just of the woman, by herself.

'Who is she?' whispered Katie, and Nic opened her mouth to say she didn't know, but it looked as if it was someone she cared about, when they both heard a car door shutting and they froze for a split second, staring wide-eyed at each other. They'd missed the sound of Miss Durham driving up.

They shoved the photographs, willy-nilly, into the drawer, shut it, and scrambled out of the room, across the porch and through the door. At the last moment, Nic caught the door just before it slammed behind them. They rushed down to the lake, into the water and waded and ran and splashed as fast as they could to Paradise.

They never did solve the mystery of those photographs, and the scare was enough for them never to break into anyone's house again – not while anyone was still living there, at least. The following summer, they explored the ruins of the Miramac hotel instead. And the summer after that, Katie was more interested in boys than in solving mysteries, and they had moved on to reading sexy romance novels that guests left behind at the campground.

Now that she was grown, Nic sometimes wondered if what they'd really been doing that summer, and the summer after, was trying to solve the bigger mysteries of their lives. The disappearance of Katie's mother; why Shane had cancer; why Nic's parents had screamed at each other and then acted as if nothing was wrong. They were looking for those answers in the lost cats and buried treasure and ruined buildings. A logical clue that would explain everything.

They hadn't yet learnt that sometimes things just happened that way.

Chapter Thirty-four

I emerge from the water sputtering, pushing my sodden hair out of my eyes, and Bryan is right beside me. He shakes his head like a dog, scattering droplets that catch the sun, and I have to catch my breath because I remember the minute I realised I was falling in love with him.

It wasn't big or dramatic. I was spending about half my non-working hours over at his apartment anyway because we were sleeping together and trading the dog back and forth, a convenient arrangement that meant that we both had our space but were available whenever one or both of us needed a distraction. For all that Nic said about not shitting where you live, I was finding it pretty much ideal for a time when we weren't allowed to travel or socialise much. 'Bubbling,' they called it.

It was a Saturday morning in October. We went for a workout in the park together and then he made us breakfast. We were sitting on his sofa and Eebie was on his lap. I was scrolling on my phone; he was reading a magazine. The living room speaker was playing old jazz, Ella Fitzgerald singing 'These Foolish Things Remind Me of You'. It was a perfectly ordinary day.

I looked up from my phone at the same time that he looked up from his magazine and our eyes met.

The sun from the window hit his face at a slant and turned his brown eyes into a shade of amber, and every part of me just went *wow*.

He kept looking at me. And I kept looking at him. And finally, I said, 'What?'

And he said, 'I think I've accidentally attached my future happiness to you.'

And then he burst out laughing. And I, who in a normal moment would have got up from the sofa and run away, started laughing too. Eebie, startled, began to bark. Bryan leant over and kissed me. And we went on with our day.

But it stayed with me. I couldn't get rid of it. The sunshine on his face. How it felt when he kissed me.

These foolish things remind me of you.

I had accidentally attached my future happiness to him, too.

And now I remember it.

Like I remember it all: every single choice I made to get me here to the present moment. All of the love and trust and giddy newness of it, and all the pretending, the denying, the running away, the pain, the lies.

'Are you OK?' Bryan asks me.

'Yeah! It's just – it's cold.'

'Do you feel better?'

'Yeah,' I say. 'I really do. We need to shout "fuck" together a lot more often.'

'It's a date.' He turns and wades back towards the shore. I follow him, my mind racing.

I should tell him that I remember. He's my boyfriend and I'd forgotten our entire relationship. But how can I tell him about Nic's ultimatum? How can I explain why I never told him about that night on the beach, when Nic confessed that she loved me – and my own cruel, cowardly reaction?

I can see now why Nic said my memory loss was convenient. It neatly removed eighteen months and with it, my culpability in the death of our friendship.

And it gave me an incredible gift. It means I can set things right.

I have so many things to set right.

We reach the shore, dripping, and I say, 'We're going to have to change now before we go to Dad's.'

'So how do you like feeling your feelings?'

'It's scary.'

'All the best things are.' He grins at me and I want to kiss him, and then I remember that I can't.

Chapter Thirty-five

While I'm changing into dry clothes, I go through my memories of the morning of the accident. It was only a few days ago, but it feels like another lifetime.

It was midsummer's day. When I woke up, Bryan was already out of bed and Eebie was asleep beside me, stretched over Bryan's pillow with his backside, as usual, in my face. I lay in bed for a few moments, trying to figure out how to act. What to do about Nic and about Bryan. How to handle Nic's ultimatum without losing someone I loved, for ever.

I had no idea. I went through it and through it, and came up with no solutions at all. If I chose Bryan, I would lose Nic's friendship. If I chose Nic, I would lose Bryan. And I might lose Nic's friendship anyway.

For nearly a year, I'd tried not to think about my feelings for Nic. I'd let other feelings grow instead, because they felt safer. And now ... no feeling was safe.

I found Bryan on the porch, drinking coffee, a plate with toast crumbs in front of him.

'You're up early,' I said. I kissed him on the cheek.

'You were up late.'

'Is there more coffee?'

'Plenty. I thought you might need it.' He poured me a cup. 'How'd you sleep?'

I joined him at the table. It's a scratched and sanded wooden table, which once was painted blue, and shows it in the crevices in the bevelled edges and turned legs. I think it belonged to my grandmother or even my great-grandmother, like almost everything else in this house – the furniture, the paintings on the wall, the bedlinen, the books, the glassware and dishes, the very air.

'Not great,' I said. 'I've got a bit of a headache.'

'You had a few beers, I guess. You and Nic had a lot to catch up on.'

'Yup.' I lied. The truth was, I drank half a bottle of wine when I got back from the campground, sitting on the beach by myself, trying to work out what to do. How to choose between Nic and Bryan. How to work out some loophole, some magic escape, so I didn't have to choose at all.

'Do you want me to cook you breakfast?'

'No, thanks, it's fine.'

'Aren't you hungry? You hardly ate last night.'

I didn't feel as if I'd ever be hungry again. Or at least never enjoy eating something – to see food, smell it and anticipate pleasure. That didn't seem like something I deserved any more.

I shook my head. It felt as if he could see everything on my face. I waited for him to ask me what was wrong. Why I didn't want him to come with me to see Nic, when she was supposedly my best friend, part of my family.

What did I think was going to happen? I hadn't spoken to her in nearly a year, because, if I spoke to her, I would have to face the enormity of what I'd given up. And yet I told Bryan for that whole year that she was my best friend. Pretended that everything was fine. All because I couldn't face the pain that I'd caused her, or the pain that she was asking me to cause my brother, or the pain of being too afraid to risk changing our friendship for ever for something as ephemeral as love.

And now all that pain was right here, filling the air. And I knew that Bryan could tell that something was wrong, but not what.

'What time is it?' I asked him.

'It's about nine.'

It was already late. I didn't have much time left.

'I've got a headache. I think I need to take it easy.'

He nodded. 'I thought I'd cycle over to that old cemetery you told me about.'

'What are you going to do there?' I ask.

'Walk around, sit and soak in the atmosphere. I like being surrounded by history.'

'My dad can probably tell you something about it. He loves history.'

'I'll ask him later. Do you want to come with?'

He was smiling, cheerful, like someone on vacation in a beautiful place with the person he loves.

'Maybe after this headache goes.'

'I'll pack a cooler and put it on the back of the bike. We can have a picnic.'

'You go ahead. I need to drink this coffee and maybe take a couple of aspirin.'

He kissed me on the forehead, and I went upstairs and curled up on the bed and waited to hear him leave the house. I heard the squeaky shed door open and I heard him wheeling out the bicycle. It was the old bike because that one had a rattly fender on the back wheel, which my dad had been meaning to fix for years. It's a summery sound, the sound of picnics and jaunts to the beach, the sound of towels and bare, sandy feet, the sound of kids on makeshift Fourth of July parades and long aimless afternoons.

The rattle receded into the distance.

I lay on the bed for quite a long time. It was a beautiful day – the sunlight reflected off the water and through the window, making patterns on the ceiling. A shimmering, a vision that you couldn't quite work out, like the aura of a migraine.

I wanted to lie there for the whole day and watch the light shift and change as time passed by, and everything went on without me.

But I couldn't. Last night, my best friend in the world had said, 'Either you choose me, or you choose him.'

I couldn't pretend any more that everything was all right. I had to make a decision.

I wheeled the other, newer, bicycle out of the shed. This one was cherry red and it had a wicker basket attached to the handlebars. It's the sort of bicycle that you could see in a picture, maybe of the 1950s, maybe of somewhere in France, with a woman in a flowing skirt pedalling along with the basket full of flowers and a long baguette.

I mounted the bicycle the way my mother taught me when I was very young: one foot on the pedal, one foot pushing off the ground, propelling the bicycle forward and then, once it's in motion, swinging my leg up over and perching myself on the seat. I've always got on a bicycle this way, although my brother does it the way our father does it – he straddles the bicycle in a static position, puts one foot on a pedal, the other foot steadying, and goes. My father was always stable, my mother was always one foot in flight.

When I was a kid, I thought for a while that riding a bicycle was the only thing I learnt from her. Now I was finding out that wasn't true.

Today, I was going to have to leave someone. I only had to decide who. By the time I reached the main road, I had to decide to turn left and join Bryan in the cemetery, or turn right and meet Nic in the campground.

Whatever direction I chose, everything would change. I would lose someone that I loved. Either way, I would hurt myself. But my choice would hurt Bryan, or it would hurt Nic. And I had only myself to blame.

I focused my eyes on the end of the drive and pushed one leg down, and then another, trying to listen to my body and not the sound of the wheels on the road. When you've got a big choice to make, your body is supposed to know what you should really do. I heard a talk on it once, some professional training day. They said it's about listening to your gut, but really it was about listening to your brain. Hormones and enzymes, electrical impulses from your hippocampus. I thought it was a whole load of bullshit.

Though maybe it wasn't, because by the time I reached the stop sign I knew what I was going to do.

But still, I paused. I closed my eyes for a second. I took a breath – the last breath before I consciously tore myself in two.

Then I pedalled forward, into the crossroads. And there was a rush of noise, maybe a scream, and a big, solid, hard something thrust the bike out from underneath me. I glimpsed the asphalt below me, I saw the trees above, I was flying, and then I was nowhere, pushed out of the world that I knew.

Now I'm back. And I have more decisions to make. But the amnesia has given me the opportunity to make the right ones, this time around.

Chapter Thirty-six

First, I have to talk with my dad.

Bryan wants to drop me off at the house and then come back to pick me up later, but Tessa co-opts him to help her change cellphone providers, a complex procedure that apparently takes most of the afternoon. My dad and I go for a walk.

My dad and I have always gone for walks. Apparently it started when Shane was a baby and I was a toddler, and the only place we would sleep was in our double buggy. He wheeled that buggy all over town, at all hours of the day and night, up and down hills, through every street of our suburb. He says that half the time, he was probably sleepwalking. He also says that those hours upon hours of walking the streets taught him the value of walking, not just as exercise or a trick for lulling crying babies to sleep, but as a form of meditation. As a family, we started hiking very young – adventures of an hour, or an afternoon, or a weekend. Sometimes we got lost but my dad never cared. He was happy to be walking anywhere, even if it was in the wrong direction.

But he always found the right direction. That's my dad.

Unlike me. I rush off in any direction, whatever seems best at the time, which usually means whatever seems easiest.

When, on that day when the family all sat in his living room with plates of cake on our laps, Dad told us that he had been diagnosed with a progressive disease – a disease that would, in the span of years, erode his ability to move and talk, and eventually kill him – he was calm and he was kind. He put our worries first, answering questions and reassuring us that he was following all of his doctor's orders. He told us that his symptoms at present were minor and that the medications would help him live as normal a life as possible for the longest possible time. He was honest with us, but he was smiling in a way that was meant to tell us that it was OK, that it was nothing that we could not handle.

It was the same way I remember him breaking the news about my brother's childhood leukemia, and my mother abandoning us, and the death of Nic's father. Or when my grandmother died, or our cat, or when he broke his ankle and couldn't take us to Disney. Every problem, big or small, temporary or permanent, is met with the same courage and kindness.

He's a good man, my father. I'm nothing like him.

Dad and I walk down towards the river, where there's a path along the bank, winding through trees, a popular spot for joggers and people wheeling their own babies around. I watch him carefully. I can see a hesitation in his usually regular gait. A tremor in his hand. He hides it well, for now.

My dad moved here to Casablanca when he married Tessa. He practised corporate law in Connecticut, but in Maine he opened a general law practice and did a little bit of everything until he took early retirement. He knows everyone in town and he says hello to them all, and sometimes stops to re-introduce me to people who apparently I have met at some point or another, so a walk that should take about ten minutes takes more like half an hour. I wonder if any of these people – former clients, neighbours, his barber – know how sick he is. My father is truthful, but also he does not complain.

And I'm lying to him by not admitting that I've got my memory back. I only hope that I'm able to make it up to him – that the ends justify the means.

Finally, we reach a less populated section of the trail and I'm able to say the words I've been rehearsing in my head.

'Dad, I know you've been worried about me after my accident, but I also know that there's something wrong with you that you're not telling me.'

'Oh, sweetheart. There's no need to—'

'You and Tessa are adapting her uncle's camp to live in. And when I asked about it, you changed the subject. And also, I notice you, Dad.' I reach for his hand and hold it, lift it up so we can both see the faint tremor.

'There is plenty of time to talk about this, Kitty. Right now, you need to get better.'

'I am better,' I say truthfully, but to preserve my lie I continue. 'And I might never get my memory back. You're protecting me, I know, and I appreciate it, Daddy. But I need the truth. Please.'

He leads us to a bench in a sunny spot, where we sit, side by side.

'So,' he says. 'It started in early 2020.'

'Tell me everything,' I say.

And for the next hour and a half, in between interruptions when we see yet again another person who he knows, he tells me the story of his illness, from the earliest symptom to the final prognosis.

The first time he told me this, just after his diagnosis, my initial response was denial. I sat on his sofa next to Nic and my brother, and I made my father repeat himself, and asked him if he was sure, if he hadn't misunderstood the doctor, if he didn't want some more opinions. Then, after making my father justify his own terminal diagnosis, I burst into tears. I couldn't stop crying and eventually Shane had to drive me to Nic's house, where she poured Jack Daniel's into me and I calmed down enough to argue with my brother.

And then I went back to Philadelphia, to my own life.

Now, as he speaks, I listen as hard as I can, because now I remember all of it, but with my silence he's telling me more than he did the first time around. Pretending that I'm ignorant gives him space to share.

'But you mustn't be upset,' Dad tells me, in typical impossible optimism. 'Tessa and I have plans in place. And I've got a great doctor. And your brother has been hugely supportive.'

Like Shane promised to be, when we first found out. I didn't trust him when he made those promises. To give me a little credit, it's hard not to think about Shane as he was when he was my little brother, who was fragile, who I had to protect. But he's grown up now, and he has followed through, with not only my dad but with Jeannette.

'And how have I been?' I ask.

For the first time in this conversation, he hesitates.

'I've been angry.' I make the suggestion for him. Of course I know the answer.

'You've been shaken,' he says.

'I made it all about me.' I interpret his words.

'No, no, no, of course not. You were upset. You are upset. I understand. I'm your last parent left and you want me to live for ever.' He tilts his head, as he does when he is thinking. 'And, correct me if I'm wrong, but I think you've idealised me, Kitty. When you were little, you thought I could do anything. And even now that you're grown up, you expect me to live for ever. My illness has fundamentally shaken your world view.'

'You never came up with that on your own.'

'It's Tessa's theory,' he admits.

'And she formulated this theory because, for all intents and purposes, I was behaving as if your sickness was all about me and she was trying to be compassionate towards me.'

He struggles for a little while, as truthfulness wars with tact. Finally, he says, 'You're my daughter and I love you.'

By which I understand – I was a monster.

We get up and walk a little further, not talking much, but I at least am thinking a lot. For the first time, I'm considering whether my amnesia might have been, in some way, something I subconsciously chose. In the hospital, Nic said that it was convenient and it is true that it conveniently started not too long before my dad started showing symptoms, which is something I haven't been good about handling.

'Shane's been good, then?' I ask eventually.

'He's been great. He's come to almost all of my appointments, and he's on top of my therapy and medications. He visits a few times a week.'

'What can I do?'

'Spending time with you is enough, sweetheart.' He pulls me into a hug and I squeeze him, hard.

'I can work from home, you know,' I say to his shoulder. 'I can move here to Maine.'

'And live where? Paradise isn't winterised.'

'I'll figure it out. I can rent a place. Or I can stay with you and Tessa for a little while.'

He draws back a little and pats me on the shoulder. 'That's really sweet, honey, but have you discussed it with Bryan?'

I haven't. Because I have been monstrously selfish, and I continue to be.

'Also, not to ick you out,' he says. 'But Tessa and I don't want you staying with us. We might not have as much time together as we thought and we're trying to have as much sex as possible before we can't any more.'

'Oh, my God, Dad.' I grimace, but I'm laughing.

He kisses me on the cheek. 'I don't want you to stop your life because of me.'

'You stopped yours to raise me and Shane.'

'No, I didn't. Raising you and Shane was all I wanted to do and, besides, I'm your dad. It was my job. It's not your job to take care of me. Maybe one day I'll need you and I promise that if I do, I'll ask. You can visit all you want, and Tessa and I can come out and see you, too. But right now . . . you need to live your own life.'

'Can Tessa look after you?'

'She wants to.'

'That's not what I asked. Can she?'

'She will. That's what we vowed to do. In sickness and in health. And we'll get help when we need it.'

He takes both my hands and peers at me. And I see something in his face relax as he sees something in mine.

'Welcome back, Kittycat,' he says.

Then he hugs me again and we begin walking together.

Chapter Thirty-seven

Ma was at an all-day church event and Nic had the house to herself. She should be working on her research – she even went as far as to open her laptop and log on to the university portal. She looked at her guitar, sitting idle next to the pegs of winter coats. The fiddle in its case. But then she found herself in the kitchen, clearing up the detritus of their morning. She wiped down all the surfaces, let the dogs out, swept the floor, put away the last bit of bread before it went stale, went outside to tell the dogs to stop barking, put the jam and milk back in the fridge – first sniffing the milk to make sure it hadn't gone bad from being on the countertop all morning in midsummer – then let the dogs back in.

She had to pause twice to answer her phone. Then she tackled the living room – plumping cushions, vacuuming the rug, folding the throw back onto the sofa, collecting butterscotch wrappers from under her mother's chair.

She let the dogs out again.

When Nic was small, her mother had done this every day of her life. Sometimes, Nic had 'helped' clean with a broom or a useless feather duster, or had made an extra mess while cooking.

Nic had learnt that that was what women did.

When her father died, her mother had taken on the repair jobs and running the campground, and when Nic herself had needed less attention because she was at school, her mother had cooked for bake sales, for charity dinners, for elderly neighbours. Jeannette had done this work every day of her life until she couldn't any more because she had dementia far too early, and it was too dangerous for her to be alone.

'When you get married and have children, you'll do the same,' Ma had told her. To child-Nic this sounded exciting, but to teenage-Nic this became a threat.

Nic went to university – the first person in her family – so she could have a different life. For her bachelor's she studied music and teaching so she'd have something to fall back on. And then she got a master's in ethnomusicology. She dated women as well as men, went to concerts and queer bars, got herself an apartment in the heart of the city.

She had all of the doubts of a chronically overthinking bisexual person in queer spaces: *am I gay enough? Am I pretending to be? Do I just think I'm attracted to women because I want to avoid being in a marriage like my parents'? Do I just think I'm attracted to men because society tells me I should be?*

And after it all, despite all of this effort to be different, Nic was treading the same path as her mother.

Literally – from one room of this patched-together house to another.

She stopped. 'What the hell am I doing?' she said aloud to the house her father had built.

And of course as soon as she said it aloud, she knew exactly what she was doing. She was doing the same thing she'd been doing for a year now.

She was not allowing herself to feel.

She called in the dogs, got them settled in their beds, took her car keys and left.

She parked the car on the dirt shoulder of the road and walked straight into the woods, where it was darker, quiet, cooler, and everything smelled of moss and fallen needles of pine. The narrow dirt trail snaked between trees and grey rocks, and started climbing right away. A chickadee spoke its name over and over

— *chicka-dee-dee-dee-dee-dee-dee*. She heard her own footsteps and, soon, her breath in her ears.

She climbed faster. Roots grew across the path, making a sinuous staircase. Generations of footsteps and handholds had worn their bark thin. In late summer she would climb this hill to pick wild blueberries at the granite top of the mountain, loading the tubs into a backpack to keep her hands free for the climb down. Now she carried nothing. She wasn't even wearing the right shoes. She wore shorts and sandals, nothing to protect her from falls, insects and poison ivy.

It didn't matter. She wanted to get as far away as she could from everything and everyone, somewhere that she wouldn't have to cater to anyone else's needs or feelings, where she wasn't a friend or a daughter or a girlfriend or a caretaker. Where she could finally be simply alive and nothing else.

She tried to concentrate on the rhythm of her steps and her breaths. This path was always longer than she remembered but she was good at carrying on, keeping her head down, getting done what needed to be done. Muffling herself in busy-ness as if she were wrapping herself in layers of cotton.

But with every step, some of those layers fell away. Keeping busy and never having time to think was protecting her. But it was also keeping her tethered to a place where everything was haunted by the past and dreams never worked out.

She belonged at Morocco Pond, but she had never fitted in there. She loved playing music, but she did not like an audience. She loved a woman, but that woman did not love her enough.

The sun broke through quite suddenly, framed by evergreen branches. She stepped over the bed of a sometime stream, grabbed hold of a branch and heaved herself up over a short, sheer rockface, scraped her knee, gathered her balance and stood.

She wasn't quite at the top. This was the spot where you stopped and rested, and looked at how far you'd come – a slab of granite that jutted out over the side of the mountain and gave a clear view of the valley below. Seen from above, the carpet of trees spread outwards and upwards over the other hills, split by the grey crayon line of the road. In the distance, she could see Morocco Pond – a sapphire set in green. That water was in her veins.

Nic sat on the sun-warmed rock. It glittered with flecks of mica. She caught her breath and picked a bit of dirt out of her grazed knee, and wished she had a bottle of water. She watched a bird circling on an updraught. Around and around. Maybe an eagle, maybe something else. Maybe looking for prey or a mate, or another place to go. It was too far away to tell.

It turned once more and then plummeted, leaving the sky unpopulated and blue.

All at once, out of nowhere (but really out of everywhere and everything), she began to cry.

Not the stifled, stunted crying that she'd done when she'd visited Katie. This was a great sob, ripped out of the bottom of her lungs, followed by another and another. For her lost dad, her fading mother. For how she'd broken a good man's heart. For her best friend and even for that night when Nic had revealed her true feelings, feelings that Nic was now the only witness to.

For herself, the person who inhabited this strong and tired body – this body that could create love and lose it. For the way she thought she'd understood herself, but maybe she never had, and maybe she never would again.

No one was watching, no one could hear her, and she howled into the air, let the tears stream down her face and drip onto her neck, her hands lying limp by her sides, while she gazed out into nothing.

It was hard to know how long she cried for. She poured it out to the mountain and the sky and the trees, everything she'd been trying so hard not to feel. The sobs didn't stop so much as trickle down into nothing. An undignified hiccup and a wipe of the back of her hand. A single white cloud had come into view.

'I don't know what to do,' she said to the cloud. 'I don't know how to be.'

Behind her, a twig snapped.

Quickly, she turned. Someone stood behind her – not on the rock, but on the path, at a polite distance. She wore sunglasses, a hat, carried a backpack. She looked familiar but Nic couldn't place her until she said, 'Have you been hurt?' and she recognised the voice. Audrey, who'd inherited the Durham place.

'No,' Nic said. 'No, I'm OK. Not hurt. Just having a cry.'

She tried to dry her eyes and nose with her hand, but that didn't do it so she used the hem of her T-shirt instead.

'It's a good place for it.' Audrey stepped closer, reached into the pocket of her pants and held out a red bandana handkerchief. 'Here, use this. It's clean.'

Gratefully, she wiped her face and hands. The bandana smelled of detergent. 'Thanks,' she said. 'I'll wash it before I give it back.'

'No worries.' Audrey handed her a water bottle.

'How'd you know what I needed?' Nic said, laughing shakily. She unscrewed it and drank deep. It felt as if she'd sweated and cried everything out of her, and she was a fragile shell.

'I've been there.'

Undignified, she sniffed. 'I'm sorry to interrupt your hike.'

'You haven't.' Audrey stepped onto the rock. 'Nic, right? From up at the pond?'

'Right.'

'Do you want to tell me about it?'

Nic's breath caught in an echo of her sobs. When was the last time someone had asked her that?

'I don't think so,' she said. Audrey nodded.

'OK. Well, if you want to, you know where to find me.'

'Thank you.'

'I mean it.'

Nic gave her the water bottle. Audrey slipped it into the side pocket of her backpack.

'Do you feel better, though?' she asked.

Nic considered. 'I don't know if it's better. But ... I can feel.'

'Good,' said Audrey. She smiled at her, a lopsided smile that Nic remembered from the first time they'd met. 'See you later.'

She continued along the path, upwards. Nic wiped her face again, then put the bandana in her own pocket. She stood up. After several deep clear breaths, she started her descent.

Chapter Thirty-eight

After visiting my dad, we go back to Paradise and I tell Bryan that I need to go up to my room and have a nap. I'm not normally a person who ever naps – I hate going to sleep as, to be honest, it seems like a waste of time – but Bryan accepts this as reasonable because I've got a brain injury.

But I don't sleep. I lie on my bed and I breathe deeply, and I do what Bryan told me to do. I think about that night, just over a year ago, when Nic told me that she was in love with me and I ran away.

For months, I tried my best to not think about it. Everything was changing already. There was a pandemic; I wasn't working; my dad was sick. The last thing I needed was for my whole world to be upended. The only stable things in my life were Nic and Paradise. I needed Nic to stay the same for ever. I needed our relationship never to change.

But I knew how she felt. Of course I did. How can you know someone for most of your life and not know who they loved?

And I did think about how it would work, the two of us. Sometimes when we were talking, or lying together on the beach, I would look sideways at her lips. They had freckles on them in the summer. A deep dip in the top lip. I wondered what they would taste like, and how her short hair would feel under my hand.

Sometimes when we were in my bedroom at Paradise, changing out of our bathing suits, our feet sandy and our shoulders burned, Nic would turn away from me and I knew why she was doing it – to be less vulnerable to my gaze. And her modesty would make me want to see her more. Put my hand on her hip, turn her around and into me, taste salt and sun cream on her neck.

When we were university students she called me that time, to tell me about kissing a woman – Maya, who she dated for a while. I went to a loud and sweaty party that same weekend. I met a woman and let her take me home, let her show me what to do to her and what she could do to me. I thought about Nic.

I couldn't talk to Nic about any of this. But she knew. Of course she did. Or I assumed she did. Every once and a while we had a moment where one of us could have said something, and we pulled back. We had an unspoken agreement to keep the status quo. It was for the best.

The only surprise was that she said it out loud.

No. There were two surprises. The first was that she said it out loud and the second was that my gut reaction was unalloyed fear.

I sit up on the bed and swing my feet over the edge, listening. Furtively, I get up and creep to the bookcase by the side of the bed, kneeling beside it. I haven't looked so long that I'm not sure which book I want; it's one of the Nancy Drews. I've got a set of twenty hardbacks in pride of place on the first two shelves, every one with its matching blue spine. Taking care to stay quiet, I pull out book after book, flipping through the pages. I finally find what I'm looking for in *The Secret of the Old Clock*, wedged between pages seventy-eight and seventy-nine.

I take it out and study it. It's a photograph of a woman holding a long-stemmed rose. She is middle-aged and is wearing glasses, a dark top, a string of pearls. She's leaning against a glossy bar in a restaurant or a hotel; I can see shelves of bottles behind her. She's gazing at the person who's taking the photograph and smiling.

I don't know the woman. I'm not sure where or when the picture was taken. Though the photograph has been dried and flattened from being inside the book for so long, it still bears wrinkles and water-stains from when, many years ago as a child,

I shoved it inside my bathing suit to hide it when I stole it from Lydia Durham's camp.

I glimpsed the photo that day when Nic and I heard Lydia Durham returning, so I took it more out of instinct than on purpose. But when I got back to Paradise and was alone, I pored over it. Every single detail on the front and on the back, where the letter *A* was written in blue ballpoint. No date, nothing else.

Then I shoved it inside a Nancy Drew and tried to forget about it. But I never have, even though it is a picture of someone I've never met, whose name I don't know.

Because in the background of the photo, over the strange woman's left shoulder, blurred and moving so that she is not instantly recognisable to anyone except for someone whose every memory has been honed to an edge, it's my mother.

She is holding a glass in her hand. She in the act of half turning away to the side, out of frame. Her auburn hair is loose around her face and she is laughing. She is too far away to touch and she is happy.

In that breathless second in the empty house, I saw her and I stole the photo. It's the only photo I have of her. My dad has some, of course, in family albums, but I never look at them. It's too painful to see her pretending to be in love with my dad, pretending to care about little me and baby Shane. Why would I want to look at lies?

But this photograph is real. She isn't posing, she probably didn't even know it was being taken. This is the woman who gave birth to me and raised me for seven years, I loved her so much.

Then she disappeared.

I creep downstairs. Bryan is sitting on the porch swing. It's built for two. Before she left us, I remember my mom and dad sitting on it, watching the sun set. Nic and I used to sit on it too, on rainy afternoons, each of us with our books, each of us resting with our backs on the arms of the swings, our toes touching under our shared blanket.

Why can't love be simple and straightforward? Why does it have to be layered all through with the past and the future?

He looks up when I come onto the porch and he smiles at me. He always smiles at me the same way. I fell in love with him when we were stuck in one place, when neither one of us could go anywhere but towards each other. Neither one of us could leave.

'Good sleep?' he asks.

'Can I join you?'

'Of course.' He scoots over a little and I sit beside him. After a moment, I lean sideways and he lifts his arm so that I can nestle against him. He holds me.

'This is nice,' he says, and I remember a night in Philadelphia when he said the same thing, when we were cuddling a lot like this on the sofa in my apartment, Eebie fast asleep on the rug at our feet, a thunderstorm raging outside. Rain ran down the window and lightning flashed, but we were dry and together, and it all felt so obvious.

'Why didn't you leave this morning?' I ask him. 'And don't give me anything about kicking a kitten.'

'Because ... because honestly I think that last night was the first time in our relationship that you've been truly vulnerable with me.'

I lift my head. 'Really?'

'Yeah. You've always been so positive and upbeat. You're like this force of nature sometimes. It's almost good to know that you're struggling, too.'

'So you stayed because I'm confused?'

'No,' he says. 'I stayed because I love you. Even if you don't remember it, that doesn't change how I feel. And I'm not going to leave you.'

I bite my lip. I should tell him that I remember. But I can't, until I've sorted things out with Nic.

'Do you like it here?' I ask him instead.

'It's beautiful. I see why you love it so much.'

The porch overlooks the lake, which today is a deep electric blue, under a lighter and brighter sky. The air is so clear that it feels like you could count each individual tree on the distant mountains.

I invited Bryan here because I wanted to show him how perfect it was. I wanted to share this part of myself with him, in a way that I've never shared it with a boyfriend before. I wanted him to see all the beauty, and love it so that he would love me.

This was one reason why I didn't tell him about my split with Nic before we came. I didn't want him to judge me for how I'd treated her.

Suddenly I want to give Bryan something – something real, in return for loving me, for being so patient, for coming with me to Maine. I sit up. 'Have I met your parents?' I ask, though I know the answer.

'Not yet.'

'Do you want me to meet your parents?'

'Of course I do.'

He has suggested it, several times. But every time I've had an excuse. It seemed like too much. It was easier to bring Bryan into my world, than risk stepping into his.

I think of my mother in that photograph, turning away.

'Let's invite your mom and dad for the Fourth of July,' I say.

Bryan's face relaxes and it's only then that I can see that he's been tense, holding something back. Maybe for longer than I knew.

'Are you sure?' he asks.

'Yes!' I say, even more sure now that he likes the idea. 'The Fourth is great here at Paradise. The more, the merrier. Do you think they'll be able to get a flight?'

'I'll call them,' he says, getting up. He looks so pleased.

I'm starting to get things right.

Chapter Thirty-nine

There is no culinary skill whatsoever involved in making Rice Krispie treats. You melt marshmallows and butter, throw in some cereal, spread it in a pan and cut it.

However, Nic has never been able to make them. I don't know why; either she melts the marshmallows too much or she puts in too much butter, or she puts the Rice Krispies in at the wrong time. I have no idea. She's never really been one to measure anything, so maybe that's why. Whatever the problem, Nic's squares always turn out too chewy or too soggy or too stale, and yet Rice Krispie treats are her favourite thing.

I've told her many times that she can buy them, ready-made and perfect in blue plastic wrapping, but she says that's more expensive. Me, I say how is it more expensive if you get to actually eat them instead of throwing them away? But Nic grew up with a mother who always made everything from scratch, who baked her own bread and made her own cakes, who bought food cheap in the summer and canned it to last the long winter, who when times were tight made dessert out of stale bread sprinkled with sugar. Nic has memories of being given slightly squished Twinkies by one of the RV people in the campground, a harried mom with so many children she probably thought Nic was one of her own. To hear Nic tell it, it was better than Christmas. Whereas Shane and I used to turn up at the campground on summer Wednesday mornings without fail, because that was when Nic's mom was making her pies.

Anyway, I never had a mother to make me cake or pie, or even

stale sugar bread, so I've made Rice Krispie treats a lot. When I
was young, they were my staple item to bring to school for the
PTA bake sales, because my dad, though he kept us fed, never
had any time to make sweet things. I would make a batch in a
Pyrex dish, cut them and wrap them in plastic wrap and foil, and
carry them in on a plate. Sometimes I pretended that my mom
had made them. Not aloud, but to myself. When I slipped them
on the table, I'd mutter something like, 'My mom needs the plate
back,' to see how it felt.

And all of this sounds a little sad, but, the thing is, it wasn't
ever sad because I also knew that Rice Krispie treats were my best
friend Nic's favourite thing. I think they're junk food-y enough to
feel like a guilty pleasure to her, and yet you make them by hand,
so they are technically homemade, so not a guilty pleasure at all.
It's the sort of convoluted thinking that would make no sense to
anyone else but Nic, but which I understand perfectly.

Once for her birthday I made her a three-tier cake out of
Rice Krispie treats, standing on little pillars, coated in chocolate.
She said it was the best cake ever – even though really it was
just cereal stuck together with melted marshmallows and butter,
covered with a whole bag of melted Hershey's Kisses.

So in the late morning of the hottest day of the summer so far,
I make an extra-large batch of Rice Krispie treats as a peace offering. I layer them in a Tupperware box in between sheets of baking
paper, because I don't want them to melt together. 'Wow, those
look good,' says Bryan, wandering into the kitchen barefoot and
wearing a pair of shorts, buttoning up a shirt. I catch a glimpse of
his stomach and chest.

'They're for Nic,' I say, turning my attention quickly to the
Tupperware. It's all old in this house and the lids never fit. 'I
need some girl time.'

'Of course.' Bryan reaches into the box and I playfully slap his
hand away. 'Oh, come on, one?'

'One.' He grins, takes one from the top and bites into it.

'Before you go, have you got a minute?' he asks, chewing. 'My parents have told me that Isaac is also coming. My youngest brother?' he adds when I apparently baulk.

'Oh, yes,' I say quickly. I remember who Isaac is, but I didn't expect a sibling as well.

'If it's too much, or too soon, they can send him to Polly's instead. It's no problem. They suggested it, actually, because they don't want you to be overwhelmed with company while you're recovering.'

'It's fine,' I say. 'Of course it's fine!'

'Are you sure? I mean – you don't remember, but you have been reluctant to meet my family before. It's a lot all at once.'

'I am absolutely sure.' I hold out the Tupperware box. 'Here, take another one of these before they melt.'

The campground, on a hot, sunny day, feels listless. A few residents are sitting in the shade under the limp awnings of their RVs, and someone's playing a radio, but it seems like most people have already decamped to the beach or maybe gone somewhere with air conditioning.

It's only when I give my usual perfunctory knock on the screen door and hear the dogs howling in response, that I realise that the last time I was here, I had a whole conversation with Jeannette. Until she called me by my mother's name, I didn't even notice that she had any memory issues at all.

I'm selfish. I'm a coward. I can't do this.

Nic appears in the doorway and she stops, gazing at me through the screen. It was only a few days ago that we stood about this far apart on the beach and she told me that I had to choose between her and Bryan.

And my response to that was to get myself hit by an ATV and forget everything about it. No wonder when she visited me in hospital, she said that my amnesia seemed convenient. No wonder she's hesitant to speak with me now.

'I've brought a present,' I say, and hold up the box.

'What is it?'

'The severed heads of your enemies.'

She opens the screen door. The dogs frisk, or rather wallow, around her feet. I give her the box and she looks inside.

'They're your favourite.'

'You remembered that, at least.'

She seems unwilling to let me inside so I say, quickly, 'You've been avoiding me. And I don't know why. I don't care why, frankly. I miss you and I want us to make up. Whatever it was that I did, I'm sorry.'

'How do you know it was something you did?'

'Let's face it, we both know it was something I did. And I'm sorry.'

I hold my breath. This is my chance. The only way I know how to get back to how we were before all of this happened – by ignoring that it ever happened in the first place, pretending I still don't remember, until she's remembered how precious our friendship is.

But I'm telling the truth about being sorry.

'Wanna go swimming?' I ask.

Our special swimming hole is in the Bear River, half a mile upstream from the pond. It's an easy walk from the campground, along a trail used by snowmobiles in the winter, but hardly anyone goes there so it has the aura of a secret. If you go off the trail about twenty yards, you reach a place where the river tumbles over boulders in a natural waterfall into a rock-lined pool. The water is cold, much colder than the lake, and clearer. It floods with snowmelt in spring and dries to a trickle and puddle in August, but in the middle of the summer it is perfect. From here you can't hear the children laughing on the beach or smell the summer barbecues. You hear crows arguing, the breeze in the pine branches, the water's endless flow.

Nic drops her towel on a dry rock, kicks off her sneakers and pulls off her shorts and T-shirt. She's always been wiry, but in her one-piece I can see that she's lost weight. Her shoulders and elbows are sharp, her hip bones visible.

I did this to her.

She steps down from rock to rock until she reaches the bottom of the cascade, then steps directly underneath the water so it washes over her head and streams down her body.

'Feel good?' I shout over the noise of the falls.

'So good. Get in here.'

I shuck off my own clothes and do what I always do – launch myself off a rock into the air to splash into the dead centre of the pool. I come up spluttering and swearing.

'You're an idiot,' Nic calls to me from the waterfall. 'How do you know it's going to be deep enough?'

'It always is. You can see when the water's too low.' I tread water, while Nic slips into the pool and swims. It's lovely to watch her swim; she's graceful and economical, as natural as breathing. She makes several circuits of the small pool while I watch, never glancing in my direction, her attention fully taken up by her swimming. It's one of those moments where we could be twelve again, nineteen, twenty-six. We'll be old ladies one day and still swimming in this river.

I hope.

Finally, she pulls herself back up onto the rock under the waterfall and sits there with the flowing water massaging her shoulders. I join her and she budges over so we both can sit with our feet in the pool, being part of the water's journey on its way to the lake and the sea.

'It might not be deep enough one day,' she says, later, when we're lying on a rock in the sun, spread out on towels, our heads propped up on our shoes. 'You might jump in and break a leg. Hit your head.'

'My head's harder than the rocks,' I say.

'You might forget everything the next time.'

'Never going to forget you,' I say, nudging my elbow into her arm. She flinches and moves a little bit away. 'Are you angry with me?'

'Why would I be angry with you? You made me Rice Krispie things.'

'Do you want to tell me why you've been avoiding me?'

I hold my breath. She doesn't answer.

What if I had made the choice to be with her that June, last year, before I allowed myself to fall in love with Bryan? How would my life be different?

But I do love Bryan now. And I can't erase that, even with amnesia.

Overhead, a crow flies through the patch of blue sky, cutting it in half.

Chapter Forty

Nic's father drowned in the lake when she was twelve. He liked risks and he took too many with his money, but on the day he died he wasn't doing anything risky – he wasn't boating without a life jacket, or swimming drunk, or diving off a rock, or swimming on the far side of the lake, where there was no one to hear him if he got into trouble. There was no undertow, no dangerous fish, no very great depths. The skies and the water were calm.

He'd simply gone for a swim, like he did every day when the water was warm enough and had done since he was a child – a habitual and steady crawl back and forth along the line of the campground beach. 'It cleared out the cobwebs,' he used to say.

He swam out of his depth, but only barely. Often, Nic liked to join him, though he always made sure that she swam closer to shore. She'd try to stay out as long as he did, swim as far, match his strokes, though he was bigger and faster.

The day he drowned was an overcast day, but not cold or windy. Although it was high summer, not many people were on the beach. He left the house in late morning wearing his swimming trunks and carrying a towel, and at lunchtime her mother sent her down to the beach to call him in. She found his towel on the sand and she squinted out at the water, but she couldn't see him swimming. She thought maybe he'd walked up the beach, or got into one of his buddy's boats, or gone back to the campground and forgotten his towel. So she went back and told her mother, who covered his lunch with Saran wrap and went out to look for him herself.

It was her mother who found him, carried by the waves about a quarter of a mile along the shore. Nic only found out when her mother came running back into the house and picked up the phone to call an ambulance. Still, she couldn't make sense of what her mother was trying to say, even though the words were plain and clear and stark.

She tried to go and see for herself, but her mother wouldn't let her. She stayed inside the house and then in a little while, Bill Stone came over to collect her and take her to Paradise, where she stayed overnight.

They said he'd probably had a cramp. The week of his death and his funeral was the worst of Nic's life, though everyone was kind. 'We have to get through it,' her mother told her, and that was what they did. But there was an empty space where he used to be. There would always be an empty space.

The day after his funeral, she went down to the campground beach for her swim. It was sunny and busy; they kept the campground open through everything, because Ma said it wasn't fair to ruin other people's vacations, and, to their credit, most of the regulars helped out, bringing food, running errands.

Nic dropped her towel on the sand and walked to the water's edge, and she couldn't go in. She couldn't even get her toes wet. It wasn't that she feared dying like her father, it wasn't even that she had anything against the water, or begrudged it for taking her father's life. It was only water.

But still. She couldn't swim in it.

This continued for a while that summer. When they asked, she told Katie and Shane that she just didn't feel like going in the water. Shane seemed to accept this and went in anyway, but Katie stayed with her on the shore, reading books under her umbrella, or wading in the stream by the side of Paradise, where you could find all sizes of frogs. The stream, apparently, was fine.

She wasn't sure if this was only for a summer, or if it was for ever. She didn't much care, she thought. Not being able to swim was the least of her losses.

One day Katie turned up at the campground carrying a plastic bag. 'Put on your bathing suit under your clothes,' she told Nic. 'And sneakers, not sandals.' Katie was bossy like this sometimes.

'I don't feel like swimming today,' Nic said, although the tin thermometer on the side of the house said it was eighty-five degrees, and it was muggy too.

'Who said we were swimming?' said Katie. So Nic did what she said and she told her mom she was going to Paradise (her mother was more insistent about knowing where she was, these days). But instead of going down the road, Katie crossed it and struck out onto a snowmobiling trail in the woods.

'We're going on a hike?' Nic asked, wishing she had a water bottle if so.

'You'll see.'

They only walked for ten minutes, maybe less, before the trail met up and ran alongside a fat, running stream. 'What's this, Bear Creek?' Nic asked.

'Yeah, I think so,' said Katie, and kept walking. The trail was narrower here, so she went ahead of Nic. In another ten minutes or so she went off the trail for a few metres and stopped, and Nic, coming up beside her, could see why. The creek made a waterfall here, foaming over boulders and into a nearly round pool. Skinny-legged insects danced on its surface. A slab of rock lay beside the pool in a ray of sun between the trees.

'What do you think?' Katie asked. 'We can just sit here if you want.'

And Nic realised that her friend had found this for her – a place that was near to home but that was not the lake that had taken her father, a pool deep enough to swim or to cool down. A place of running, cold, fresh water – a waterfall that no one knew about but the two of them.

'Hell, no,' she said, stripping off her clothes to her bathing suit. 'I want to swim.'

They kept that place secret; they didn't even tell Shane. And gradually, between them, the story became that it was a place they'd found together, that was equally theirs.

But Nic always knew that it was Katie who'd found it first, and she had given it to Nic. Just like Nic was the person who had named Paradise, and given the name to Katie.

Nearly twenty years later, Katie brought her Rice Krispie squares as a peace offering and the two of them hiked out to this place in the creek together.

It was exactly like it had always been, and it was entirely different than it had always been. They swam and sat side by side under the waterfall, and Katie asked why Nic was angry at her.

How could she explain that she wasn't angry at this Katie – that she was angry at the other Katie, the one that only she remembered. Not the friend who loved her, but the woman who didn't love her enough.

But they were the same person.

The sensible, rational thing to do would be to explain to Katie what had happened. Tell her about confessing that she loved her and how much Katie's response had hurt her.

But what if it happened all over again?

Finally, she said, 'My mother has dementia. She had her stroke and got diagnosed at the beginning of 2020, so you might not remember that.'

'Oh, God, Nic. I'm so sorry. Poor Jeannette.'

'She hardly remembers anything about the last twenty-odd years. Most of the time she thinks my dad's still alive. But the thing is, the blessing for her, I guess, is that she doesn't know that she can't remember. Most days, she focuses on what's in front of her and she's content. In a weird way, she might even be happier than she used to be. Sometimes I sort of envy her. I sort of envy you. It must be great to forget all the stuff that went wrong.'

'It's not that great,' Katie said. 'You forget the happy things, too.'

'It might be a price worth paying. I've never been able to leave the past in the past.'

'We have so much past together, you and me,' said Katie. 'We have to hold on to that, no matter what.'

Nic got up and began to gather her stuff. Katie stopped her, with her hands on her shoulders, and said, 'I need you. I will always need you. You're my best friend. You're the reason why everything makes sense. You're like my family, but it's even better than that, because you're the person I choose. I couldn't bear to ever lose you. So whatever I did, *everything* I did, I accept that it's totally my fault. I love you and I will always love you for the rest of my life.'

Nic could not think of what to say. She could not say, *you didn't need me enough.*

Or, *I don't know if you chose me or not, because you were hit by an ATV.*

Or, *accepting that you don't remember means that I go back to ignoring this part of me, the part that loves you.*

And standing there, looking Katie in the eye, close enough to kiss her, with Katie's hands on her bare shoulders, she realised – none of these responses were even true any more.

Katie might get her memory back, or she might not. Either way, the accident had changed everything. It had reset things between them. And this was an apology, of sorts.

'Do you promise that if you do remember, that you'll tell me first? Before anyone else?'

'Of course,' Katie said, and then she dropped her hands and they started walking back to the campground.

Maybe, Nic thought as they walked, Katie's amnesia was what *could* make things right. Maybe it was what erased Nic's ultimatum, what made them remember who they used to be and how precious that was.

Maybe forgetting was the only thing that could save their friendship.

But that would mean that Nic would have to forget a huge part of herself. Cut it away and go on living as a shadow of what could have been.

Chapter Forty-one

Ma was crocheting. Nic had discovered recently that crochet kept her in one place for a little while. She only wandered or got distressed when she had nothing to do. She had always crocheted, so she had muscle memory – she had used to crochet scarves and mittens during the winter when the campground was shut and she couldn't do so many things outside. Now, she crocheted granny squares. Each one was about four inches by four inches, of various colours of yarn, and they took no concentration or memory at all. She would crochet a square, then put it in a basket and forget about it, and then start another one. When there were enough, Nic planned to join them all together into an afghan and give it to someone as a gift.

The radio was on, but it wasn't loud. Ma was humming under her breath. It reminded Nic of when she was a little girl and would spend afternoons with Ma when her dad was out with his buddies, playing music or gambling or both. There had been plenty of tension simmering underneath the surface then, too, but this afternoon, it was only on Nic's side.

She didn't know if it was right to forgive Katie, to pretend that everything was as it had always been. It felt like a cop-out. But what else could she do?

Suddenly, she didn't want to be the only one who remembered everything.

'How'd you fall in love with Dad?' she asked.

'Hmm?' Jeannette looked up from her purple yarn and her hook.

'How'd you know that you wanted to marry Dad?' Nic asked again.

'Oh, Gene asked and I knew. That's all. I knew he loved me and I never regretted it.'

'Do you know how Dad fell in love with you?'

Ma smiled. It was one of her good days. Nic had learnt the good days were easier if she just let her mother remember what she could, and stopped trying to remind her of the present. Maybe that was what Shane had noticed when he came by.

'I don't think I did much. He loved my buttermilk cake.'

'But that's not how you met. You met at—'

'The homecoming football game when I was a sophomore working the concession stand and he was a senior playing for the opposite team. He was from Westbrook, don't you know.' She put down her crocheting. 'Oh, he had the biggest smile. Such sparkling eyes. And a chipped tooth, right in the front. It made him look mischievous.'

Nic remembered him using the sharp edge of that chipped tooth to cut fishing line. When she was little, he told her that the dentist wanted him to get it fixed but he wouldn't because it was way too handy, especially for a man who kept on forgetting where he'd laid his tools. She'd believed him. Now, she understood that cosmetic dental work had been too expensive.

'I knew right away that I wanted him to ask me out,' her mother said. 'I had a date for the homecoming dance – that was Steve Bouchard, the one whose father ran the lumber yard, and, believe me, Steve Bouchard was hot property in those days, but I would have traded a dozen Steve Bouchards for one Gene Leblanc.'

Nic had heard this many times before, usually more or less in the same words. It was always lovely to hear how her parents had met and liked each other – aside from the arguments, money troubles and differences of temperament, she believed that they'd liked each other, in their own way, right up until the day that her father died – but that wasn't the reason why she'd asked.

She was trying to work out now, in retrospect, why she had thought it was OK to date Shane while she was in love with Katie. What sort of rationalisation had gone on in her head, that she'd thought she could make herself fall in love with him as much as he'd been in love with her.

It had been easy to date Shane, that was true. Everyone had believed they should be together. They had seemed predestined, natural, like Lego bricks clicking together. For years they were friends, and then they'd gone to the same college, and they'd spent so much time together people had assumed they'd been a couple. And then they'd become a couple.

But she could see now that her ease with Shane, the fact that they had grown up spending summers together and knew everything about each other, belied the fact that they had never learnt how to communicate with each other. Shane had never been someone who talked about emotions. But to be fair to him, Nic had never drawn him out, either. She'd talked to Katie about her feelings, because she always had. When she'd had a tough day, she'd called Katie. When she'd been gathering the courage to apply for her masters, and then her PhD, she had gone through everything with Katie.

Maybe that was because she'd been dating the wrong sibling, or maybe it had been her own failing. Most likely, both things were true.

She should have been brave enough to say something years ago. Before everything had got so complicated – before she'd said yes to Shane, before Katie had ever met Bryan. She couldn't put all the blame on Katie.

'How did you get Dad to ask you out?'

'I didn't do a lot. I gave him my number and we talked on the phone, and then he came to visit and I made a cake for him special.'

'So that's your love advice, huh, Ma? Make a buttermilk cake.'

'Ayuh, that about sums it up.' Her mother looked up at Nic. 'Where's your husband?'

'I'm not married, Ma. Shane asked me, but I said no.'

'Oh, that's too bad. He's a lovely young man.'

'Yes, he is.'

'Why did you say no?'

She hesitated. *Fuck it*, she thought. *Ma isn't going to remember.* On good days, Ma could recall almost everything about her past life, but even on the best days – and this was one of them – she couldn't remember what had happened the day before.

'You remember Katie?' Nic asked.

'Of course I remember Katie.'

'Did you ever think that there might be something more between us than just being friends?'

Ma frowned. 'What do you mean?'

'I'm in love with her.'

'People use that word these days for everything,' her mother commented. 'They love chocolate or a pair of shoes.'

'I mean it as *love* love – I mean like being queer.'

Her mother frowned. 'Gene never went in for all that stuff. He said a man with a man, or a woman with a woman. It's unnatural.'

That wasn't surprising, though it did hurt. She loved her father – idolised him in many ways. But she'd heard how he'd talked, especially if he'd been drinking. Once on stage, he'd sung a song, a 'comedy' version of a country classic with the title 'Mama, Don't Let Your Babies Grow Up to Be Homos'. His audience had laughed, and Nic, only seven or eight years old, allowed to stay up past her bedtime, laughed too, though she wasn't sure what was funny. She got the message, though: being gay was something you should not be.

The song, and the moment, had stuck in her mind for all this time. Her father singing it and herself laughing along. Yet another reason never to tell anyone she loved about her feelings. Yet another reason to deny them to herself.

'What about you, Ma?' she asked. 'How do you feel about gay people?'

'I always figured live and let live.' She shrugged. 'None of my business, what people do in their own bedroom, if they don't want to live like everyone else. Like Audrey.'

'You know Audrey?' Nic asked in surprise. She didn't think her mother had been wandering around the pond unsupervised.

'Of course I know Audrey. At the hotel. Everybody does.'

The hotel, that had been closed for over thirty years. Ma was misremembering again. Nic got back to the subject at hand.

'You think that queer people should be allowed to live their lives how they want?' she said, prompting her mother.

'Live and let live,' Jeannette repeated. 'The Church doesn't like it, but we're also told to forgive and love everybody.'

'So you're OK with it, if I like women?'

She was coming out, she realised. She had never had this conversation with her mother before. Not in so many words. She had mentioned Maya, talked about her girlfriend, never actively hidden anything, but also never explicitly said to her mother that she dated women as well as men. 'Girlfriend' could mean so many things. She kept her romantic life private and an hour's drive away, in Portland. Her mother had never demonstrated any curiosity about it, so it had seemed easier to just let it slide. And then when she'd started dating Shane, why bother to bring it up?

But also, she realised, that it meant that her mother never knew this important thing about her, while she could still remember it. That seemed wrong, almost deceitful.

'You're gay?' Ma said.

'I'm bisexual.' Her hands were sweating. She wiped them on her jeans.

'I feel sorry for you. It must be very lonely.'

What had she expected? A Pride parade? Her parents both

grew up in backwoods Maine, voted Republican, were devout Catholics, and had rarely left the state.

'I'm not lonely because I'm bisexual,' she said. 'I'm lonely because I fell in love with my best friend and she doesn't love me back the way I want her to. And because the only person I could talk to about this, really talk about it, is the person who's broken my heart. And she doesn't even remember doing it. So I have to keep everything to myself. And sometimes I think I'm going to explode with it. I'd like to stop, and rest, or get drunk, or have a breakdown or something. But I can't, because I'm just like you. I have to keep working and keep everything ticking over, because if I don't, it'll all fall apart.'

'It all falls on the women.' Her mother sighed. 'It never finishes. I have so much to do.'

'Yeah. Anyway, that's why I'm sad. My heart hurts and I can't think of a single thing to do that will make it any better.'

Jeannette nodded. She sucked on her back teeth, which was her usual audible sign of sympathy to humans or animals. A broken heart or a sick chicken, all the same. *Tsk.*

'I'm sorry you feel bad,' she said. 'Do you want a cookie? I think I have some cookies.'

'It's all right, Ma. I don't want a cookie. We have some blondies, though. I made them yesterday. Do you want one?'

'No, I don't eat those things.'

Nic got up anyway, put a blondie on a plate and lay it on the table beside her mother's chair. Ma picked it up and took a bite.

'That's good,' she said.

'It's your recipe. I put in extra pecans, like you wrote on the recipe card.'

Ma took another bite. 'My daughter, Nicole, makes a good blondie. You should get her to make you some, sometime. Do you know her?'

Nic sat back in her chair.

'I don't really know her,' she said.

Chapter Forty-two

Someone knocked on the door at seven-thirty, sending the dogs braying. Nic, fresh from her post-run shower, answered it, expecting one of the campground residents. But it was Bryan. He had a little fluffy dog on a lead.

She hadn't encountered him since that day in the supermarket, when she'd seen him for less than two minutes, but she recognised him immediately. Still, she pretended. It was second nature by now.

'Morning,' she said, as the bassets crowded around her calves, wagging their tails and sniffing the little dog up and down. She checked behind him, but Katie wasn't with him. 'Are you looking for a camping spot? We're all filled up this week.'

'No, I came by to talk with you. I hope it's not too early. I'm Bryan – Katie's boyfriend? We met in Casablanca, before her accident.'

He seemed friendly. Not like someone who knew his girl-friend's best friend was in love with his girlfriend, and who had come to have it out. He actually looked a little sheepish.

She wanted to hate him and thought she probably had good reason to, but, also, she was curious.

'Oh, of course,' she said. 'I'm sorry, the house is a mess, but I can bring some coffee outside if you want to sit at a picnic table?'

'That would be great. Thank you.'

'How do you take it?'

'Black is good, thanks.'

She went back inside. The house was not a mess; Ma had been

doing her spring cleaning in late June. But Bryan was a stranger and she knew nothing about him, and she had enough of her father in her to know you never invited two types of people into the house – someone to whom you owed money, and someone whose intentions you didn't understand. Those people, you talked with outside.

Why was he here? Had Katie got her memory back and told him what was going on between them? Did he want something else?

The bassets followed her outside, keen to see their new fluffy friend. 'Who's this?' she asked, crouching down to greet the dog.

'Eebie. He thinks he's enormous.'

'Just like Statler and Waldorf think they're fast.' She sat across from him at the picnic table and put the coffees down.

Bryan smiled. 'Katie said you named all your dogs after Muppets.'

'It's my fault. I was a Sesame Street fiend. Before I was born, my dad named all his dogs after playing cards.'

'It's nice and busy here.' He looked around at the campground. She noticed Doreen watching them – Bryan in particular. Doreen always had an eye for the men.

'Sure is. It's a relief, after a year out of business. What can I do for you, Bryan?'

He nodded, as if she'd given him permission to stop with the small talk. 'It's about Katie. It's awkward, really.'

'Has she got her memory back?'

'No.'

Right, so there wasn't going to be any kind of a showdown.

'I was wondering if you had any opinion about her amnesia,' he continued.

'Opinion?'

'She's forgotten the pandemic. And her dad's diagnosis.' He spoke thoughtfully, with consideration. 'It makes me wonder whether her amnesia might have a psychological element that the accident could have triggered. Maybe, subconsciously, she's chosen not to remember something so painful.'

Nic bent over and fussed the fluffy dog. Because the painful things included her.

'What do you think?' Bryan asked her, after a moment.

'I never studied psychology. Have you?'

'No. But it's plausible, right?'

'It sounds like the premise of something bingeable on Netflix.'

This was, of course, more or less exactly what she'd accused Katie of: conveniently forgetting what she didn't want to remember.

'I don't want to believe it,' he admitted.

'Why?'

'Because if Katie's loss of memory is a choice, that means she also chose to forget me.'

Nic pressed her lips together. 'That hurts,' she said. Meaning: *that hurts me.*

'Hell, yes, it does.'

'Why are you telling me this?' she asked. 'You hardly know me.'

'Because you're Katie's best friend. You've known each other for most of your lives. You know everything about her.'

'Maybe.' She dared to look him in the eyes. 'I know that you're the first boyfriend she's ever brought up here. And that she's structured her life deliberately so as never to commit to anyone.'

'That's one of my worries,' said Bryan, who seemed to have not picked up on the challenge in Nic's words. 'Before this happened, she said that our relationship had changed her. That she'd never stayed still for long enough to put down roots. If she's forgotten that choice that she made… that we made together… does that mean she's back to the person who she was before, who never wanted to commit to anyone?'

'Hmm,' said Nic, noncommittally.

'But as long as I've known her, she never wanted to meet my family. As if meeting them would be a step too far, like it would be too permanent and it spooked her. And then the other day she just invited my folks here, out of the blue. So does she remember something? Or has the accident changed her in a different way?'

'This has become a very deep conversation.'

'You're really the only person I can ask.'

Carefully, she said, 'Are you asking me if she's said anything about you to me?'

'No. What you talk about is your business. You're best friends. I wouldn't make her choose her loyalties.'

If that's true, it makes you a better person than I am, she thought, and felt sick.

'Then what are you asking?'

'I'm not sure. I think... I'm asking you to help me to help her get her memory back.'

'Because you think she's faking it?'

'No, that's not what I mean. She really doesn't remember. She's in a lot of pain about it. She seems lost and that's not the Katie I know. The doctor said we have to wait, but I have to do something. When she first got back from the hospital, she said we should cut our losses since she didn't remember anything and we hadn't moved in together or got married.'

'She said that to you?' She huffed a humourless laugh. 'Yes, of course she said that to you. That's one hundred per cent Katie.'

'I'm not prepared to let her go. And I know that she has the capacity to love me, because she did love me, right up until the moment she was hit by that ATV.'

'How can you be so sure?'

Her tone was more than a little rude, but Bryan didn't seem to notice.

'Because she told me. Because I could feel it. Because knowing Katie, I know that she only chooses to do what she wants to do. And she still loves me. She doesn't look at me like she'd look at a stranger.'

'Why did she love you?'

He winced, maybe at her use of the past tense. 'It's easier to tell you why I love her.'

'I know why you love her. But I can't help you unless I know why she loves you.'

'Did she ever tell you?'

'No.'

'She loves ...' He seemed to be struggling. 'It's so hard to define what love means, in words.'

'It's wanting to share everything with someone,' she said. 'It's feeling as if when you're not touching them, you're incomplete. It's thinking of them first thing every day and last thing every night.'

Bryan looked at her with surprise. She was surprised, too. She had not meant to say any of that, least of all to him.

'I ... don't think that's quite what I mean,' he said. 'That might be a good definition of love for some people, but it's not really mine.'

'What is yours, then?'

'More about being vulnerable, and about trusting the person you love to be true to themselves. Katie trusts me. I think even without her memories, she still trusts me. She just doesn't know why. That's why she invited my family here, to show that trust.'

'And you trust me to help you get her back,' she said. 'Even though you don't know me.'

'It's easier for me to trust people than it is for Katie. But, yeah. I do trust you. I think you have her best interests at heart. And I think if you didn't think she loved me, you would have told me to get lost the minute I knocked on your door.'

She had not drunk any of her coffee. She tapped the cooling mug. She thought about his definition of love.

'If Katie trusts you to let her be true to herself,' she said, slowly. 'Does that mean that if she never remembers you, if she decides – as she said – to cut her losses, that you would let her go?'

'Yes,' he said right away. 'But I'd like the chance to fight for her first.'

'I'll get us some more coffee,' she said, standing up. She picked up his empty mug and her full one, and went into the house.

God, she wanted to hate Bryan for talking to her like this. *Her*, of all people.

But how could she hate him, when she'd tried to force Katie into choosing between them?

Katie had never told him the whole truth. Even when she'd had all her memories, all she'd said to him was that she and Nic were best friends and always had been.

Because that was the way that Katie had felt all along. That was the only explanation. Her way of loving Nic was not the same as Nic's way of loving her.

And Nic's choice now was to live in the past, or try to figure out what she wanted and what part of that she could actually have.

She had a little cry, then, over the kitchen sink. Then she dried her eyes, splashed her face with water, rinsed out the mugs and refilled them.

When she went outside, Bryan was chatting with Doreen. Of course. She had plunked herself right down across from him and looked like she wanted to eat him up.

'You flirting with another man right in front of Dale?' Nic called.

'Oh, Dale knows I'm all mouth and no follow-through.' Doreen grinned and took a drag on her cigarette. 'I just like a little eye-candy now and then.'

'Sorry,' Nic said to Bryan, who shrugged good-naturedly.

'Actually,' said Doreen. 'I was behaving myself. We were talking about the lake. He said there was some weeds growing up at the Stones' camp and I was saying it's erosion. That geologist fella gave a talk over Zoom about it. The more people build around the lake and cut down trees, the more rain that falls because of climate change – that all causes erosion. Nitrogen gets washed into the lake, weeds grow – you'd think it was a good thing because plants – but, pretty soon, the whole thing gets choked up. It happened up at Little North Pond. Pond dies. Of course, Morocco is much bigger. But it could go the same way. I'll get Dale to go up and have a look one afternoon.'

'Thanks.'

'No problem. Then again, there's not much one person can do.' Doreen stood up, with a grunt. 'Now I better go back to my husband, before he gives me the stink-eye. Say hi to Katie. You ever see Shane? We allowed to talk about him yet?'

'You can talk about him,' said Nic.

'Now *he* is a piece of eye-candy. No offence.' Doreen waved and went back to her RV.

'Nice lady,' said Bryan.

'She's a menace. But, yeah. She's a nice lady. She helps me out a lot.'

'Katie said you were running this place and looking after your mother, and doing a PhD all at the same time.'

'Trying to. Mostly failing.' She sighed. 'Listen, I don't know how I can help you. I'm not a doctor and I don't know anything about memories. My mother's losing hers more and more every day. I'm just about holding it together.'

'Yeah, you're right. You've got a lot on your plate. You can see that I'm desperate. It helps to talk to you. I really don't know what to do.'

'Just be there for her, I guess,' she said.

'That seems like so little.'

'Actually, in Katie's world, that is a lot.'

He looked so sad, this person she didn't know. This person whom Katie loved.

'My mom says that my dad fell in love with her because of her buttermilk cake. You could try that.'

'Got a recipe?'

'As a matter of fact,' Nic said. 'I do.'

Chapter Forty-three

It's been raining hard and steadily since late morning. Outside the lake-facing windows, the water is a sheet of grey. Bryan has returned soaking wet from walking Eebie, so he takes a shower while I build a fire in the stone fireplace. Well – I'm trying to. Eebie, who has already tracked wet pawprints all over the sofa, thinks that the kindling is meant for him to play with. He keeps snatching it and chewing on it. I take a stick and toss it across the living room.

'Fetch,' I tell him.

He looks at me and goes back to chewing his own piece of wood.

'Eebie. Fetch.' I point at the stick. Then I try taking the stick he's chewing and after several minutes of tug-of-war, I manage to get it and toss that one, too. 'Fetch!' I say, and he scampers after it and picks it up, and immediately lies down with it and starts chewing again.

'Stupid dog,' I say happily.

'He knows exactly zero tricks,' Bryan says from the doorway. I look up and he's wearing a towel around his waist and rubbing his hair dry with another towel, and damn he is good-looking. My mouth is practically watering.

'Sorry,' he says, realising how very much undressed he is and retreating to his bedroom.

There's no need, I don't call after him. *I remember every inch of your body.*

But the thing is, I promised Nic that if I got my memory back I would tell her first.

Which was a stupid thing to do. But how could I not? In that moment, it was either agree with her or say, *well, actually, I've got it back already and I'm pretending I haven't so that we can be friends again.*

And now I'm thinking that all of my relationships are based on untruths and silences. For years, Nic and I both failed to talk about the massive truth between us. And then I didn't want to face that truth, so I never told Bryan about it. Shane refuses to show any weakness around me and my dad wants to protect me from everything.

Eebie drops his stick in my lap. I remember how Bryan and I tried and tried to teach him some tricks and utterly failed. This dog lives in his own world. He won't come when he's called, which is why he needs to be leashed outside, and it's probably why he got lost in the first place.

'It doesn't matter,' Bryan would say. 'That dog doesn't need to do any tricks. His job isn't to perform. His sole purpose is to give us love.'

Bryan had a rough time at the start of the pandemic. His family was on the other side of the country. His mother, Cherry, recently finished cancer treatment and she had a weakened immune system. His sister was working in Covid wards and had to stay separate from her children. On warm summer evenings when both his and my windows were open, I could hear him talking to his family via Zoom. Though I couldn't hear the words they said, I could hear them laughing. Always laughing.

But when I knocked on his door one night in July, a couple of weeks after coming back from Maine, hoping for a booty call if I'm honest, he was slow to answer and when he did, his face was streaked with tears.

'I heard you talking on Zoom five minutes ago,' I said. 'You sounded so happy.'

'I have to act happy for them,' he said. 'I don't want them to worry about me all the way over here, by myself.'

I had never in my life seen a grown man allowing me to see him so vulnerable and alone. It reminded me of my own father after my mother left, keeping it together for our sake.

It should have made me want to run as fast as I could in the opposite direction. I don't know if it was because we were so isolated from everyone else, or if it was because he was different. Or if it was because I was different. I, who had so recently broken my best friend's heart.

Instead, I took his hand. And from that moment, things started to change.

The fire is crackling, the dog is snoozing, the rain is tapping on the windows as it blows across the lake. I poke through a pile of old puzzle books on the bottom of a bookshelf and leaf through one, looking for a blank crossword. I see my dad's handwriting and my grandmother's, and my own in pink glitter pen, which dates it to my tween years. I stop at one puzzle, half-finished in capital letters.

This is my mother's handwriting.

I tear that page out and toss it into the fire. And find a stack of Shane's old comic books instead.

I'm engrossed in the adventures of Spider-Man when Bryan comes in from the kitchen. With him comes a waft of baking, vanilla and brown sugar and cinnamon, and he presents me with a plate before sitting beside me on the floor in front of the fireplace.

It smells delicious. It looks like ...

'What is this?'

'It's supposed to be cake. I think something went wrong.'

I turn the plate around to look at what he's made from all angles. It is a large slice of something that is brown and somehow both flat and lumpy at the same time. There's icing on it, but that's melting off and pooling on the plate.

'I'm not much of a baker,' he admits. 'And we didn't have any buttermilk so I just used butter and milk.'

'I'm not much of a baker either, but I think buttermilk is not made of butter and milk.'

'Now you tell me.'

I pick it up and take a bite. 'It's ... well, it tastes good.'

'I think you're being nice to me.'

'Why'd you decide to take up baking?'

'It seemed like a good day to try.'

'Did you make this for me?'

'Yeah. I did.'

'I will never look a gift cake in the mouth.'

'You are, however, still chewing that first bite.'

'It's a little dense.' I swallow. And swallow again. 'Delicious.'

'You are lying.' He reaches over and swipes a little icing off my plate with his finger, which he licks, and then grimaces. 'You are definitely lying.'

'Not lying! It's so nice that you made me cake! And it is delicious. Look. Eebie agrees.' I break off a lump of cake and hold it out to the dog.

Eebie lifts his head and sniffs the cake. Then, quite deliberately, he gets up, turns his back to me and then flops back down.

'Oh, my God,' says Bryan. 'I am never, ever going to recover from this.'

'He's just picky.' I am laughing so hard that my stomach hurts and I have to put my hand over my mouth to stop from spitting cake everywhere.

'Katie, that dog spends about seventy per cent of every day licking his own ass.'

Before I can think of what I'm doing, I lean over and I kiss Bryan on the mouth. Not a long kiss, but a full one, icing on my lips and all. And it's just the way it always used to be.

Then I recall the last time I kissed him and then apologised, and how hurt he was by it.

I kiss him on the cheek and I smile at him. *These foolish things remind me of you.*

'Thank you for making me cake,' I say. 'It's the worst cake I've ever had and I think it's great.'

He smiles back at me and goes in for another kiss.

A horn sounds outside, over the sound of the rain. Bryan pulls back. 'Who's that?'

The horn sounds again. I get up to look out the window and Shane's truck is parked outside, running, with Shane behind the wheel.

It's raining hard enough that I have to put on a waterproof before I go out to see what he wants. He rolls down the window.

'Get in,' he says.

'Is something the matter? I'm having a romantic afternoon in there.'

'I've got something to show you.'

'Just a second.' I run back inside. Dripping, I tell Bryan that I'm going out with my brother for a little while. 'I'll be back later for more cake.'

Shane's got the defroster and wipers turned up to full and he's playing Jeff Buckley. 'What's so urgent?' I ask him.

'You'll see.' He turns the truck around and drives the way he came.

As we pass the campground, I ask, 'Have you spoken with Nic lately?'

'A little.'

'How are you doing?'

'Fine.'

'What did you do with the ring that you bought?'

He side-eyes me. 'She told you, huh.'

She has not – or not since the accident, at least. But I let him think so, because I want him to stop avoiding the issue with me. He and I never talk, and that's another thing in my life that has to change.

'It's not your fault that it didn't work out,' I say.

'Hell, no, it's not.'

'And it's not hers, either. It would have been worse if she'd said yes, and then—'

'Didn't I say I didn't want to talk about this? Ever?'

He turns up Buckley singing 'Lilac Wine'.

I watch Shane as he drives. I can see a continuity between the man he is now – tall, broad, with five o'clock shadow and a floral tattoo peeking out under his shirt at the wrist – and the boy he used to be, sickly and too pale, bouncing up and down in bed as he watched Road Runner cartoons. I know rationally that he's a grown man, a civil engineer, and healthy. But it's instinct and habit to see him as a sick child – my little brother who needs protecting.

Shane and I used to drive around like this all the time when we were teenagers. Especially when it was raining and there was nothing to do, we'd climb in Dad's car and go for a drive. At first I would drive, but then, when he got his licence, whoever got the keys first got to drive, and whoever got to drive also got to choose the music. We drove around our suburban streets or into town. We listened to whole double albums or we surfed radio channels. We stopped at gas stations or general stores, bought junk food and kept on driving. We didn't talk much on those trips either, but they made me feel closer to Shane anyway. Like we were on some sort of adventure together.

I forgot about that until just now. We spent all that time together side by side, as almost-adults, before I went away to college. And we never talked about a damn thing.

We go along the back roads towards Ranger Lake. Usually this is a pretty drive, through the notches between mountains, but the rain obscures the view and spatters the windscreen with mud. Ranger is much bigger than Morocco Pond. It's not too far from a major road and it was featured as the setting of a Hollywood movie, all of which means that it has much more of a tourist footprint. Ranger has things like boat rentals, a visitor information centre, a bar and a restaurant.

Shane pulls into the parking lot of the Ranger Diner – a log-cabin type structure with a picture of a moose on the side and a sign proclaiming *BEST BLUEBERRY PANCAKES IN MAINE.* There are hardly any cars in the lot, but then again it's mid-afternoon, not really pancake time, and today is a terrible day for tourists.

'Are we going for coffee?' I ask, as he turns off the engine.

'Might as well.'

'I thought you wanted to show me something.'

He checks his phone and puts it back in his pocket, then shrugs on a jacket and gets out of the truck. Shane and I didn't grow up in Maine, but he looks like a total native, with his baseball cap and LL Bean jacket, not to mention the truck. I remember when he used to dress in denim and Chucks, and listen to Blink 182 and Nine Inch Nails.

I follow him into the diner, which has steamed-up windows, a long counter across the back featuring pies under glass, and rustic-style tables and chairs. 'Hi, sit anywhere,' says the woman behind the counter. Instead of taking a stool at the counter like I expect him to, Shane walks straight towards a table in the corner of the room where a woman is sitting by herself.

She's wearing a plain white shirt and gold-rimmed glasses, and her greying hair is cut in a bob. She's got a mug in front of her, but she is looking down at her hands folded on the table. As soon as we come close, she looks up.

And I know her. Even though I haven't seen her for nearly twenty-five years, or keep any photographs of her, I would know her anywhere.

It's my mother.

I turn around and walk right back out of the diner into the rain. Shane's truck is locked so I do the only other thing I can do, which is to start walking down the road. There's no sidewalk, so

I walk on the sandy shoulder. My sneakers soak through in less than a minute.

'Katie!' Shane's shouting behind me, but I ignore him until he catches up with me, then I turn and face him.

'What the fuck, Shane.' I'm too angry to shout it.

'She wanted to see you. I knew if I told you, you wouldn't come.'

'You got that right.'

'She's our mother.'

'She lost the right to call herself that when she walked out on us and never got in touch again.'

'She never got in touch with you again. Because you never let her.'

'Have you been talking to her this whole time?'

'Not the whole time, no. But since the pandemic. I contacted her to make sure she was OK and we stayed in touch.'

'Does Dad know you've been talking with her?'

'Yes. He says it's a good idea.'

'Why?'

'Because she's *our mother*, Katie. Just go and drink coffee with her for ten minutes. Please.'

I pull out my phone, sheltering it from the rain with my other hand.

'Who are you calling?'

'Bryan. So he can come get me.'

Shane sighs.

'OK. Get in the truck.'

We don't speak all the way back to Paradise. This time, I don't make an effort to break the silence. When we arrive, I get out of the truck and my brother drives away.

'Hi.' I call out, the screen door slamming behind me. I leave my wet shoes and jacket in a heap by the door.

'In here.' It sounds like Bryan's in the bathroom. 'Is everything OK?'

'You'll never believe this. Shane brought me to see our long-lost mother. Are you in there? I need a towel.'

The bathroom door is open. Bryan is standing at the sink, wearing a pair of jeans and nothing else. Half of his face is covered in shaving foam. The water is running in the sink, steaming up the mirror.

I stop.

He meets my gaze in the mirror. 'Shane did what?'

'It doesn't matter.' I step into the bathroom. My hair is dripping down the back of my neck. I don't care. I touch his back, between his shoulder blades, downwards, the place where his spine curves in. His skin is warm.

'Katie...'

'Shh.'

'What are you doing?' he asks.

'Can't you tell?' I slide my palm around the side of his torso to rest on his stomach, and his intake of breath is gratifyingly sharp. I rest my fingertips on the top button of his jeans.

He grabs a towel and wipes the shaving cream off his face, and then turns to face me, his arm around me. I smile and arch my back, pressing into him, lift my chin so he can kiss me, tug the top of his jeans open.

Instead of kissing me, he says, 'What did you say about your mother?'

This is not sexy.

'I don't want to think about it. I just want to get back to where we were before Shane turned up.'

'And we will, sometime, I hope. But right now, you need to tell me what happened.'

I sigh and drop my hands to my sides.

'Shane's been talking to our mother. He brought me to see her in this diner up at Ranger Lake.'

'And did you talk with her? What did she say?'

'I got one glance of her and walked straight back out. She doesn't deserve any of my time or attention.'

'OK,' says Bryan carefully. 'How do you feel?'

'I feel terrible! That's why I wanted to seduce you.'

'Wow. Flattering.' He reaches for his shirt, which is hanging on a peg. 'I'm going into town to buy some buttermilk. I'll be back in about three-quarters of an hour. I left some hot water for you if you want a shower.'

He puts on his shirt and leaves the bathroom. A few minutes later, I hear the door closing behind him.

Chapter Forty-four

Nic had dealt with a blocked sink in the campground bathrooms and as she ran back towards the house through the rain, her phone rang in her pocket. She ducked under the shelter of the porch roof to check who was calling.

It was Katie. She took a deep breath before answering it. 'Hey.'

'Hey! So I'm sorry about the late warning, but tonight's the Fourth of July Eve lobster feed at Paradise.'

'Tonight? It's the second of July – it's a day early.'

'Yeah, we moved it up last minute because Bryan's family is coming tomorrow and they don't eat shellfish. Can you and Jeannette come?'

Aside from 2020, they did this together at Paradise every year on the third of July. They feasted on lobster and corn on the cob, with blueberry pie for dessert. Even before Nic started dating Shane, Nic and her mother were always invited and they always went. Usually the date was written on the calendar in advance. Not this year.

'Um. Mom hasn't made a pie.'

'We'll get some pie. Dad and Tessa will be there and they would love to see you. They asked specially. And it wouldn't be the same without you and your mom. But if you don't want to be there with Shane, I understand.'

'Shane told you what happened between us?'

'I got it out of him.'

It wasn't Shane she was worried about so much as being in the same room as Katie and Bryan. And a lot of tools for dismembering crustaceans.

'What do you think?' said Katie. 'We've already ordered the lobsters. Dad's going to pick them up on the way to Paradise. It feels so important to do something normal, you know?'

And Ma loved lobster, and company would do her good. And Nic needed to start doing things again. She hadn't seen Katie since they'd gone swimming. Katie had texted her, but she'd avoided answering, knowing all the time that she wasn't making anything better.

If being in the same room with Katie and Shane was too much to handle, she could always use her mother as an excuse to leave early.

'Sure,' she said. 'We'll be there.'

'Great! See you at six. If it keeps raining like this, you might have to take a boat over.'

As she ended the call, a text came through from Audrey. Only the third text she'd ever received from her – the first when they'd met outside the Durham place, and a second one after they'd run into each other on the mountain, saying **Hope your day's better**. Nic had put a thumbs-up reaction to it, and she'd meant to reply, and bring Audrey's bandana back, but there always seemed to be something she had to do and it had dropped from her mind.

Hey Nic, it's Audrey. Do you play gin? Or drink it? Do you feel like doing either tonight? This rain is driving me nuts.

'Oh!' she said. No social life for weeks, and suddenly two invitations at the same time.

I like doing both! But I have plans tonight. Sometime soon?

You're on. Ax

The rapidity of the reply made her smile. That was something to look forward to. Unlike her plans at Paradise for tonight, which she was deeply unsure about. She put her phone back in her pocket and went into the house. 'Hey, Ma, it's lobster tonight!'

Her mother, who had been folding and refolding laundry in the living room in front of the TV, was nowhere to be found. 'Ma?' she called, mentally checking whether she'd remembered to hide the car keys, cursing the fact that they lived next to a lethal lake and a forest that, with a little bad luck, stretched uninterrupted from here to Quebec. 'Where'd you go?'

A noise from the office. Shit, she had forgotten to lock the inner door and it was ajar. Nic went in and found Ma sitting at the desk, shuffling through papers. Nic's research notes, that she'd spent most of yesterday afternoon getting in order. She hadn't done any research, of course. Just rearranged her papers.

'Ma! What are you doing?'

'Doing the bookings for the campground.' Ma held up one of Nic's notations, glanced over at it and threw it in the wastebasket beside the desk. 'I don't know what this rubbish is.'

'It's my work!' She ran to the wastebasket to retrieve her notes. It was already full of crumpled paper. She smoothed out a sheet: her transcription of 'Le Moineau et le Martinet'. 'Ma, this isn't rubbish – you can't throw it away. This took me months to put together.'

'We have people arriving to stay, we don't have time for this nonsense. Where's my invoice book?'

'I do that on an app now. Ma, please leave it.'

'Where's my invoice book? Where'd you hide it? What is all this stuff?' Her mother picked up a folder and knocked over a water bottle on the desk. As if in slow motion, Nic watched the water glug out of the bottle, directly onto her open laptop.

Her laptop where all of her work was stored. Her recordings, her research, her proposals. Every single bit. She'd backed it up, but how long ago?

She leapt forward and grabbed the bottle with one hand and her laptop in the other. The bottle was empty. The laptop was dripping. As she stared in horror, she saw the screen go grey and then dark.

'Fuck!' she yelled, and snatched a beach towel from a shelf and started dabbing at the computer. 'Ma, what the hell!'

'I was looking for—'

'I know what you were looking for, but you're not even supposed to be in here! This is my work!'

'But I—'

'Every time I try to do anything, every time I want something for myself, it gets ruined. This is my office, Ma! It's not yours any more! You're not allowed in here!'

'It's my house! It's my house! *It's my house!*'

Her mother stood behind the desk, fists clenched by her sides, elbows digging into her waist, glaring at Nic, yelling at the top of her lungs. In another part of the house, the dogs were howling.

'It's my house! My house! You get out of here!'

'Ma...' Nic discarded the laptop and the towel, and held out her hands.

'Get out of here! Get out of my house!'

'Jeannette? You OK?'

Shane was standing in the door from the outside, which wasn't locked either. He came in, past Nic, and put his hand on Ma's shoulder. Ma stared at him, but she didn't pull away.

'Hey, good to see you, Jeannette,' he said gently. 'Everything OK with you?'

'I was... oh, hello, I was doing something. I don't remember.'

'Let's go have an iced tea. I'm parched. Can you fix that for me?'

He nodded at Nic as he guided Jeannette through the office into the house, leaving Nic with her sodden towel and her dead laptop. Alone, she dried off the desk and she fished the rest of her papers out of the wastebasket and tried to get her heart to stop from hammering.

She shouldn't have left her laptop out. She shouldn't have had a bottle of water on the desk. She should have put all her papers away. She should have backed up more religiously. She should have locked the door to the inside. This was all her fault. And she had yelled at her mother. Her own mother. Again.

She sat down among the wreck of her life and cried.

In the living room, Shane was sitting with her mom on the sofa. They each had a glass of iced tea and they were watching a cooking show on TV.

'There's a glass in the kitchen for you,' said Shane.

'Thanks,' Nic said. 'Ma, I'm sorry for yelling.'

Ma shrugged. 'Everyone messes up.' It was what she always used to say to her dad when he'd apologise for gambling away all their money or forgetting to make a mortgage payment.

Shane followed her into the kitchen. 'Are you OK?'

'Yeah. Thanks for looking after my mom.'

'She doesn't hold grudges any more. Not like she used to.'

'Well, that's one benefit.' She got a bag of rice out of the cupboard. 'My laptop is trashed. I'll try the rice trick.'

'Rice trick never works. I can take it to my guy in Portland if you want.'

She put the laptop and the rice into a big plastic Ziplock bag anyway. 'Why are you being so nice to me?'

He looked baffled. 'You and your mom are family to me. You have been, my whole life. Nothing's going to change that.'

'God!' She flopped down at the table. 'You are so much nicer than I am, you know that?'

He shrugged, like that had always been obvious. 'Are you coming to Paradise tonight?'

'I planned to.'

'That's why I dropped by. I wanted to make sure it was OK if I was there.'

'They're your family, Shane.'

'Yeah, but you and Katie are joined at the hip, so.'

'It's fine. It's like you said – we're all family. And I really appreciate your help today. I don't want to get upset with Ma. You know I don't.'

'You need a break,' he said. 'Listen, I'll stay with your mom until it's time to go over. Why don't you take a rest, or get some work done, or whatever.'

'Do you mind?'

'I'd like it. I was going to ask if you'd mind if I came to visit more often, anyway.'

She bit her lip. 'Shane, we're over, though. We're not going to get back together. I'm sorry.'

'I know. I just had to get that through my head before I could see you again, you know?' He held out his hand. 'Friends?'

'Friends,' she said, and shook.

She was past believing that friendship was ever that simple. But they could try, at least.

Chapter Forty-five

She knocked on the screen door and Audrey appeared. She had on rolled-up jeans and an Amherst hoody, her hair up on top of her head, a pair of glasses on top of that. Hoop earrings, silver rings on her fingers.

'Hey!' she said, clearly pleased. 'I thought you were busy tonight.'

'I am. But I'm unexpectedly free this afternoon. Are you still up for playing cards?'

'Always.' She held open the door. 'Get in quick, before you get any more wet.'

'I don't think that's possible.' Nic came inside, dripping. She took off her raincoat and gazed around her. 'Wow.'

'I've made some changes. Though my aunt probably never let you in here. She never let anyone in.'

'I've been in here before, but that's got a story to it.'

'She let you in?' Audrey took her coat and hung it up on a peg near the door. 'She didn't even let me in. I never saw the inside of this place until I inherited it. She invited my brother, but never me. But then she left it to me in her will and cut him out entirely. My mom just about fainted with shock.' Audrey shook her head. 'Crazy old lady.'

'I... we broke in. My best friend and me. One day when your aunt was out.'

Audrey laughed. She had a nice laugh. 'What did it look like?'

'It was pretty dismal. You've done a nice job.'

The kitchen wall had been knocked through, so the cottage

interior was all one room and bigger than Nic remembered from their secret spying mission all those years ago. Audrey had painted everything white: wooden floors, walls and ceiling. The furniture was sparse, mismatched, covered with throws and blankets. Rag rugs scattered the floor and the light came from several lamps. One side of the cottage had a kitchenette with what looked like an original butler's sink, a propane stove and open shelves; the other had a large stone fireplace. The front, facing the lake, was mostly made up of windows opening onto the screened-in porch. A white-painted ladder led up through a hole in the ceiling.

'It's all cosmetic changes inside for the moment,' Audrey explained. 'I didn't have enough money to put in new plumbing and electrics this year, so it's pretty basic. And everything in here is from garage sales. I put in a bedroom under the eaves, and that's even more basic. I don't have power up there so I get to enjoy reading in bed by candlelight and listening to the rain.'

'I like it.'

'Thanks. It's an adventure, anyway. And a nice way to get away from campus. I live half a mile from where I work and sometimes it feels like I sleep there too.' She took a couple of glasses off a shelf. 'Drink?'

'Sure.'

'Something soft or will you have a gin?'

'Gin. Definitely gin. It's been one of those days. But I can only have one, because I'm having dinner with my ex's family tonight and I need to be on best behaviour.'

'Got it. Strong one or weak one?'

'Strong one.'

'I'm sorry, I don't have ice, but I keep the gin and tonic in the fridge.'

Nic nodded and watched as Audrey sliced lemon, poured drinks. They brought the glasses over to a pair of chairs in front of the window, a rocking chair and an armchair, with a spindly and scarred table sat between them. A glass Coke bottle held a few wildflowers.

'You're my first guest this summer,' Audrey said.

'Wow, really? I'm honoured. Thanks.'

'My partner was meant to join me for the holiday. But they have to work.'

Nic filed that away – both the fact that Audrey wasn't single and the fact that she didn't sound too happy about being by herself on the Fourth of July.

'Thanks for coming over,' said Audrey. 'I owe you a drink. You were right, that electrician didn't mess me around or try to upsell me. He made everything safe for now and I'm going to get him to rewire the whole place next year. Cheers.'

'Cheers.' They drank. 'When did you meet my mom?'

'Which one is your mom?'

'Jeannette Leblanc. Tall, skinny lady, grey hair on the sides, usually wearing a flannel shirt. She owns the campground.'

Audrey shook her head slowly. 'I don't remember her. I've been pretty busy fixing this place up. Did she say we'd met?'

'She has dementia. She says a lot of things. She probably was thinking of someone else. Or making someone up – she does that sometimes.'

'I'm sorry.'

Nic shrugged. 'It is what it is,' she said, and sipped her drink.

'I didn't want to pry,' said Audrey. 'But now I'm curious. You said you've got plans with your ex and their family tonight. Is that OK or is it complicated?'

'It's more complicated than you can imagine.'

'That's tough.' She opened a drawer in the table and took out a pack of cards. 'Well, you don't really know me, but I'm always here if you want to talk.'

'That's nice of you. Thanks.'

'I also like to play cards, if you don't feel like talking. Should I deal?'

They played a hand of gin. Nic won.

'You didn't say you were good at it,' Audrey said.

'It was luck.' Nic shuffled. 'Another game?'

They played again, and this time Audrey won.

The rain was still pouring down and yellow lamplight reflected against the windows. To anyone walking by, Nic and Audrey would be all lit up, sitting across from each other, as if on a stage.

'We need a tiebreaker,' said Nic.

'I know about shitty break-ups,' said Audrey, while she was dealing. 'I've had a few. It can really mess you up.'

'This one was all my fault, so being messed up seems like a luxury I don't deserve. I'm sorry you went through that.'

'Thanks,' said Audrey. She picked up her hand and fanned it out, perusing her cards. Then she glanced at Nic above them. 'And I was flirting with you a little, too, that time we first met. I'm sorry if that was inappropriate.'

'Because you have a partner.'

'Well, that, and because I wasn't sure if you like women.'

'I like women.' Nic's heart was suddenly pounding.

Audrey raised her eyebrows, but said nothing. She looked at her cards. Nic drew a card from the pack, discarded, and they played a game in silence. Her heart was still pounding. She wondered if Audrey was flirting with her now or if it was just a way of establishing that they had this thing in common.

She won.

'You've got best out of three.' Audrey got up, brought over the tonic, and refilled their glasses. 'I don't know if I dare play you again.'

'One more,' said Nic. Her hands felt clumsy, so, instead of shuffling properly, she cut the cards and mixed them together, again and again.

'My ex is a guy,' Nic said. 'But I've been in love with his sister for years.'

She'd said it. Out loud, to someone who she knew, and who wouldn't forget.

'Is she straight?' asked Audrey.

'I'm not sure how she defines herself. She's in a relationship with a man.'

Audrey raised her glass. 'Congratulations.'

'Huh?'

'Queer rite of passage.'

Nic frowned. 'I've spent most of my life in the woods here, so you're going to have to explain.'

'There's not a single gay or bisexual person alive who hasn't had a hopeless crush on someone straight.'

'It seems so stupid when you say it like that.'

'It's not stupid. It's actually quite logical. We develop hopeless crushes on people we can't have because it's much safer than being vulnerable and our true selves in a real relationship.' She raised her eyes to heaven. 'Mine was Daisy Wincowicz. She was a cheerleader. I didn't have a hope in hell. I think she has six kids by now.'

'Mine was a cheerleader too.'

'It's the little flippy skirts. You have good taste. Was she your first love?'

'Yeah.'

'So she was your queer awakening. Like Daisy was for me. It's hard to let that go.'

'It sucks, doesn't it?'

'Sure does. But she opened your eyes.'

'Yeah. So...' Nic put down the cards. 'So my feelings served a purpose, even if she didn't love me back. I never thought of it that way.'

'Bingo.'

'I've got a fuck of a lot to learn,' Nic said.

'Don't we all,' said Audrey. 'Are you going to deal? I feel lucky.'

Chapter Forty-six

On her way to Paradise from the Durham place (having drunk two gins, after all), she heard a sound ahead of her and saw that the underbrush by the side of the drive was moving.

She stopped, thinking maybe a deer was about to cross the road, or – more dangerously – a skunk. Once, years ago, she'd seen a porcupine ambling along the yellow centre line of the road, armed to the teeth with quills, ignorant of vehicles, unafraid of anything. She'd made a wide detour.

The brush parted and a moose appeared. It stepped elegantly with its long legs over the ditch and into the road.

Despite the rain, he was in no hurry. He was vast, blackish brown – a bull with antler rack sprouting wide from his head. She counted five points on each side. The animal was probably nine feet tall, probably weighed half a ton and could flatten a truck. She didn't dare move, hardly dared breathe.

Long patrician nose, dipped down at the end, curling nostrils, ears flicking away a fly. The moose walked across the road not twenty feet in front of her. She was close enough to hear a huff of his breath, close enough to catch a whiff of his murky animal scent.

A small, gleaming black eye looked directly at her. She held her nerve, did not step back.

This enormous animal was aware of her presence but didn't alter his course or quicken his mammoth steps. The two of them were alone on this road. This encounter was theirs alone.

He paused. She held her breath.

Then he continued on his slow, stately way. He reached the other side of the road. Slipped between two pines. Aside from damp footprints, he was gone as if he had never been. This powerful creature, this force of nature – a memory.

A message.

Things spooled out, disappeared, left your life for ever. Sometimes you were their only witness. Not everything was in her grasp, or able to be held and kept. Some things, you had to let go.

She arrived at Paradise after everyone else. The first thing Nic did was hug her mom.

'I'm sorry,' she whispered into Ma's ear. 'I love you.'

Ma patted her on the back. 'There, there, it's OK,' she said, and Nic knew she didn't remember any of it. But Nic had to say it, for her own sake.

Then she was swept up into the Stone family, as always – hugs and kisses from Bill and Tessa, with delighted exclamations of gladness that she could make it, as if everything was normal, as if she'd never turned down the possibility of being a real and permanent part of the family, as if everything between her and Shane was all in the past and had maybe never happened.

Once again, she marvelled at the capacity of this family to pretend that nothing at all was wrong.

Bryan said to Jeannette, 'You've got to talk to me about baking,' and gave Nic a wink.

Katie, in a yellow dress with her hair up and make-up covering the remains of the bruises under her eyes, poured Nic a large glass of wine. 'Shane said you had a meltdown this afternoon.'

'That's an understatement.'

'Get this wine down you. We'll look after your mom.'

'Katie, you and I need to—'

But she never got to finish the sentence, or indeed any sentence, for some time. Tessa came through with a platter of bright-red cooked lobsters, and that was the signal for everyone to go to the big wooden table near the picture windows.

Lobster, of course, was not only the Maine state dish and a large part of the economy but it was also a ritual. The lobsters were dismembered at the table, dipped in melted butter. The shells were tossed into a communal bowl until it was a heap of red carapaces. Lobster was also expensive, even in Maine, and had never graced the Leblanc family table. For something so seemingly rarefied and elegant, you ate it with your hands and it involved boiling an animal alive and then pulling it to pieces.

Nic had had her first taste of lobster with the Stones, and she had eaten it enough with them since to know how their particular ritual went. Katie ate hers quickly, piece by piece as she unshelled it, not bothering with the fiddly legs and tail fins, which she gave to Nic; Shane was methodical, taking every single bit of meat out of the lobster and putting it in his butter to soak until he was finished, and then eating it all at once. Tessa mostly liked the tail, so she gave her claws to Bill, and Bill liked the claws best, so he gave his tail to Tessa. Jeannette, as always, ate her lobster thoroughly and with great relish, sucking meat from the legs and drinking the juice from the claws, even eating the greenish tamale that nobody else liked, not even Nic.

There were some differences this year. The subtle one was that Tessa had to help Bill with his lobster, especially with navigating the crackers and the pick. Nic noticed that everyone else was ignoring this, just like they ignored Jeannette's occasional non sequiturs or the fact that Nic and Shane were being ridiculously polite to each other.

Bryan had never had lobster in the shell before, so everyone gave detailed and often contradictory instructions to him.

'Start with the knuckle.'

'No, twist off the tail.'

'You'll need your cracker for the claws.'

'These are soft shells. Just use your thumbs.'

'Don't worry about the body – it's a lot of work.'

'Are you kidding? The body is the best part!'

As befitted his role as the newcomer to the family, Bryan took all of this advice good-naturedly and agreed to let Jeannette help him out when he couldn't get the meat out of the knuckle or the vein out of the tail.

'This is carnage,' he said, elbow-deep in juice and bits of shell. Nic watched as Katie caught his eye across the table and they smiled at each other.

It hurt. But Nic didn't look away. She let herself feel it. She could survive it. It was going to hurt, and maybe one day it wouldn't.

She wiped her mouth, drank some more wine and all at once she realised that she could stop torturing herself.

It didn't matter whether Katie ever got her memory back or not. It didn't matter who she had chosen, before she was hit by the ATV. They would have to talk about it, whether Katie wanted to or not, but ultimately it didn't change anything.

Nic had been the one who had disturbed the status quo between them. Which meant that Nic was the one with the most to lose.

She had to do what was best for herself. And that meant giving up what no longer served her.

For all her life, from the moment she'd clapped eyes on Paradise, she had adored Katie and pined after Katie, and envied her family and wanted to be part of it. She put her life on hold when Katie was not around. She dwelled and felt comfortable in Katie's shadow.

But it wasn't where she could live any more.

Chapter Forty-seven

After dinner, the dishes have been done, the lobster shells thrown away, and Dad and Tessa are sitting in the kitchen with Jeannette, and Shane and Bryan are on the sofa drinking beer and talking about baseball, with Eebie asleep on Shane's lap. I open a new bottle of wine and take it out to the porch where Nic is sitting on the rocker watching the rain.

This year's lobster feed has, I think, been a rousing success. Everything seems almost back to normal. Dad is in good health, Bryan is having a great time, Shane hasn't brought up our trip to Ranger Lake, and Nic seems relaxed, much more so than she's been recently. It's as if nothing ever happened between us to split our friendship apart.

'At this rate, we're going to need to build an ark,' she says, holding out her glass. I fill it and sit down beside her, like I have a thousand times.

'Your mom's doing really well,' I say.

'She's better in company. She'll be exhausted after. I think it takes a lot out of her, to follow everything and pretend.'

'And you and Shane seem to be getting along.'

'He's a nice guy.'

'He's pissed off with me,' I say.

Nic snorts.

'Did he tell you?' I ask.

'Of course he didn't. But I don't know why I'm surprised. It's not as if this house is short on unspoken subtext. Why's he pissed off with you?'

I swig my wine. 'He's in touch with our mother. And he tried to get me to talk with her.'

'That sounds like a good idea.'

'What? Are you kidding me? Why would I want to talk with her, of all people?'

'You might get some answers.'

'I don't need any answers from her.'

Nic is looking at me and I say, 'What?'

'I think the answers might help you. Anyway, it would be good for you to face some of this stuff.'

'No way. You know how I feel about her. Why would I put myself through that?'

'What does Bryan think?'

'He'll support me whatever I decide to do,' I answer, which is not exactly what he said, but he's said that before so I'm assuming it still counts.

'Did he make you a buttermilk cake?'

'How did you know about that?'

'I gave him the recipe.'

'It was meant to be *that* buttermilk cake?'

'It's my mom's love potion.'

Nic holds out her glass, which surprisingly is already half empty, as is mine. I refill them both and put the bottle on the floor between us. I'm going to need that wine, because now that things are back to normal between me and Nic, and we're friends again, I have to tell her I have my memory back but that everything is OK.

'Earlier you started to say that we needed to talk,' I say.

'Right,' says Nic. 'We do. But before that. Do you remember all those photographs we found in old Lydia Durham's house?'

'I can do better than remembering.' I nip upstairs, fetch the photo from the Nancy Drew book and bring it back down to Nic. She peers at it.

'You stole one?'

'That's my mother.' I point her out. Nic studies her. I don't know that she's ever seen a photo of her before.

'And that's the woman in all the other pictures,' she said. 'There were dozens of them, weren't there? All of the same woman. And your mother knew her.'

'I don't know,' I say. 'Maybe she did. Maybe she's just in the background.'

Nic examines the photo some more. Her dark eyes intent, her brows drawing down. You can always see when Nic is thinking hard, trying to puzzle something out. She loves following clues, making sense of things, making stories whole.

I love her so much.

She looks up. 'Can I borrow this?'

'Of course. Take it. I'm not even sure why I stole it in the first place.'

'Thanks.' She gets up and slips the photo into the back pocket of her jeans. 'OK, now we need to talk.'

She shuts the door from the porch into the camp, and then sits back down beside me. I'm expecting something about being a bit jealous of Bryan – I saw her watching, tonight, when I touched him on the shoulder in passing. I'm expecting us to discuss how we'll carry on our friendship when I've got a boyfriend, or something like that. Something about moving forward, and her forgiving me, and putting everything in the past.

But instead, she says, 'I know you've forgotten about the last eighteen months on purpose.'

Chapter Forty-eight

I can't reply for a second while my brain catches up with her words.

'On purpose?' Has she figured out that I've got my memory back and she's about to accuse me of lying to her? 'What do you mean?'

'It's been a tough time. It's not just what's happened in your family and between you and me. People have been getting sick and dying, and this country is more divided and unequal than ever, and the whole world has felt uncertain and like it's falling apart. It's frightening. I'm not saying you faked your amnesia. But I am saying that you were pretty strategic about what you forgot.'

'Yes,' I say carefully. 'I think I probably have been.'

'But the thing is, that you seem to think that everyone else can forget about what happened, too, and start as fresh as you want to. And that's not fair. So we need to talk about what happened between you and me. I need to talk about it.'

'OK,' I say. My heart is hammering.

'Last June, after I couldn't get engaged to Shane, I told you that I was in love with you and I have been for as long as I can remember. And you freaked out and refused to talk to me about it. You blocked me and left me to deal with it by myself.'

'I am so sorry,' I whisper.

'I was so lonely. I felt like I had lost everything. Because you couldn't handle my emotions and it was easier for you to run away.'

'Nic. I should never have run away from you.'

'Damn right you shouldn't have. And for over a year, now, I've been blaming myself because I should never have said anything out loud. But that was wrong. I don't need to feel ashamed of how I feel. I don't need to feel ashamed of how you feel, either.'

'No,' I say. 'You have nothing to be ashamed of.'

'I *am* ashamed that I got upset and jealous, and I gave you an ultimatum. I said you had to choose between your friendship with me and your relationship with Bryan. And I shouldn't have done that. A real, equal friend wouldn't do that. So I'm sorry about that and even if you don't remember it, I owe it to myself to apologise to you, so that I can let it go.'

'We can both let it go' I say desperately. 'We can move on and start again. Nothing needs to change from before.'

Nic shakes her head. 'No, Katie. Everything has changed.' She stands up. 'But actually, some things have never changed. Our friendship has never been equal. It's always depended on me adoring you and never saying anything about it. You've always been moving and I've always been here, waiting for you, like a loyal puppy.'

'That's not true.'

'You know it is. And that was fine when we were children, but we're grown up now.'

'Nic, I've always needed you.'

'And I've always needed you. But I had to live without you for a long time. Even before you cut me out of your life.'

'We can move on from that.'

'Yes. But not together. I have to let some things go. I have to let you go, at least in the way that I've always thought about you. And I need to work out how to do that by myself.'

She puts down her glass, which is still half full.

'It's getting late. I'm going to take my mother home.'

She leaves the porch, leaving me behind, stunned.

When I manage to get up and follow her, she's announced her departure. This precipitates a long round of goodnights, and then

Shane says he'll drive them both to the campground because it's raining so hard. Bill and Tessa say they're going to head home too, which precipitates another long round of goodnights, and I can do nothing but hug and kiss everyone, and act like everything is OK, that my best friend hasn't ended our friendship again, and for good, just when I thought it was healing.

When everyone's left, I start collecting glasses and bottles, and Bryan stops me. 'What's wrong?' he asks.

I have no words for this. I've lost Nic. It's all ruined and it's all my fault. I can't tell Bryan right now and risk losing him, too. I can't risk showing him this terrible, faithless, ugly view of me. Not right now, when it still hurts so much.

'Nothing's wrong,' I say. 'Actually everything is great.'

'Then why do you look like that?'

'Like what?' I try to smile normally, but, from his expression, I am failing.

'You look stunned. Like an animal hit by a car.'

I swallow the pain. 'I remember everything,' I say.

His eyes widen. 'You do?'

'It ... sort of came to me. And. It's a lot. Pandemic. My dad.'

'But you remember us?'

'I remember everything about us.'

He embraces me and holds me close against his chest. He's practically thrumming with happiness.

I should have told him earlier. It was cruel not to tell him earlier, as soon as it happened, instead of making him wait.

Bryan loosens his hold, leans back to look into my eyes. 'Something's still wrong, though. You're still not yourself.'

'It's ... I'm feeling overwhelmed. I guess I still need some space to get used to everything.'

'That's OK.' He kisses me. 'If you remember us, then everything's going to be OK.'

I nod and kiss him back. But everything is very much not OK.

Chapter Forty-nine

At 9.45 a.m. on the third of July, while she was driving to Casablanca to get groceries, Nic's phone rang and the name that came up on her screen was Pierre Robichaud. She pulled onto the shoulder right away and answered.

'Mr Robichaud? It's so good to hear from you! I've been calling and calling – I've left a lot of messages. I haven't been able to track down any more information about the "Le Moineau et le Martinet" song and I'd love the opportunity to speak with you again. How are you?'

'Uh, hi,' said a voice on the other end, and it wasn't Mr Robichaud. It was a woman. 'Is this Nicole LeBlanc?'

'Yes. Um ... who's this? This is the number I have for Pierre Robichaud.'

'Yeah, it's his phone, but I'm his great-niece, Marissa. I've been sorting out all his stuff and his phone had a bunch of messages from you on it, so I wanted to call you back.'

Oh, no. Oh, no.

'How is he? Is he OK?'

'He passed away last summer. He had liver problems and then he got Covid. He didn't use his phone much and he left a lot of stuff to deal with so I'm just getting around to it all as I can.'

'I'm so sorry,' Nic said, staring at the trees by the side of the road, feeling yet another dream dying around her. 'That's very sad.'

'Well, he had a long life.'

'When I couldn't get hold of him, I looked for obituaries in the Maine papers but ...'

'We ran one down here. We're in Florida. Anyway, now you know. I got a few more calls to make, then I'm going to cancel this phone contract along with everything else.'

'Did he leave any documentation about his music?' Nic asked. 'We have an archive up here at the University of Maine that I know would be interested in anything you have. Any recordings, notation, photographs, and even any memories you could write down for us would be useful.'

'We got rid of that stuff when we took him down here to live with us.'

'You donated it?' she said, without much hope.

'Threw it in the dumpster.'

'He said there was a notebook that his grandmother gave him, which was full of songs.'

'Wouldn't know. It was a big mess, let me tell you. He was blind so everything was thrown in a big pile and his roof had been leaking for years. House is still on the market; no one wants to buy it. OK, well, I got to go now, so—'

'Do you have any memories of the songs he used to play? I'm looking for information about one in particular – he said it came from I'm guessing your great-grandmother. In English it's called "The Sparrow—"'

'I'm not really into music, sorry. OK, you take care now, bye.'

Nic threw the phone onto the passenger seat. Well, that was it. Two years of research down the drain, thrown in a dumpster.

The song was going to remain unfinished for ever. Like her parents' lives, gone or changed too early. Like the house she lived in, with its patched-together rooms and its uneven floors. Like her relationship with Shane, which was over, really, before it had ever begun, or her love for Katie, which would only ever be one-sided and sad; the mysteries they'd never really solved as children.

Last year – last week – she would have been crushed. She would have raged and cried, tried not to blame her mother's sickness for delaying her research. Or worse, she would have done what she did when Katie rejected her, and felt nothing at all.

But today, here on the side of the road, she could just be sad and think about what was lost.

Chapter Fifty

Dad and Tessa arrive just after lunch the next day, the third of July, ostensibly to bring up groceries and help get the camp ready for overnight guests, but really it's because Tessa is so curious to meet Bryan's family.

'It's too bad they're only staying two nights,' Tessa says, handing bags of hamburger and hot dog rolls to Bryan. I'm holding an umbrella up over the trunk of her car to keep her dry.

'They couldn't pass up the chance to do a little tour of the Maine coast while they're here,' says Bryan. 'I hope it doesn't rain the whole time.'

'Supposed to be nice tomorrow,' says my dad, who isn't carrying anything but doesn't like to miss out on conversation. 'Hopefully we can have a barbecue and watch the fireworks.'

'The weather is terrible,' I say. 'The beach is flooded. And the chimney is leaking. It's sort of a mess here.'

'They don't care. My dad says happy families are at their best when things aren't perfect.' Bryan, laden with groceries, goes inside.

He and I need to talk, I know. We need to have the mother of all talks, and then I need to find Nic and talk with her, too. But not now, I tell myself. The holiday is going to be too busy and crowded with people, and, besides, he deserves time with his family and he's so happy I have my memories back. I don't want to ruin it for him. We'll talk properly when we have some time to ourselves.

Now that I've had a little breathing space, I'm not sorry to have the excuse to put off the conversation. What Nic said to me brought back the horrible, hollow ache I felt last summer, after she confessed her feelings for me, and after I made the decision to stop answering her calls and texts because thinking about it made it feel much worse.

Last night she said that our friendship wasn't equal. As if her feelings about me – the length of time she's had them, her willingness to give up everything for them – meant that I had some power over her.

But I don't want that power. I never did. The thought of it makes me feel angry and sick. It was easier to pretend never to notice her feelings about me. But that pretending was what made it all so bad. It's what is making it bad right now, although I'm hiding it.

It's all too messy. Much messier than the leaking chimney.

Back in the kitchen, I say to Tessa, 'I love you very much, but please don't start talking marriage and babies with Bryan's mom, all right?'

She pretends to pout. 'I thought Nicole and Shane were going to give me some grandchildren. Now you're taking away my hope?'

'You guys need to adopt a cat or something.'

'You hear her, Bill? Another vote for a cat.'

Dad says, 'Speaking of Shane, he says that you tried to meet up with Cynthia.'

Proving that Shane tells Dad much more than he tells me. I make a noncommittal sound and bend down to put the beer into the fridge.

Bryan's been checking out the window every thirty seconds. He says, 'There they are.' He opens the umbrella again and goes out to meet a car that's pulling up outside. Even before it's completely stopped, the passenger door is opening and Bryan's mother is getting out and hugging Bryan, clasping her arms around him and rocking him back and forth, even though he's about a foot and a half taller than she is.

I grab another umbrella and join them. Bryan's mother rushes over to me and hugs me.

'Katie, I'm Cherry,' she says.

'It's great to meet you. Bryan has told me so much.'

'We are just thrilled to be here.'

On my other side, her husband claps Bryan on the back and then shakes my hand. 'Daniel,' he says. 'Nice to meet you.'

'This is Isaac,' Bryan tells me as his brother, lanky and unkempt, with a beard that's not quite there yet, climbs out of the back seat. He stretches and I can see that he looms over both his parents and even Bryan.

'Amnesia is based,' Isaac says. 'I wish I could forget most of last year, too.' His mother elbows him. '*Joke*, Mom.'

'It's OK,' I say. 'My memory's come back.'

This causes a small joyous uproar, as Bryan's parents and mine exclaim their happiness. Dad gives me an extra-long hug and a kiss on the head. He doesn't say anything about knowing all along, and I'm grateful.

'They're so nice,' I whisper to Bryan as we carry their bags to the camp. And that is nearly the last thing I get to say for the next several hours, as our parents introduce themselves and launch straight into conversation. Cherry and Daniel (but mostly Cherry) tell us about their journey (full of crying babies), and who's taking care of their cats (their neighbour, Janice, whose hobby is growing giant vegetables), and compare their first views of Maine to Michigan (hard to tell, in the rain).

'I know I talk a lot,' Cherry says to me. 'But I don't know what Bryan's told you, so I want to tell you everything.'

Bryan is grinning ear to ear.

'Also, she talks a lot,' says Isaac, and then, 'Ouch.'

His parents love Paradise. We give them a tour of the house and by then the rain has eased up. Finally it stops, leaving the air clear. Isaac goes straight into the pond, but Daniel and Cherry want to be taken over the entire property and told everything about its history and family stories, and so now I do get to talk, but about happy memories. Bryan keeps us well supplied with beer, and, before I know it, he and his dad are grilling burgers, and Isaac is rolling a joint to smoke behind the camp and his parents are pretending not to notice that he flew from Michigan with weed in his bag, and I'm in the middle of a family and one of them.

I don't know why I was so reluctant to meet them before. Well, actually I do. If I didn't meet Bryan's parents, I could pretend, even subconsciously, that I had one foot out of the relationship.

But from now on, that is going to change.

Paradise has three bedrooms. We've given my dad and Tessa's bedroom to Bryan's parents, and before dinner Isaac moved his stuff into Shane's old bedroom where Bryan has been sleeping – though we only found that out when he disappeared during the washing-up and I found him lying on the bed, fully clothed, earbuds in, asleep.

Five rounds of good-natured cheating at cards later, Dad and Tessa go home, promising to be back in time for breakfast. Cherry and Daniel get ready for bed and Bryan and I are left sitting on the sofa, each finishing a final beer. Eebie is asleep on my feet. Ruefully, Bryan eyes the pile of blankets and pillows that we left on the end of the sofa, intending to make it up for Isaac.

'I'm going to drag my brother out of there by the ear,' he says.

'He's just like Shane at that age,' I say. 'Anyway, he's too long for this couch. And so are you. I can sleep here.'

'There is no way you're sleeping on the sofa in your own home because of my family. My mother would literally die of shame and then she would strangle Isaac herself. Which I think she almost did, earlier, when he started running around the house with Eebie, both of them barking.'

He gets up and begins to unfold a blanket.

'Sleep in my room,' I say.

'I said, I'm not letting you sleep on the couch.'

'I meant, with me.'

He looks at me, thoughtful. 'Are you sure? You don't mind?'

'Of course I don't mind. You're my boyfriend.'

'But I've been trying to give you space. I didn't want to go too fast.'

'I'd like you to.' I stretch, and unexpectedly yawn before I can cover my mouth.

'Just sleeping,' he says. 'We have plenty of time for everything else.'

I wouldn't mind a bit of everything else – it would take my mind off hating myself. But even I understand that we need to have at least one heart-to-heart before we jump straight into intimacy.

If he even wants that, after finding out the truth.

'And cuddling, please,' I add.

'Definitely cuddling,' he says. 'You go ahead up. I'll let out Eebie and come up in a little while.'

I get up, then pause. 'Nic said she gave you the recipe for the famous buttermilk cake that made her dad fall in love with her mom.' It gives me a pang to mention Nic, but somehow it's better than if I don't mention her.

'Oh. Oh, yeah, that.' He's embarrassed. 'Well, it was worth trying.'

'Sure was.'

'I'm glad you like my parents.'

'Of course I do.'

'You did very well meeting them for the first time.'

'Oh. Well. They're very easy to get along with. Like you.'

'Flirt,' he says.

I go up to bed alone, and fall asleep alone. But in the morning when I wake up, he's lying beside me, awake.

I gaze over at him. His hair is tousled, his eyes are soft. I can feel the warmth of his body, even though we're not touching. He's wearing a T-shirt, whereas usually he sleeps naked. His cheek is on my grandmother's pillowcase, I can hear waves lapping outside my window, the sun is shining through the curtains, and this moment right here is exactly what I wanted when I invited him to come to Paradise with me.

These foolish things remind me of you.

I love him. He's not going anywhere. Why have I been so afraid?

'Hey,' he says softly.

'Hey.'

He reaches over and smooths my hair away from my forehead. 'Tell me how you're doing.'

How I'm doing is I want to scoot over and press up against him. I want to take off his T-shirt and touch his skin. I want to kiss him and have him hold me.

I curl my palm around the side of his face. 'I knew you,' I say. 'Even when I woke up and didn't remember anything, some deep part of me knew that I could trust you.'

'You can trust me.' He takes my hand that's touching him and he kisses my palm. 'Is there anything you need to tell me, Katie?'

I shiver. I could tell him right now. I want to tell him. I want to talk about my relationship with Nic and why I never talked about it with him, and ask his opinion of what I should do. I want to tell him how good it feels to be part of his family as well as mine, about how being vulnerable with him is scary but I want to learn how to do it. I want to thank him for supporting me even when he doesn't know he's been doing it.

Then I hear people stirring downstairs and I realise that this is totally the wrong time to have this conversation. We have a houseful of people. Dad, Tessa and Shane will be here soon, and it's the Fourth of July.

Bryan's family is leaving tomorrow morning and we'll be alone again. Then we can do all the talking we need to do. I can show him all the terrible things about myself, all the mistakes I've made.

Today, it's time to enjoy the present.

'No,' I say. 'Everything is great.'

Chapter Fifty-one

When she was at Audrey's camp playing cards, Nic had invited her to the campground for the Fourth. 'Usually, it's mayhem. It might be a little less busy this year. Anyway, there'll be all the hot dogs you can eat and a good viewing spot for the fireworks. If you haven't got plans.'

'I wasn't going to do anything,' said Audrey. 'Except sit here and feel a bit sorry for myself because my girlfriend has to work.'

'Well, you're very welcome, if you change your mind,' said Nic, but she didn't expect it to happen, and she knew she shouldn't be disappointed, because it wasn't exactly a date or anything, and Nic was definitely not ready to develop another crush on another person who was unavailable.

The Fourth of July was by far the busiest day at the campground; they were always booked up and the people who were there invited their friends and families to swim and barbecue, and play cornhole and horseshoes. Some of the residents of the nearby camps came over, too, bringing food to share. It was outdoors and well-ventilated, and, after all, her father had designed the place to be great for a party, with a big, open common area in the middle, a stage, hanging lights, a workable PA for music, and barbecue pits. After all the rain, the public beach was flooded, so the campground was the biggest gathering spot at the lake. And although every year, Ma grumbled that they could make twice as much income and maybe upgrade the place a little if they started charging people an entrance fee for the holiday, she never did. It didn't seem right.

Nic hardly had any time to sit down. This was what her mother had done for all of Nic's life – greeting people, handing out sparklers to the kids, emptying rubbish, supplying ketchup and relish and cookies, making sure the hounds didn't steal any hamburgers. Most of the campground residents pitched in, but there was still a load to do. Ma had had to watch Nic out of the corner of an eye when she was a child, and now Nic had to do the same for Ma. Holidays showed you how everything changed and yet how everything stayed the same.

After their conversation at Paradise, she should miss Katie. But to be truthful, Katie and Shane had never spent the day of the Fourth at the campground. It was always a family day for them at Paradise. When they were older, they'd come down in the evening after the fireworks; before they were twenty-one they'd steal a couple of bottles of beer and they'd listen to music and dance.

So although she always missed Katie, although there was a permanent empty spot in her heart, she didn't miss her more than usual. She had enough to do, anyway. And it was a relief not to have to worry about drama or tension, about what she was and wasn't allowed to say out loud. There was an ease in the worst already having happened.

Nic had just cracked open her second beer of the afternoon and was sampling some of Doreen's homemade spinach dip when she saw Audrey walking into the campground. She wore denim shorts and a white button-up shirt, and carried a canvas bag. Nic snagged another bottle of beer from the cooler and wove through a cornhole game to meet her.

'You came,' she said, feeling a foolish smile spread across her face.

'I felt like I needed to see what the big deal was about.' Audrey accepted the beer. 'I brought my famous caramel popcorn balls.'

'What's famous about them?'

'They'll break your teeth in thirty seconds.' She clinked the neck of her bottle with Nic's and looked over the campground. 'This is great. You're right – it is mayhem.'

'We had a year off last year, but it seems to have come back twice as strong. It almost feels like the world could be normal again. C'mon, I'll give you the grand tour.'

Doreen and Dale were sitting outside their RV on lawn chairs, along with Jeannette and the dogs. 'Hey.' Doreen waved them over. 'You're Lydia Durham's niece.'

'For my sins. I'm Audrey.'

'Doreen, and this is Dale, and this is Nic's mom, Jeannette Leblanc, who's the queen of this whole place. You remember Lydia Durham?' Doreen asked Ma.

'Sure. Nice lady,' said Jeannette.

'My mom has memory problems,' Nic whispered to Audrey.

'You're not Audrey,' said Jeannette. 'Audrey wears glasses. She doesn't look anything like you.'

'Which Audrey are you talking about, Ma?'

'You know. Audrey at the hotel.'

Doreen said, 'Listen, I want to talk to you about the Morocco Pond Association. We need help with the water quality and erosion survey. C'mere.' Doreen patted the lawn chair beside her.

'We've got our names down to play the winners at horseshoes,' Nic said quickly, threading her arm through Audrey's. 'But we'll be back after.'

'Make sure you are. We need some fresh blood!'

'Quick thinking,' said Audrey, as Nic steered her away.

'Yeah, but now we actually have to play horseshoes because Doreen will be watching us like a hawk. I hope you brought your competitive spirit.'

'Always.'

They sat on the sidelines of the horseshoe pit, watching the game in progress and drinking beer.

'Audrey at the hotel?' said Audrey.

'She probably meant the old hotel that used to be up here. It closed down before I was born. It's weird – she can't remember anything, and then something from the past pops up and she recalls it perfectly.'

'It must be difficult.'

Nic shrugged. 'Today's not the day to talk about it.'

'What's the stage for?' Audrey asked, nodding at it. 'Do you have concerts here?'

'Not so much these days. When my dad was alive, there was music most every weekend. Either his band or his friends', or sometimes he'd just play his fiddle and people could sing along.'

'I vaguely remember my aunt complaining about it. One of the many things. You don't have music here now?'

'Someone will hook up their Spotify playlist to the PA after the fireworks. It's going to be noisy here till late.'

'But not live music? You don't play?'

'Oh, no, not me.'

'You said you were a musician, though.'

'Not in public if I can help it.'

'Shame,' said Audrey, and gave her a little side glance that made Nic feel as if she were blushing.

'Thanks for coming,' she said.

'Thanks for inviting me. Is this where you grew up?'

'It was indeed.'

'Must have been a fun place.'

'It was. Sometimes. Some of the kids were mean.'

'They were just jealous,' Audrey said, nudging her.

'Ha! Queer bookworms are always an easy target, I think.'

'From bitter experience, I can confirm this. My school years were hell. Anyway, you stayed.'

'I might sell it,' Nic said, for the first time out loud. 'Doreen and Dale make Ma an offer every year – a good offer – and she always turns it down. But eventually, she's going to need more help than I can give her and the money from the sale would help.'

'And what would you do?'

'Get my PhD? Have a life?'

'Crazy shit like that.'

'Crazy shit like that, yeah. But right now, it's important for me that Ma gets to stay in her house for as long as she can. Doreen and Dale would let her, if they bought the campground. They told me that. I'm going to do everything I can to help Ma out. She deserves a good life.'

Audrey was gazing at her, her expression thoughtful. She had hazel eyes, a finely-shaped mouth.

'You're so lucky,' Audrey said.

Nic laughed. 'I don't have a real job, I live in a homemade house that belongs to my mom and I fail at every relationship I try.'

'I would've given anything for a place like this, full of family and friends who accept me.'

'Well. I'm not out to everyone.'

'But to your mother?'

'If she remembers.'

'My family never got to grips with my sexuality,' said Audrey. 'At first I said "screw them" and went off and did my own thing, but, as I get older, I wish something could change. Especially after the past year, which has been so isolating.'

'But you can't live a lie,' said Nic.

'No. But I miss them. Jobs, houses, relationships – everything else is fixable. Not family.'

'Loneliness is fixable though,' said Nic, quietly, gazing back at Audrey. And then someone called Nic's name and it was their turn to join the horseshoe match.

As the beach was flooded, they had to set up lawn chairs along the edge of the treeline to watch the fireworks, and still the water was close enough for them to toe off their sandals and dip their bare feet in it. Some of the teenagers waded out to perch on the big driftwood tree, which was surrounded by water. They lit sparklers and waved them around like miniature stars.

'Usually they're set off from the public beach,' Dale explained to Audrey. 'But this year the fellas are setting them off from a party boat on the lake. See, there it is – you can see that fool Charlie Abraham's cigarette. They're gonna kill themselves one day, but they haven't yet.'

The sunset was still lingering over the mountains in streaks of yellow and navy when the first rocket went off – a fountain of gold and then a boom. Statler answered it with a long, loud howl.

'Don't worry, he's just singing,' called Ma, and Statler was drowned out by another whistle and boom. Lights across the fading twilight.

Fireworks were always the same and always different. Sound and fury, momentary beauty that melted away into darkness. Their whole point was their impermanence. Some of the teenagers on the log were trying to take photos with their phones, but, to Nic, she might as well try to catch a peal of laughter, or a heartbeat.

Jeannette carried her lawn chair up from the beach but instead of setting it up in front of Doreen and Dale's RV, where it had been before, or back to her own porch, she plunked it down in front of the stage, front and centre.

'You going to listen to the music, Ma?' Nic asked. She hadn't had enough beer to be drunk, but she was buzzed from the holiday and the people and, yes, from feeling Audrey looking at her. So much for not feeding another impossible crush.

'I'm just waiting for Gene to start playing.' The bassets came and lay down at her feet, and Ma stroked their ears.

And Nic was a child again, a little kid whose whole world was this place, whose parents knew everything and would never die.

'Just a second,' she told her mother. She went into the office and reached for her guitar, but then she changed tack and took out her fiddle, the one that had been her dad's. Without letting herself overthink it, she brought it outside and climbed the four wooden steps to the stage.

She wasn't planning to play for anyone but her mother, and then just one of her father's favourites, one of the old Cape Breton songs. But as soon as she set foot on the stage, people stopped talking. She heard someone say, 'Shh.' And suddenly everyone's attention was on her.

'Oh,' she said, and stepped back with the impulse to get off the stage, but then she saw her mother, still in the lawn chair with the dogs at her feet, and instead she took a deep breath.

'I'm just going to play one song,' she said, surprised at how her voice carried from up here. 'It's in honour of Pépère Robichaud, who taught it to me. And my ma, who throws this party every year.'

Someone whooped, and some people clapped, and Nic positioned the fiddle under her chin, lifted her bow, and played.

She played 'Le Moineau et le Martinet', as she'd played it alone to herself. Incomplete, without the words – just the two verses and the chorus. And then she played the chorus again, but this time slowly, drawing out the notes, hearing in her head the sad story about the two birds who sang together until one had to fly away. Thinking about the flowers and fountains over the lake, mirrored in the water. The beauty that was gone and never would be captured again, but that was all the more beautiful because it was vanishing.

She finished and held the fiddle still, listening to the silence that the music had left. Then she lowered the instrument and left the stage.

'More!'

People were clapping and whistling. Someone patted her back and someone else said, 'Play us another one!'

She shook her head and went to join her mother. Doreen and Dale had pulled their chairs up too, and Audrey was sitting on the ground next to the dogs. 'Did you like that, Ma?'

'It was a sad one,' Ma said.

'Yeah. It was a sad one. Next year, maybe I'll play a happy one.'

She sat on the ground next to Audrey. Waldorf put a saggy head in her lap and Audrey handed her another beer.

'That was beautiful,' she said. 'You should play in public more often.'

'I only know half of it,' Nic said. 'The rest of it's been lost.'

'Well,' said Audrey. 'That's OK. You'll just have to finish it yourself.'

Chapter Fifty-two

'You have to come again next year and stay longer than two days,' I say to Cherry, hugging her before she gets into the car.

'Next year?' says Bryan, beside me. 'You're planning for the future, all of a sudden.'

'We're all planning for the future,' says Cherry, holding up two hands with fingers crossed. 'See you soon, baby.' She hugs Bryan, and then a whole round of goodbye hugs starts over again.

Isaac is standing to the side, as usual, but he's not scrolling on his phone and he doesn't have earbuds in, and he's smiling to himself. I nudge Bryan and point at his brother.

'What have you got in your pockets, dude?' asks Bryan.

'Nothing, dude.'

'Are you sure?'

Isaac turns and reveals that one pocket of his oversized army surplus jacket is full of Eebie.

'I just wanted to borrow him.'

'Not a chance,' I say, swooping in. Isaac, grinning, gives him back.

'You are *just* like my brother at your age,' I tell him.

Isaac shrugs. 'Your brother's sorta cool.' He folds himself into the back seat and puts in his earbuds.

We wave as Bryan's family drive away. Cherry opens the window to hang out and wave for a little bit longer. And then they're out of sight. Bryan drops his arm and turns back to Paradise.

I draw a deep breath and sigh it out, happy.

'That was perfect,' I say, following Bryan inside. 'The weather was great, the fireworks were on point, our families totally love each other. And now, even better, we have some time to ourselves.'

Bryan doesn't reply. He goes into the bedroom that Isaac has vacated.

I call out to him. 'We don't have to strip the beds and do the laundry just yet. Let's chill out a little bit first. Maybe go for a walk?'

He doesn't answer.

'Bryan?' I go to the door of the bedroom. The bedclothes are a mess, tangled and half pulled off the bed, but Bryan isn't doing anything with them. He has pulled out his suitcase and put it on top of the chest of drawers.

'What is going on?' I ask.

'I'm packing.'

'What?'

'I was waiting till my parents were on their way.'

'What for?'

'I'm going. I can't stay here.'

'Why not?'

'Because this isn't what I want.'

He's taking clothes out of the drawers and putting them into his suitcase.

I have a sudden vision of an empty closet. Swept clean of everything except for my mother's scent.

'Hold on. You did this the other day, decided to leave, and you changed your mind.'

'Things are different now.' He packs some T-shirts. I feel sick.

'What do you mean? We've just had a wonderful time! Things have been going so well!'

He stops and gazes at me. 'Have they?'

'Yes!' My heart is hammering. 'Tell me what's wrong.'

'I'm not stupid, Katie. I know that you're hiding things from me.'

His voice is cold, his face expressionless. I've never seen him like this before. It's terrifying.

At my feet, Eebie barks.

'I ... was going to tell you,' I say.

'Were you?'

'Yes! I was waiting for your parents to leave. So we could have some time to ourselves, to talk.'

He frowns. 'That's interesting. Especially because you got your memory back days before you told me, when we had all the time in the world to talk. And you kept on pretending.'

'How did you know?' My voice is small.

He turns away and starts packing again. The last of his clothes in the drawers, and then a sweatshirt hanging from a hook on the wall. Then he turns to me. 'I love you, Katie. Do you think I wouldn't be able to tell?'

'But – why didn't you say?'

'I was waiting for you to tell me. I was waiting for you to open up about it. About anything. What's going on with Nic. What's the deal with you and your brother. Why you found it easier to pretend you didn't remember our relationship. I thought you needed space and I was OK to give it to you. I thought that once you told me you'd got your memories back, you'd be ready to discuss what's really happening. But you didn't open up to me. So now I'm leaving.'

He walks past me to the bathroom, where he starts collecting his belongings. I follow and so does the dog, who is still barking.

'You can't go.'

'I have to.'

'Bryan. Please. I'm sorry.'

He tosses his toothbrush into his toiletries bag. 'Why didn't you tell me right away? Why have you been lying? What else are you keeping from me?'

'It's ... complicated.'

His face isn't blank now. It's angry. 'No, it's not complicated. It's simple. You lied to everyone.'

'My dad knew,' I say.

His frown deepens. 'That's supposed to make it better?'

'It wasn't a lie,' I say. 'It's . . .'

What is it?

'I made a mistake,' I say.

'It doesn't even matter,' he says. 'It's not about your memories. It's about you, keeping everything inside and not letting me in. I opened up my whole life to you, Katie. I don't think it's unreasonable for me to ask you to do the same for me.'

He goes back into the bedroom, throws his toiletry bag into his suitcase and zips the case up. I remember how in Philadelphia we laughed with each other, competing at our ability to fit two weeks' worth of clothes in a carry-on bag. Which we didn't even have to do, because we were driving, but it was a game.

Bryan lifts his suitcase.

'I love you,' he says. 'But it's over. Eebie can stay with you for now. If you decide you don't want him, I'll take him.'

'Of course I want him! I want you to stay!'

Bryan nods without agreeing. He carries his suitcase through Paradise and outside to the car, where he beeps the trunk open.

I have become the person who follows the person they love and pleads with them to stay because they are afraid. I have become the person who feels that if the person they love leaves them, they will stop being able to breathe.

The person I love is leaving me.

Yet another person I love. It is my fault.

He squats down and pets Eebie, who is whining now. Scratches his ears, kisses the top of his head. I remember how tender he was with this little dog. How he rearranged his whole life so that he could look after him. How he rearranged his whole life so he could accommodate me.

Did I do the same for him? Or did I just take and take?

'Please, Bryan.' I don't even know what I'm saying, I just know that I have to stop him driving away. 'Give me a second chance. I remember everything about us. I love everything about us. You're the first man I've ever fallen in love with. This is new for me.'

He picks up Eebie, gives him to me, and opens the driver's side door. I hold on to the window frame with my other hand. I remember watching my mother climbing into a waiting car while I watched from an upstairs window and couldn't say a single thing.

'I fucked up,' I say. 'Don't I deserve a second chance?'

He's got tears in his eyes. I take this as a little bit of hope.

'Maybe,' he says. 'If it was just about the memory. If you meant it for the best, to make everything easier for yourself and your family. But it's not about that. It's about what I deserve.'

'What do you deserve? Tell me! Please tell me, so I can fix it.'

He swallows, hard. 'I deserve what my parents have. What your parents have, too. I deserve someone who lets me in. And you don't do that, Katie. You never have, not really, and I'm not sure that you ever will.'

'But—'

'Please let go of the door,' he says softly.

I do.

He closes it. He starts the car.

He drives away.

Chapter Fifty-three

On the fifth of July the campground was a mess, but Nic got up a little later than usual, went for a run, settled her mother at Doreen and Dale's with coffee and leftover apple pie, and then walked the dogs before she tackled any of the clean-up. As always, Waldorf stopped by a water-filled ditch by the side of the road and attempted to pull her into it so that he could sniff out frogs. She set her feet wide in her running shoes and kept a tight hold on the leash. Statler just plopped down on the road to wait for his brother to stop being a fearsome death machine.

The thing about bassets was that they never ever did anything except what they thought was necessary in that moment. Much like the Leblanc family, she thought, and smiled.

A car approached and she stood on the outside of Statler so he'd be seen. She recognised it – a silver car with Pennsylvania plates that had been parked outside Paradise since the day before midsummer. Was it time, now, to talk with Katie again? Redefine the parameters of their friendship – if there was a friendship any more?

She raised her hand in a wave, but the car didn't slow down or stop. As it got closer, she saw that it was Bryan behind the wheel and he was alone.

He drove past her. He didn't wave back.

Audrey was outside her camp, deadheading roses, earphones on. When Nic and the dogs approached, she took off her earphones and called a hello.

'I was going to come by later,' she said. 'See if you needed help with the clean-up.'

'We've got it covered, but I found something that you might be interested in.'

She'd found it this morning after her run, when she'd pulled on a pair of shorts. They were the same ones she'd worn three nights ago at Paradise, and the photo that Katie had given her was still in the back pocket. She'd forgotten all about it after the discussion that followed. But glancing at it again, she'd noticed something she hadn't seen before.

'Katie stole this picture from your aunt's camp when we were kids,' she said, handing it over. 'It belongs to you, I guess.'

'Who is it?'

'Well. That's Katie's mother in the background.' She pointed to the figure. 'That's why Katie stole it. But when we broke in that time, your aunt had a whole drawer full of photos of this woman.'

'She did?' Audrey put down her shears and studied the picture.

'I'm guessing you didn't find them when you inherited the place?'

'No. There wasn't much personal stuff. Just a lot of ancient *TV Guides*.'

'You never met this woman?'

'No. My mother might recognise her. I don't talk to her much, though.'

The dogs, realising that they were here for the long haul, lay down on the grass. Waldorf grunted.

'The thing is,' Nic said. 'Dale recognised her when I showed him this morning. Do you remember yesterday when my mom was talking about Audrey at the hotel – the old hotel that's fallen down now? Dale said that this woman in the photo was Audrey. She worked there, a housekeeper or something. He worked there one summer when he was a kid.'

'Did your mother recognise her?'

'She's tired today.' She hadn't recognised Nic. Audrey glanced up quickly and obviously saw something in Nic's face, because her brow creased with sympathy and crinkles appeared in the corners of her hazel eyes.

'Anyway,' said Nic, wanting to move this on from herself. 'Look here. That's the bar at the hotel, I'm pretty sure. This wooden part, with the carving at the end. It was still more or less intact when we saw it. And, Audrey, your aunt had dozens of pictures of this woman. She was in some of them. They were together.'

'My aunt Lydia didn't like anyone.'

'She liked someone,' said Nic, and turned the photo over to show Audrey the *A* written on the back, in blue ballpoint.

Audrey was silent for a while, gazing at the photo.

'My mother always hated my name,' she murmured. 'She said she gave it to me to please her sister. But then Aunt Lydia never liked me. She didn't like girls at all.'

'But then she left you her camp.'

She and Audrey exchanged a look.

'No,' said Audrey. 'We're queerwashing this. She was not—'

'Or maybe, you belonged in your family more than you think.'

Audrey put the photo in the back pocket of her own jeans. 'You're a good detective, you know that?'

'Well. Or maybe I just know how to interpret the past in a way I can live with.' She looped the canvas bag off her shoulder. 'I brought your bag back, too. There's something in it for you.' Audrey pulled out a box of sparklers. 'We had a lot left over and I thought you might like a bit of sparkle in your life.'

'Always! Hold on, I'll get some matches.'

Nic hadn't intended to light the sparklers right now, in the daylight, but she tied the dogs' leads to a slender tree. Audrey emerged with a lighter. She lit two sparklers and gave one to Nic.

They didn't say anything. They watched the fire in their hands spit and spark, eat its way down the wire until it fizzled and went out, leaving blossom-ghosts of light behind their eyes.

She didn't know who moved first. It could've been either or

both of them. But the sparklers went out and her hand caught Audrey's, and they were kissing each other.

Nic closed her dazzled eyes.

'Wow,' said Audrey after who knew how long, her hand still holding Nic's.

'Wow,' Nic said.

They kissed again, and this time Nic liked it even better.

'I can't come in,' she whispered after a while. 'I've got the dogs.'

'That's OK,' said Audrey. 'I think you and I have a lot of our own baggage to deal with right now, anyway.'

'I have so much baggage.'

'My relationship is splitting up.'

'I'm a package deal with my mother.'

'But this was ... it is.' Audrey leant closer and kissed Nic's cheek, her other cheek, the bridge of her nose. Her top lip. Right out in the open, on the lawn, where anyone could see.

'It is,' Nic agreed. She stroked her thumb against the palm of Audrey's hand and enjoyed the other woman's little intake of breath. 'How about ... next summer?'

'Next summer sounds good.'

They smiled at each other. Nic felt dizzy with Audrey's proximity, her lips, the sudden change of everything from past to future tense, from *could have been* to *could be*.

She stepped back. 'Cards tomorrow night, though?'

'I'll beat you this time,' Audrey promised.

Chapter Fifty-four

When it rains, the water falls on the mountains and it rushes through the trees, downwards through ferns and reeds, across roads and under culverts, over rocks and churning mud, to empty out into the lake, raise the water level, eat the land, swallow the beach, lick at the roots of birches.

It hasn't rained for two days now but the stream by Paradise is swollen and fast, brown with mud and flecked with foam, even higher and wider than it was before. The past catches up with you. The ground under a young spruce has washed into mud. The tree has toppled over across the stream, but the water flows over it as if it isn't there. Its roots reach out into the air like fingers reaching out for connection.

Shane told me once that eventually, maybe soon, the changing climate will create a storm so great that the stream banks will disappear, the water will rise and the ground under Paradise will wear away too. The house, foundationless, will collapse and sink into the lake, and it will be as if it never was.

Eventually. Maybe soon.

After Bryan left, I went into the house. I didn't know what else to do. I walked from room to room, the little dog following at my heels. These were the curtains my grandmother chose. This was the drawing of a loon that my father framed and hung. This was the vase that held the flowers that I picked as a child, daisies and black-eyed Susans and goldenrod that shed yellow pollen on the table. The stacks of games we played, the books I read, those summers when Nic and I tried sleuthing and spying, the soft-edged playing cards that I used to play solitaire with, over and over, while my brother was in hospital and my mother had gone. The sheets on the unmade beds, still holding the shapes of the people who slept in them.

This was the place I was always safe, where I could escape from everything. Now it's too full of memories. Now it's one storm away from collapse.

He's gone. I never thought he would leave me. I thought he was safe.

I tucked Eebie under my arm and I left Paradise, walking fast towards the campground, more by instinct than by reason. I needed to speak with Nic. Because I broke her heart, I know I did, and that was my fault. But if I could talk to her, apologise, own up to everything, maybe she would forgive me and I would not be all alone.

I thought about all the ways that Bryan looked at me over the past few days. He knew all along. Every time he asked me what was wrong, every time I could have told him the truth, and I didn't. I wanted to go back in time and do it right. Forget about it all again.

I was barefoot, still in the shorts and sweater I pulled on when I got out of bed to say goodbye to Bryan's family. I didn't notice the rocks digging into my feet or how the road was already hot under the morning sun.

I thought I was all right with being alone. I thought it made me strong to move on, to keep myself safe, to tread lightly on the surface of things.

I thought I was safe if I loved just a little.

None of it was safe and I have missed so much.

I reached the end of the drive and was about to turn right, to walk to the campground, when I saw Lydia Durham's old place and the two women standing in front of it.

The dogs were tied to a tree. Nic was standing close to Lydia Durham's niece and the two of them were kissing.

My feet stumbled and stopped. I turned around and ran back to Paradise.

And now here I am. Kneeling in the mud by the side of the flooded stream, with a tiny dog clutched to my chest.

I want to drive and drive, go somewhere else where I don't have to think. But I don't have a car, and what good would it do? I want to pretend, but I can't. I want to forget. I want to escape. But there's nowhere to go and pain follows you anyway. Bryan, who loved me, has left me. Nic, who loved me, has found someone else. My mother disappeared. My father is disappearing.

They loved me. I didn't love them enough in return.

I wish I could cry and let these tears be carried along with the water, wearing the earth away.

Chapter Fifty-five

Shane and I are driving again in his truck. He hasn't yet asked me why I called him and I'm trying to get up the courage to tell him.

Eebie's on my lap. I haven't put him down since Bryan gave him to me. He's looking out the window as if this is an enormous treat.

'Feels like it's going to rain again,' my brother says, eventually. 'Heavy. A thunderstorm.'

I nod. We drive on.

'Feel like telling me where we're going?'

'I just wanted to drive,' I say, hugging Eebie closer.

He nods. I know he knows there's something wrong. But he won't ask me, in the same way that he'll never answer when I ask him how he's feeling.

'Do you ever think about the cancer coming back?' I burst out, and he glances over.

'No.'

'Really?'

'A little, maybe. But it was a long time ago and I was a kid. Most people don't know about it and I try not to think about it.'

'Does it help? Not thinking about it?'

'Help with what?'

'Everything.'

He drives for a little while, then says, 'Sometimes.'

'Bryan left me.'

He slows down the truck, but he doesn't pull over.

'Why?' he says.

'Because I got my memory back and I didn't tell him.'

'Why not?'

This is not a good time to lie. It's also not a good time to tell Shane about why Nic and I fell out, and why she wouldn't marry him.

Because that, I can see now, was also my fault. If Nic and I had the conversation about our feelings a long time ago, if I hadn't avoided it so assiduously, maybe she and I would have been together and she never would have dated my brother in the first place. Or if we hadn't ended up together, she would have been able to come to Shane with a full heart, like both of them deserved. I think about how often I encouraged her to give him a chance, about how often my family teased him about asking her to marry him. It must have been painful for both of them.

'The reason I didn't tell is complicated and it's not really something I can talk about right now, not until I've really worked it all out in my head. But I will say that I fucked up. And I was too scared to make it right, until it was too late.'

'I fucked up my relationship, too.'

I turn to him. 'How did you fuck up, Shane?'

'She didn't love me enough. And I knew, and I asked her anyway.'

'You asked her because you loved her.'

'I shouldn't have tried to change things. I couldn't stand things the way they were. I knew that asking her to marry me would push her away. I knew she would say no and it would hurt. But it was the only thing I could think of to do, to make her admit the truth.'

'Is this you and me?' I ask. 'Do we push people away because that's all we know how to do?'

'I don't know,' he says. 'I hope not.'

'I think I need to see Mom,' I say. 'I need to understand why I'm this way.'

He does pull over, then. He makes a short phone call, then turns the truck around and heads back the way we came.

*

Her house is a low, yellow ranch house, single-storey, with vinyl siding and white trim. There are rose bushes and tiger lilies, and a red Subaru is parked outside. It's not far from Ranger Lake – as the crow flies, it is probably less than ten miles from Paradise.

'She lives here?'

Shane turns off the truck. We're parked on the side of the road, not in her driveway. 'That's what the satnav says.'

'Did you know she lived so close?'

'Nope. We talked by email and phone. She suggested the diner that time – I thought it was because it was a neutral place close to us.'

'Huh.'

We both sit for a minute, looking at the house. It's hard to tell whether there's anyone inside, but when Shane called she said she'd be in, so.

'It looks so normal,' I say. 'Not like someone who'd run off and join a cult, or whatever.'

'Who told you she joined a cult?'

'Nobody. I just liked that explanation better.' I take a deep breath and get out of the car, and walk up to the door before I can chicken out.

She opens it before I get the chance to knock. She was sitting down last time I saw her and it's a bit of a shock to see that Shane and I are both taller than her.

'Katie,' she says. 'Shane. Thanks for coming.'

Her voice hasn't changed from when we were small. I didn't even know that I remembered her voice. But I do.

I remember it with my entire body.

'Come on in,' she says. 'Do you want some coffee?'

'No,' I say. We follow her into the house, which opens up right away into a living room. There are two sofas in an L-shape, an armchair, a glass-topped coffee table. Beige carpet, a print of a desert sunset on the wall. It's very clean and tidy, with marks on the carpet showing that she's just vacuumed. Shane and I sit on a sofa and she sits in the chair opposite, facing us, like it's a job interview.

She didn't used to wear glasses. She used to have long hair. She used to be skinnier. Her hair used to be redder. She's wearing a little bit of make-up, not a lot. Her fingernails have been shaped and polished in a French manicure, and she is wearing a ring on her wedding finger. Presumably it's not the one our dad gave her.

'You brought your dog,' she says. 'What's his name?'

'Eebie.' He wags his tail at his name, but I keep him on my lap. Probably a good idea – he'll stop me from making any rash moves.

'It's good to have you here,' she says. 'Thanks for coming to see me.'

'Why did you want to see us all of a sudden?' I demand.

'It's not sudden,' she says. 'I've written to you. I've tried to pass on messages through Shane. He tells me you're doing well for yourself.'

'I'm fine.' I say the lie, then realise I've done it. 'No, I'm not fine. But that's not really your concern. I know why Shane wanted to get in touch with you and make sure you're OK, because he's that kind of person. But why did you want to see us? You were the one who chose to leave.'

The woman who is our mother takes a deep breath through her nose.

'Are you sure you don't want some coffee?'

'We're fine, Mom,' says Shane. 'Tell us what you need to say.'

'I wanted to talk with you,' she says, 'because I'm working a twelve-step programme. And the stage I'm at is making amends. Step Seven. I realise it is too late for me to make up for the two of you having a childhood without your mother. And I realise that you probably don't want me to try. But what I can do, is apologise.'

There's a lot in this to unpack. 'A twelve-step programme? What is that?'

'Mom's a recovering alcoholic,' Shane says. 'But she's been sober for, what Mom? Two years?'

'Twenty-eight months. It was alcohol and pills.' She looks up now and meets my gaze. 'I was on the downward slope when I left Bill and the two of you. I thought I was coping, but I wasn't. And it didn't get better for a long, long time.'

'I didn't know that,' I concede. 'But it's not an excuse.'

'No, it's not.'

'Did you ever think about us?'

'All the time.'

'Are you married again?' I ask. 'Did you marry the guy you ran off with?'

'No. That didn't last. But I am married again, yes.'

'Have you got other kids?'

'I have stepchildren. Two. Alex and Angie.' She points to a framed photograph on a side table. The two kids in it look like they're in high school.

'You stuck around for them?'

She nods. 'I was lucky to get to start over, a little.'

'Yeah. Lucky you.'

'I understand why you're angry,' she says. 'I'm also angry with myself. And I have been for a long time.'

'Did you actually want to see us or are you just working your steps, whatever that means?'

'I wanted to see you so much, Kitty.'

I've forgotten that she called me that too. 'Don't use that name.'

'Katie. I wanted to see both of you – you and Shane. I can't believe how grown-up you are. You both look great. Shane, you're so handsome. You look just like your dad.'

'It doesn't work like that,' I tell my mother. 'You can't just say oops, my bad, sorry, I'm doing these steps now, and then come back into our lives and be all happy families. You abandoned us.'

'I know.'

'Why did you do it? Don't blame the booze. Why did you pick up and leave in the middle of the night?'

I'm dangerously close to tears and I hate myself for it. I don't want to let her see me cry. I don't want her to have that much power over me.

'It was my fault,' says Shane, and both of us turn to him at the same time.

'It was not,' I say.

'It wasn't your fault,' says our mother.

'I was sick,' says Shane. 'It was too hard.'

'Yes,' says our mother. 'I left because you were sick. But you were a child and you couldn't help it. I was an adult and I couldn't deal with the fear and the sadness.' She takes off her glasses and polishes them, over and over, with the hem of her shirt. There are little pink dents on either side of her nose where they sat. She polishes her glasses much longer than she needs to and I wonder if this is a nervous habit, something that she has started to do in the years since I knew her.

'I hope to God that neither one of you ever has a child who gets that sick,' she says. 'It's the most terrifying feeling in the world. But I didn't let myself feel it. I thought I would die if I did. I ran away instead. And that was wrong and I am sorry.'

This is what I've wanted to hear for years. I've wanted to know why. And I've wanted to hear her say that she was sorry.

And it's not good enough.

'I wasn't sick,' I say. 'I was perfectly healthy, and I was scared, and you left me too.'

She makes as if to reach out and touch my hand, and then stops herself.

'You're strong, Katie,' she said. 'You've always been strong. Stronger than me. I knew that you were going to be all right.'

'But I wasn't,' I say. 'I'm not.'

*

There isn't much to say after that. Shane and I leave. I take her number and I don't promise to call her, but I don't say I won't, either. I don't know what I will do.

I let Eebie piss on the post of her mailbox.

We drive. It's started to rain again. The only sounds are the windscreen wipers and the tyres on the wet road. Outside, it's rain and trees and rain and trees, and a low rumble of thunder in the distance. We sit side by side.

Maybe that's why we drove around so much when we were younger, when we were both trying to work out how to grow up without a mother. Because we didn't know how to talk about what we needed to talk about. But we knew we had to be together.

'I guess we have some answers, at least,' I say after a while.

'Are you glad you saw her?'

'"Glad" isn't the right word. It needed to be done. I couldn't keep ignoring it. Have you met up with her before? You knew about her drinking.'

'This was the first time. She told me that stuff in emails.'

'And the letters she wrote you when we were kids.'

'She didn't really say a lot in those. They were mostly questions. I didn't know how to answer them.'

'It's hard to imagine her being a normal stepmom to those other kids.'

'They looked like good kids.'

'I made her out in my head to be someone evil and heartless,' I say. 'But she's just weak.'

'She's right about one thing,' he says. 'You are strong. You always have been.'

'Dad was the strong one. I just... tried to be normal. Tried not to think about it too much, and be happy. I never faced my own feelings.'

'I didn't know that you weren't OK.'

'I didn't know that you thought it was your fault.'

He doesn't answer this, which is how I can tell that he really has thought this, for all this time.

'It's not your fault, Shane. None of us ever blamed you, not at all. You were a little kid and you had leukemia. You were in a terrifying situation and you were never anything but the sweetest kid. You never made any demands of anyone. You still don't make any demands of anyone. And sometimes you should.'

'We never showed each other how we really felt about it,' says Shane. 'Me being sick and Mom leaving.'

'Why did you stay in touch with her?'

'I missed her. And I wanted to understand, I guess.'

'Do you understand now?'

'Not really.' He drives for a little bit, then says, 'Maybe Mom couldn't help it, but I'll tell you something. I will never do that to you, or to Dad and Tessa. If I ever have a family of my own, I'm going to be there for them. They are always going to know exactly where I am.'

'Whereas I've never done anything but keep on running,' I say bitterly. 'I'm just like her.'

Shane glances over at me. 'Nah, you're not.'

'How are you so sure about that?'

'You're my sister. I know.'

Chapter Fifty-six

The thunderstorm has passed but it is still raining, though not the cosy type of rain where you've got a fire lit and you're cuddled up in bed with the person you love, where you have a hot drink and a good book to read, and can hear the raindrops pitter-patter on the roof. This is a never-ending mist that makes everything feel damp and grey, weighs down the grass and the needles on the trees, stops the birds from singing and turns the lake into a flat piece of metal.

I'm lying on the sofa with Eebie on my chest. I've been lying here for hours since Shane left, dry-eyed and staring at the ceiling. I don't have the energy to get up. I tried to call Bryan, but his phone went to voicemail, and I couldn't think of anything to say to make things better, so I hung up.

Shane was wrong. He said I was nothing like our mother.

I am exactly like her.

I have run away from everything difficult in my life at every turn. I thought I was doing it to stay safe and free from pain, but it's done exactly the opposite. I refused to acknowledge Nic's feelings about me, or mine about her. And when she forced me to see them, I ran away from that, too.

Bryan didn't leave me – he tried his hardest to stay. I have been leaving him since the day he and I met.

I've never loved him so much as I do now that he's gone. And it's all my fault.

I close my eyes and I remember the day that we really met – the day he told me about on the beach, when I found Eebie on the steps of our apartment building. When I first saw the little dog, I thought he was a rat – one of those huge Philly rats that you hear rumours about – and then I thought he was a bedraggled cat. When I got up close, I saw that he was a dog. He was dirty, he was panting and shivering, and I hesitated, because how would I know how to take care of a stray dog?

Then I stopped and knelt down, and held out my hand for him to sniff. He should have been afraid of me, but he wasn't. He let me pick him up. He hardly weighed anything.

And then I brought him upstairs and I didn't even hesitate before I knocked on Bryan's door. Because Eebie trusted me to help him, and somehow I trusted Bryan to help us.

I must have fallen asleep, because when I open my eyes again it's fully dark. I sit up on the sofa and turn on the nearest lamp, blinking against the sudden light. It takes a blessed half-second before I recall everything and the emptiness hits me again. As I've been doing since this morning, I reach for Eebie, for his tiny, fluffy comfort. 'You need to go out, buddy?'

But he's not there.

'Eebie?' He doesn't come, but that's not unusual, so I get up and look around the room to make sure he hasn't curled up in one of the other chairs, or underneath a table. I look in the kitchen, in case he's looking for a snack. Then I check all the bedrooms. The bathroom. The porch.

And then again, searching for any place where a tiny dog could hide himself.

'Eebie!' I start to yell. Nothing. And then I realise – the screen door on the porch opens outwards, maybe easily enough that a small animal could escape. That's why we keep it latched when Eebie is inside. And when I check, I haven't latched it.

I run outside. Without moon or stars, and with only one lamp lit inside Paradise, it's almost impossible to see, but the dog is white. I call for Eebie, running around the camp, peering underneath it. I promise him cheese. I promise him steak.

I can't find him. Did he try to run after Bryan's car? Did he wander into the woods?

There are coyotes in the woods. Bears. Wildcats. We think we are so safe, but just a few feet into the forest, there are things that would eat the things we love.

I'm crying now – all the tears that wouldn't come before, big sobs that make me clutch my belly. But I'm still looking. I check the swollen stream. If he was swept up by that, he'd be long gone by now. Maybe the beach – he loves the beach. But the beach is gone with the flood. He could have fallen off the last step into the water. I don't know if he can swim. All dogs can swim, can't they? But Eebie isn't like any dog.

I start wading into the lake, calling. Looking for anything white. Thinking of him struggling against the water, splashing and sinking, while I was fast asleep on the sofa, so caught up in my own feelings of abandonment. I abandoned him, when he needed me the most.

'Eebie!' My face is wet; I am in water up to my waist. 'Eebie, please come back.'

Chapter Fifty-seven

Once, only once, that summer of the hotel when they were spending all their free time in the ruins of other people's lives, Nic snuck into Paradise by herself.

It was deliberate. She didn't go there to see Katie, found the camp empty and decided, on a whim, to go in – she knew before she left the campground that Katie was spending the day at the hospital with her dad and Shane. Nic walked straight to Paradise without worrying about being seen. She felt invisible. She found the spare key where Mr Stone always left it, hanging under the eaves of the little shed that housed the bicycles and the lawn chairs. She let herself in, closed the door behind her and stood in the kitchen, breathing in the silence. She wandered the rooms, pausing in each. Touching the furniture. Sitting in the chairs.

She had never been there alone before.

Nic went upstairs. She ran her fingertips over the spines of Katie's books, all the matched set of Nancy Drew mysteries, and she lay down on Katie's bed.

She had thought, maybe, that by being there by herself, she could try to feel as if she lived in Paradise. As if she belonged there as much as Katie did. Because sometimes she wanted to climb right inside Katie and ride along with her, wearing her clothes, seeing through her eyes, tasting with her mouth, speaking with her voice. Touching these books, this cushion, the slick surface of this photo frame.

But that wasn't what she wanted. Not quite. She didn't want to be Katie. But there wasn't a word for what she wanted, that kind of merging. Being one, without being each other. She felt it sometimes when they were together and not speaking. In the curve of Katie's cheek, in the quick meeting of their glance, the scent that clung to Nic's clothes. In the moments when their breathing eased and they were on the edge of sleep.

She wanted those moments to last for ever. She didn't know what they meant, or why they were fleeting. She was young and there was no language to speak it.

But what she wanted was not here. Lying on the bed, she felt suddenly ashamed. Even though she had lain here many times before, had slept here, had rolled on this bed in fits of giggles, curled up in it on rainy days with a book. It was wrong. There were no answers. Her yearning was not for this house, where she was only ever a guest. It was for something else, something that she could almost taste, something as insubstantial as smoke and as real as a water-smoothed rock.

She passed quickly out of Paradise and locked the door behind her. She didn't tell Katie about her adventure. Only many years later did she understand that what she'd been looking for, what she had been looking for the whole time in so many places, was within herself.

Chapter Fifty-eight

Nic was listening to music and sewing some of her mother's crocheted squares together, when the bassets let out an almighty cacophony of barking and howling.

'Oh, my God, you two, shut up!' she said. When they didn't stop – though to be fair they usually didn't – she got up and found them crowded around the front door, baying. She looked out the window and didn't see anyone there, just the porch and darkness beyond.

'You are the worst guard dogs ever,' she told them. 'Calm down.'

But they didn't. Statler pawed at the door. It could be a cat, or a raccoon. Thank goodness her mother slept like the dead.

'You are going to wake up the entire pond. OK, OK, I'll take you out.' She got them on their leads and then opened the door, the dogs straining.

Instead of dragging her off the porch and to the grass to do their business, or towards the garbage cans to hunt out a raccoon, they stopped and sniffed something on the porch.

She drove down to Paradise. As soon as she stopped the car, she heard screaming and sobbing. Only one voice: Katie's.

'Katie!' she yelled out in alarm. Katie's voice wasn't coming from the house – it was coming from the lake. She locked the car and ran down to the water in the dark. She couldn't help thinking about her mother finding her father drowned. Herself finding her mother wandering on the ice.

She could hear Katie crying. She couldn't see her.

She didn't think twice, she dived in and swam towards her friend. 'Katie!' She surfaced, gasping, striking out towards Katie's voice.

Katie grabbed her. 'Nic! Nic, he's gone.'

'Who?'

'Eebie. He's run away,' Katie sobbed. 'I think he's somewhere in the water, but I can't see.'

'He's safe,' said Nic. 'He's in my car. He's OK.'

'What?'

'He's fine. Come on. Come in.'

Katie clutched on to her. Nic led her to shore.

Inside, lights blazing, Nic got the entire story out of Katie after they'd both changed into Katie's dry clothes and Nic had made them each a cup of hot tea. Katie had her memory back, but hadn't told anyone. Bryan had left because he said she didn't trust him enough. Katie and Shane had gone to see their mother, Cynthia. Eebie had disappeared. And there was a lot of other stuff about the soil eroding away and Paradise being swept out to sea or something, but Nic dismissed that as hysteria. Katie was still crying.

'You promised you'd tell me when you remembered everything and you didn't.'

'Because I wanted a fresh start.'

'That is stupid. And also, completely in character for you.'

'I'm sorry.'

'Why didn't you come and talk with me when Bryan left?' Nic asked.

'You didn't want me to.'

'Katie. Be real.'

'I tried to,' Katie admitted. 'But I saw you kissing someone.'

'Ah. Audrey.'

'And I don't deserve to talk to you. I hurt you so badly, Nic. I was being avoidant and a coward. I've ruined my relationships with everyone I care about. I'm just like my mother.'

'You are not like your mother.'

'You've never met her.' Katie's face was wet and her eyes were red.

'I don't need to. Yes, you're fucked up by her leaving you. And, yes, you will do anything to avoid your problems and that ends up hurting people. But you can change that, you know.'

Katie shook her head. 'It's too late.'

'Giving up sounds like one more way of avoiding your problems.'

Katie used yet another tissue. Eebie was lying on her lap, his paws and belly muddy. His head was matted with basset slobber. He looked perfectly contented.

'I've never seen you so upset about a boy,' Nic said.

'I'm sorry I ghosted you,' Katie said. 'I'm sorry I ran away from what you were telling me. I'm sorry I rubbed my relationship with Bryan in your face. It wasn't my intention, but I can see now that it was a stupid and cruel thing to do.'

'It was hard,' Nic said. 'But eventually, I saw that he made you happy. And if you truly love someone, you're happy that they're happy. Eventually. When you can put the sadness aside.'

'Are you happy with Audrey?'

'It was one kiss. You just happened to see it. There is nothing.'

Katie raised her eyebrows.

'OK, yes, I like her.'

'I was a little jealous to see it.'

'Good.'

'It's been easy for me, with you dating my brother.'

'Like it was easier for me when you weren't dating anybody.'

Katie looked down at the dog in her lap. 'Where did you find him?'

'Outside my door.'

'He knew what I needed. He knew I was sad and he went to get you for me. He didn't know that our friendship was over.'

'I said our friendship had changed, not that it was over. Oh, my God, Katie, you are such a drama queen.'

'I'm not the one who was giving ultimatums.'

'Fair. Though also, I have already apologised for that.'

Katie rubbed her eyes again.

'So we are friends?'

'It's different,' said Nic. 'We can't be the way we were before.'

'We're not kids any more. We can figure it out.'

Nic thought about how she had dived into the lake to save her friend. The first time she had swum in Morocco Pond since the day her father died. She had not hesitated. All the answers she needed were right there.

Nearly.

'That day, that morning,' Nic said. 'When you were hit by the ATV. Do you remember the accident, too?'

'Yeah. The doctor said I might never remember that part, but I do.'

'Where were you going? Were you coming to meet me? Or were you going to meet Bryan?'

'Do you really want to know?'

'Would you tell me, if I did?'

'Yes,' said Katie. 'If you want to know, I'll tell you. I'll be honest and I won't run away.'

Katie raised her chin and looked Nic in the eyes. Nic looked back, steadily. This was how she'd always wanted the two of them to look at each other: as equals, with nothing to hide. It wasn't the way she'd dreamt about it . . . but it was something precious, anyway.

'No,' Nic said. 'I guess I'd rather not know.'

Katie nodded. Eebie was fast asleep by now, emitting tiny snores. 'I don't know what to do next,' she said.

'Of course you do,' said Nic.

'I don't have a car.'

'You can use Ma's car. She's not allowed to drive it.'

'But what if he doesn't want me back?'

Nic shrugged. 'Then at least you'll have tried going towards someone instead of running away. That's worth a shot.'

Chapter Fifty-nine

Philadelphia is muggy and loud, full of traffic and pollution and concrete. Jeannette Leblanc's air conditioning is sketchy at best and I spent most of the journey from Massachusetts onwards with both windows open, breathing in fumes. I spent twenty minutes finding a parking space and by the time I unlock the door to our apartment building and step into the cool corridor, I have sweat patches under my arms and I smell like someone's used towel.

I run up the stairs to our floor, carrying Eebie.

I should go to my own apartment and shower. I should put on make-up, a flattering top, put up my hair in the way that Bryan likes. But waiting is hell.

For the entire drive, I've been rehearsing what I'm going to say. I rejected a dozen different things before settling for the simplest one of all: *I'm sorry. I love you. I'm ready to tell you everything, if you want to hear it.*

In front of his door, I hesitate. What if he's not in? What if he didn't even come back to Philadelphia, but instead joined his family on their vacation on the coast, or went somewhere else?

What if he's not happy to see me?

Then I think about the wise words of my best friend, and I knock.

Acknowledgements

Thank you, as always, to my agent, Teresa Chris.

Thank you to Rhea Kurien, Snigdha Koirala, and all the Orion team listed in the following credits. You are a pleasure to work with. Thanks too to Charlotte Mursell for your feedback on early drafts of this novel.

The setting of this novel is based on the lake in Maine where I grew up, and partly on the camp on that lake which has been in our family for generations. I have a photograph of myself as a baby being held in my great-grandmother's arms in a rocking chair in that camp. I also have a photograph of my own baby being held by my mother in that same rocking chair. I have photographs of my grandparents laughing on the beach; my brother waterskiing; my cousins celebrating birthdays; my child with all their cousins piled up together in one bed. It was on the nearby public beach that my dad asked my mom on their first date. My father has spent every summer of his life there. So had I – until the pandemic in 2020.

When I returned in 2021, the first thing I did was to stand in the lake and cry.

My blood runs with the love of that lake, that camp, and the people who live there. And although *Paradise* is a work of fiction, and all of the characters and situations are imaginary, this novel was fuelled by that love and the longing I felt when I wasn't able to return.

Credits

Julie Cohen and Orion Fiction would like to thank everyone at Orion who worked on the publication of *Summer People* in the UK.

Editorial
Rhea Kurien
Snigdha Koirala

Proofreader
Linda Joyce

Audio
Paul Stark
Jake Alderson

Contracts
Anne Goddard
Humayra Ahmed
Ellie Bowker

Design
Charlotte Abrams-Simpson
Nick May
Justinia Baird-Murray

Copyeditor
Suzy Clarke

Editorial Management
Charlie Panayiotou
Jane Hughes
Bartley Shaw

Finance
Jasdip Nandra
Afeera Ahmed
Elizabeth Beaumont
Sue Baker

Marketing
Corinne Jean-Jacques

Production
Ruth Sharvell

RAISING READERS
Books Build Bright Futures

Dear Reader,

We'd love your attention for one more page to tell you about the crisis in children's reading, and what we can all do.

Studies have shown that reading for fun is the **single biggest predictor of a child's future life chances** – more than family circumstance, parents' educational background or income. It improves academic results, mental health, wealth, communication skills, ambition and happiness.[1]

The number of children reading for fun is in rapid decline. Young people have a lot of competition for their time. In 2024, 1 in 10 children and young people in the UK aged 5 to 18 did not own a single book at home.[2]

Hachette works extensively with schools, libraries and literacy charities, but here are some ways we can all raise more readers:

- Reading to children for just 10 minutes a day makes a difference
- Don't give up if children aren't regular readers – there will be books for them!
- Visit bookshops and libraries to get recommendations
- Encourage them to listen to audiobooks
- Support school libraries
- Give books as gifts

There's a lot more information about how to encourage children to read on our website: **www.RaisingReaders.co.uk**

Thank you for reading.

---

[1] National Literacy Trust, Book Ownership in 2024, November 2024
https://nlt.cdn.ngo/media/documents/Book_ownership_in_2024

[2] OECD. 2021. 21st-century readers: developing literacy skills in a digital world. Paris, France: OECD Publishing.
https://www.oecd.org/en/publications/21st-century-readers_a83d84cb-en.html